Completely Pucked

Anna Sparrows, M J Booth

M J Booth ♡

Dear Jess,

Happy reading!

♡ *Anna Sparrows*

Writing sometimes kinky, but always sweet & steamy LGBTQIA+ Romance

Contents

Preface   V

Acknowledgements   VI

Acknowledgements   VII

Chapter One   1

Chapter Two   9

Chapter Three   19

Chapter Four   30

Chapter Five   42

Chapter Six   52

Chapter Seven   63

Chapter Eight   74

Chapter Nine   82

Chapter Ten   93

Chapter Eleven   109

Chapter Twelve   118

Chapter Thirteen   130

Chapter Fourteen   144

Chapter Fifteen   154

Chapter Sixteen   167

Chapter Seventeen   173

Chapter Eighteen   184

Chapter Nineteen   194

Chapter Twenty   204

Chapter Twenty-One   210

Chapter Twenty-Two   221

Epilogue   237

About the Authors   245

Preface

COMPLETELY PUCKED TAKES PLACE in the Daddies Of The League shared world, but it can be read as a standalone.

This book includes age play, wetting, a child whose mother died (prior to the events of the book), custody disputes, hurt/comfort themes, anxiety, referenced/vague eating disorders/issues with food consumption and body issues.

"Let's read, shall we?"
MJ Booth   Anne

Acknowledgements
MJ

CO-WRITING WITH ANNA SPARROWS was a bucket list item I didn't know I had until it was happening. Seriously... I took a chance on messaging you that one time to request (kindly) that a character in one of your books I was mad at be rid of.. I'm still waiting for it, but we've become friends so I guess I'll let it slide for now.

Writing this was so much fun and yes, some of these guys will need their own stories eventually. I love that we are both so chaotic in our writing and planning styles that we just go with whatever happens. I'm grateful to be a part of this shared world so thank you for inviting me in to co-write!

Thank you to the beta readers for all the feedback and Joe Satoria for the cover design and putting this whole shared world together!

Acknowledgements

Anna

FIRSTLY, THANK YOU MJ for being such a wonderful co-author. The fact that you put up with my multiple 'so, this chapter went off the rails' messages says a lot about your patience and kindness. You're definitely stuck with me now, though. A few guys in this book are going to need their own stories. So...series? Pretty please?

Thank you to Joe Satoria and the other authors in the Daddies Of The League series. It has been so wonderful being a part of this group project, and a fantastic experience dipping my toes into a shared world. Extra special thanks to Joe for designing the original cover, too!

Also, thanks to our beta readers, Cindy, Megan & Erin, for giving us valuable feedback and helping us polish this into a book that I am so excited to put out into the world.

Finally, thank you, reader, for picking up our book. I really hope you love it as much as we enjoyed writing it!

Chapter One

Justin

DRIVING FOR NEARLY THREE days is rough on anyone. Now add the fact that I'm driving a moving truck and my five-year-old son is in his car seat beside me, with all of our belongings in the truck portion. Everything we own in one truck, to be unpacked in a new house, in a new state, where I'll start my new job in a month. I'm totally not at my last straw.

"Again!" Owen shouts excitedly, like the song that just finished hasn't been on repeat for the last hour alone. It's that or a meltdown. I'm choosing my battles.

Did I mention I was close to my last straw?

I glance over long enough to see him restart the video on my phone. The god-forsaken Wiggles start up for the umpteenth time. I would love to cut that tree with the limb and the nest and the feather and whatever else is living on it down. But it keeps Owen laughing and distracted about the fact that we have almost reached the new house. It's been an adventure getting us here. It took almost a week to pack everything alone, and then I thought we could have a nice father-son bonding trip, but Owen wasn't interested in stopping to look at statues or views of the mountains. He wanted to stop at every convenience store he saw, claiming he had to use the bathroom each time. Somehow, the bathroom always led to the snacks or the cheap toys some stores sell.

We made it through Tennessee before the first round of waterworks started and I found a hotel for us. After a bath and fresh pajamas, Owen was out like a light. I shouldn't have counted that as a blessing because he was up at five the next morning and we were back on the road by eight. Driving through Arkansas and Oklahoma was no better. Both of us were tired from the traveling, and I hated how little healthy food I was feeding myself and my kid. It just added to his irritability.

But now, we are only thirty minutes from the new house.

Despite everything, I smile when I hear Owen trying to sing along with the words. He isn't quite there with memorizing and speaking that fast, but A for effort, buddy. His jumbling and mixing the words brings a small smile to my face.

He's the only constant positive in my life and I love him with my whole heart. I grew up fast when he was born and his mom passed away shortly after. My family didn't see him as a gift, rather as something that derailed my plans. It didn't matter that I ended up graduating with a degree and worked my ass off to get my license just one year behind what it should have taken. So, we parted ways, and Owen and I are starting our new lives together.

I've just finished school at twenty-seven, while Owen is going to kindergarten this year.

"Daddy." Owen's voice pulls me out of my past and I look over to see he's holding out his arm with my phone. "Battery dead."

"Thanks, buddy." Taking the phone from him, I let it fall onto the seat. I'll have to dig through my bag to find the charger once we get to the house. "Are you ready to see the new house?"

"No."

Well, alright then. At least my kid is honest.

"It's going to be fun," I try. "And you'll be starting school soon, so you'll make a bunch of friends."

He doesn't say anything to that, and I try not to let him see me sigh and slump my shoulders. It'll be an adjustment, which is why I decided to move us a month earlier so he could get settled and hopefully make a friend or two in the neighborhood. It's supposed to be a nice school system, too.

We drive the rest of the way in silence, but I can tell he's getting antsy. So am I, so I can't blame him. I'm ready to stretch my legs and avoid moving anything for at least a day. We can sleep on the air mattresses tonight. I'll call it inside camping or something.

"Look, Owen. That's our house." I point to the house on the corner of Radford and Buckeye Street. Most of the houses in the neighborhood are of a similar style. A single story with a driveway on the left. The sandstone color blends from one house to another. The front landscape consists of gravel, rocks, and shrubbery. There's a tree which shades a portion of the driveway, and I back the truck in so it's easier to unpack later. For the twentieth time, I wish I'd hired some movers to help.

"Where's the grass?" Owen asks when I help him out of the truck. The sun is beating down and I can almost immediately feel sweat trickling down the back of my neck.

Owen squints against the sun, looking back and forth from me to the space around us. He's wearing a white t-shirt with his favorite Paw Patrol character and matching, light-up shoes. The shorts land just above his knees, and I smile at how pale he is compared to myself. He definitely took after his mother with the red hair and fair skin. He has my hazel-green eyes, though.

I add extra sunscreen to the growing list of things I need to make sure we have.

"There's a backyard too." I try to make it sound fun to get him excited. He has moved to closing one eye completely and his face is all scrunched up when he looks up at me.

"Can we set my pool up?"

The pool is just one of those plastic kiddie pools from a large chain store. He's nearly grown out of it; this will likely be our last year using it.

"How about we focus on getting the inside fixed up first?" We start moving to the front door as I dig for the keys in my pocket. "Do you want to open it?"

"Yes!"

Yes! I repeat in my head. This is the first sign of excitement I've seen from him in days where the move is concerned. Owen is a typical five-year-old, but I swear he's so contemplative at times. He likes to learn and ask questions, but I'll also find him sitting quietly and watching the world around him sometimes.

It takes him a full minute to get the key right and I help him by turning the knob while he pushes the door open. The house is mostly an open-floor concept. The door opens offset to the middle of the house. There is a partial wall coming from the right, creating a counter island with three chairs on the side facing us and cabinets on the other side. A sliding glass door on the opposite wall of the main entrance shows off the decent sized backyard. There is grass there, thankfully, and a five-foot wall encasing the area on all three sides. Owen will have enough space to play with his toys. We might have to choose between the swing set or pool, but that can be a problem for later.

To the left is a hallway about halfway into the space. I follow behind Owen as he explores each new room. The bathroom is the first door on the right. A selling point of this house was that the tub and shower are separate, something you don't see often in Arizona. At least not in the price range that I could afford. The second door on the right is the laundry room.

The two bedrooms are on the left side. I let Owen see both of them. One is slightly larger than the other, but either would be fine with me. "Which room would you like?" I ask Owen after he peeks his head into the closet of the second one. "You can pick, and I'll take the other one."

"I like this one," Owen says with a smile. He's missing the tooth next to his front one and it just makes him all the more adorable. "Do I still get my bed?"

"Of course, buddy." I follow him back out to the living room area. The medium-gray vinyl flooring is also different from the carpet we had in our old house. I won't have to constantly remind Owen to be careful not to stain anything. "Remember that we packed everything in the truck before we came here. We'll have to get it all out tomorrow."

"I want my toys now," Owen says. He stops in front of the glass door and immediately presses his hands to it, leaving smudges. Yeah, I might not have to clean carpet, but I'll need to keep glass cleaner on hand. "I wanna play."

I stop at the thermostat and adjust the air so it will kick on and cool down the place a little. Owen has already moved on to open all the doors in the kitchen by the time I look back. I sigh and follow behind him, closing each one as he moves on to the next. Inquisitive mind and all. I remind myself each day that I'm going to let him learn as much as he wants from life. If that means opening every cabinet and asking to look at the ones up top, I'll oblige. I was forced to "act right" way too young by my parents. I don't remember getting to be a kid very often.

"Can we get my trucks out?" Owen asks once he's satisfied with the kitchen. "I want to build a big track across the whole room."

"I'm sorry, buddy. The boxes are piled way in the back. We'll have to get it all tomorrow."

I can see the pout a moment before his little foot stomps on the floor. "I wanna play! There's nothing in here to play with."

"That's why I told you to pack a couple of toys in your bookbag, remember? We can go out and get those."

"No, I want my trucks!" Owen folds his arms across his body, and I start preparing for a meltdown while hoping I can talk him down.

"We can't get to your trucks right now," I repeat in a gentle tone. I squat down to be on his level. His bottom lip is stuck all the way out in full-on pouting mode. This is just one step away from the waterworks. "How about we walk around and see what there is? I saw a place where we could go get food just a few minutes from here? I bet they have chicken nuggets."

I can see the fight Owen is having in his little mind. Like most five-year-olds, chicken nuggets are his favorite food. But he also really loves his trucks.

The food wins out after a minute. I give myself a mental victory dance for a meltdown avoided and stand back up. He starts complaining again when I make him wear his hat. The sun is really hot here in August. I didn't account for that at all. Three minutes later, Owen is rightfully complaining that it's too hot, so I bend down to scoop him up and carry him. He isn't too heavy for me to carry yet and, even though I'm sweating myself, I won't miss the opportunity. Who knows when it will be the last time?

The restaurant is a diner just outside the neighborhood. The cool air greets us when I open the door and a bell chimes above our heads. I set Owen on the ground and take his hand. His cheeks are already turning red despite the hat.

"Well, hello." An older woman greets us with a smile. She has silver hair, wrinkles around her eyes, and is wearing a floral dress and compression socks. Every bit the grandma vibe. She immediately grabs a menu and leads us to a table. "Welcome to Ma's. I'm Ma. My husband and I run this place together."

I help Owen onto his seat before sitting on my own. The place doesn't give modern vibes at all, more a mix of 50's diner and retro with the square tiled floors, the counter that stretches across most of the space, and the mismatched chairs and tables. The tall windows let in a lot of natural light throughout the space though. I notice a group of guys, not much younger than me, it seems, sitting in a corner booth talking and laughing.

"What can I get you two to drink?"

"Water for both of us," I say.

"I want chocolate milk," Owen declares immediately.

"No, you can get water right now." I fix him with a look before turning back to the menu. It's just one side, so it doesn't take me long to see what I want. "You had a chocolate milk earlier."

"But I want chocolate milk." Owen raises his voice and I can see the few patrons in the diner glance our way, including the young guys.

"And I said no." I remain firm on that. If we have to walk back in the heat, the last thing I need is for his stomach to be upset and for him to get overheated. That chocolate milk would surely make

7

a reappearance. "I'm sorry. Two waters, please. And I'll just have a cheeseburger, and he'll have some chicken nuggets. We'll share the fries."

"Oh honey, I'm so sorry." Ma turns to me and mouths the dreaded words:

We're out of chicken nuggets right now.

Chapter Two

"...GETTING CAPTAIN?" MY ROOMMATE, Israel, asks. I grimace as I turn back to face him. It's not my fault that I've been distracted by the cute man who just walked into Ma's place with his even cuter kid.

Yeah, I know: I'm a twenty-two-year-old guy who likes kids. I can't help it. It's ingrained in me. I have a herd of nieces and nephews, for one thing, and for another...well, let's just say I get along with little ones and leave it at that.

"Gabe!" Izzy kicks at my shin, obviously irritated by my lack of attention.

"Sorry, Iz," I apologize, giving myself a mental shake. "What were you saying?"

Israel sighs dramatically and rolls his dark eyes, then looks to the others at our table with an expression that begs the question 'why do we put up with this guy?' Marshall and Noah just shrug back at him and bite into their burgers.

"I was asking who you think is getting captain this year," Izzy repeats himself, still sounding frustrated.

"Of the football team? You'd know that better than I would." I *might* be trying to press his buttons at this point.

Israel plays defense for our college football team. He's big, bulky, and grumpy as hell. He got a scholarship to play here, moving all the way to landlocked Arizona from Hawaii, and I'm pretty sure the longer he stays away from the ocean, the crankier he gets. We've been roommates since Freshman year and, now that we're Seniors, I am determined to take every opportunity I get to stir him up before we graduate and part ways.

I'm going to miss the big lug when that happens.

He growls like the bear he is and shakes his head. "I meant hockey and you fuckin' know it."

"Hey," I hold up my index finger, waggling it at him in a 'no no' motion. "Language. There are children present."

Seated beside me, Marshall sniggers. "Yeah," he says, *"you."*

Marshall is...not the sharpest crayon in the box, but he's a ray of sunshine and, though I don't quite understand how or why, he's one of the only people who ever gets a genuine smile or laugh out of Izzy.

Case in point: my roommate snorts. "Good one," he says.

I don't tell either of them that, no, the joke was actually really lame, because that would be cruel. But, across the table, I catch Noah's glance and we share a look that says it all.

"Anyway," Noah dips one of his fries into the puddle of ketchup on his plate, "who *do* you think is getting the C this year? Because Holland graduated last year."

"Didn't Bellport pick him up?" Marshall asks, then leans over the table and steals one of Noah's fries.

"No, I think it was Pittsburgh maybe?" I feel a little bad that I didn't pay all that much attention to the draft last year. But I've had other things on my mind. "We'll see if he gets any time on the ice, though. He might just warm the bench for a while."

"Cold," Noah tells me.

"Yeah, because it's ice hockey," Marshall nods.

That was *not* a joke.

I'm about to open my mouth to finally answer Izzy's question when a loud, petulant, "I want chocolate milk!" resonates through the dining space.

We all turn in our seats, drawn by the noise, and I suddenly remember my original distraction.

Cute guy with a cute kid. AKA: catnip for one Gabriel Tomas Nagy (that is, me).

The guy has unkempt light brown hair and hazel-green eyes. He's short—I know because he wasn't any taller than Ma when she led him to his table earlier— and has a kind of rounded face that makes determining his age difficult. He doesn't look much older than me, but the kid —redheaded, but with the same color eyes— has to be at least four or five-years-old.

They both look a little rumpled around the edges. The guy himself seems tired and kind of...defeated? Well, he does if the slump of his shoulders is anything to go by, anyway. Plus, he has dark circles under his pretty eyes.

But he is kind, though firm, when he denies the kid his milk, which has me holding my breath. Tired, hangry kids aren't known for handling the word 'no' with grace and aplomb.

It seems like the kid might actually be okay with the refusal, and I breathe a sigh of relief for the dude. Then Ma's voice carries over to our table. "Oh, honey, I'm so sorry..."

She mouths something at the cute guy, and I can see the moment whatever she's said registers. His face falls, and he sends a glance filled with trepidation in the kid's direction. Then he closes his eyes, takes a deep breath, and leans down to murmur something gently in the kid's ear.

The kid blinks, then his little face crumples as he lets out a loud wail. "But you *promised* chicken nuggets, Daddy!"

Cute Guy's lower lip wobbles and he looks up at Ma helplessly before trying to soothe his kid. My heart goes out to him, because if I thought he looked tired before, it's nothing on how absolutely exhausted he seems *now*.

"Uh," Noah says as I push my chair back, "what the hell are you doing?"

I'm out of my seat and dropping my paper napkin onto my half-empty plate before I even know the answer. "I'm gonna see if I can help."

"Damnit, Gabe," Izzy huffs, "leave them be."

Turning my back on my table, I ignore him and cross the space to where the little boy is still crying and begging for nuggets.

"I'm so sorry," Cute Guy is telling Ma. He glances up at me, then back at her, "I'll just...get something to go and we'll get out of your hair. It's been a long day, and I know we're causing a scene, I just..." his breathing hitches, and my heart gives a squeeze.

I drop to my haunches beside the kid's seat and make eye contact with Cute Guy to ask silent permission to interact with his kid. His eyes are wide and his expression torn between bewildered and cautious as he nods.

I gently touch the kid's back. "Hey, bud," I greet him, and the new voice is enough to startle him from his continued wailing. I smile as he goes quiet and looks at me with wariness.

He's ridiculously cute, even with skin turned blotchy pink from crying, and his eyes look really green against the red, too.

"I hear Ma's out of nuggets. But," I hold up my index finger to forestall a relapse into tears, "I'll tell you a secret."

"D-Daddy said secrets are naughty."

I consider that. "Your daddy's right. Secrets can be naughty." I can't help pausing to shoot Cute Guy a quick smile and a wink. Then I grin at the kid again. "But this one isn't, I promise. In fact, it's not *really* a secret. Everyone here knows it."

The kid squints at me. "What is it?"

"It's that Ma's mini pizzas are the best in the whole state," I tell him very seriously. "She makes the dough from scratch and everything."

"She scratches the dough?" His innocent, horrified question has me struggling to keep a straight face.

Cute Guy laughs first, and the sound makes me feel all warm and fuzzy inside. "No, buddy," he tells his kid, "it's a turn of phrase. It means that she makes the dough herself, she doesn't buy a pre-made base from the store."

"Oh," the kid nods, "*you* buy the ones at the store, Daddy."

Cute Guy blushes as he glances over at me, then up to Ma, then looks at his kid again. He clears his throat. "Well, it sounds like we have to try the mini pizzas here now. What do you say?"

The kid bites his lip, then looks up at Ma. "Do the pizzas have pepperonis?"

She beams at him and nods. "They sure do, honey. I can make sure we put extra on yours."

"Wow," Cute Guy says with exaggerated excitement. He gives his kid a tiny nudge. "What do we say, Owen?"

"Thank you," he replies dutifully.

"It's my pleasure, sweetheart," Ma says, scribbling on her notepad and then scurrying off to the kitchen.

Cute Guy slumps back in his chair, then looks at me. "Thank you," he says emphatically. "I'm sorry we disturbed your meal. Like I said, it's been a long day."

"Not a problem." Instead of heading back to my friends like I know I should, I slide into one of the two spare seats at their table. I extend my hand towards Cute Guy. The fact that he's got a kid probably means he's off-limits, but, just like when I'm on the ice, I'm going to shoot my shot anyway. "I'm Gabe, by the way."

He arches an eyebrow at me but shakes my hand anyway. "Justin. And this one," he lets go of my hand to pat his kid's back, "is Owen."

"It's nice to meet you." I cock my head. "How'd you stumble into Ma's anyway?" It's a tiny suburban diner, nowhere near the main part of town. "Did you get lost driving around Phoenix? That happened to me when I first moved here. It's how I found this place, actually."

"We walked here," Owen answers for Justin. "It was hot." He peers up at his dad. "When can I have my trucks, Daddy?"

Justin lets out a weary sigh. "After we unpack *our* truck," he answers in a tone that tells me he's repeating himself for the umpteenth time. Then he looks back at me. "We just moved here."

"It was a long drive," Owen pipes up. He picks up his napkin and starts playing with it, twisting the ends and scrunching it. "We slept in a motel." The way he says 'motel', drawing out the 'o' and the 'el', is just the cutest thing ever.

"Hotel," Justin corrects, "and yeah, we did, buddy. Daddy needed to sleep along the way." He scrubs a hand over his face and mutters, "Daddy needs to sleep *now*."

My curiosity gets the better of me, and I'm dimly aware of my friends waving their hands and trying to get my attention. I ignore them. "How much unpacking do you have left to do?"

"All of it," Owen answers again. He turns to Justin and pouts. "We can't sleep without our beds. You said I can have my bed."

Sensing another meltdown, I smoothly interrupt, "You'll get your bed. My friends" —I finally swivel in my seat to wave back at them, and they all freeze and stare at me as if sensing that I'm about to do something they'll hate— "and I will help you out."

"Wait..." Justin blinks, jaw dropping as I turn back around to smile at them. "*What?*"

***

"Dude, seriously?" Izzy bitches when I slide back into my seat and tell my friends that I've volunteered their services to help Justin and Owen. "It's like five thousand degrees out right now. I don't want to be lugging some stranger's furniture and boxes around. Especially not for free."

I glare at him and push my plate, containing my half-eaten burger, towards Marshall who leaps upon it happily. "Iz, c'mon, man. Look at him" —I point towards Justin who, while he tried protesting, seemed infinitely relieved to hear that he wasn't going to be unloading a moving truck on his own— "and tell me he doesn't look like he needs it. He's just traveled cross-country with a five-year-old on his own. He's *this close* to a breakdown."

Iz sighs and folds his huge arms over his chest, arching a bushy, black eyebrow at me. "I get it: we've been *voluntold* to do this because you think he's hot."

"And," Noah steals a fry from my abandoned plate, waggling it in the air between us, "you have a savior complex."

"I do not."

I don't.

I have a Daddy complex.

Well, Daddy instincts. And when I see some cute, helpless guy desperately in need of someone to take over and help them with their adult stresses, I just can't help myself.

"You do," Izzy insists with finality. "Plus, we all know you're a sucker for little kids."

That accusation I can't actually deny. I shrug. "I can't help it if they all remind me of my nieces and nephews."

He huffs. "You don't have to spoil every single kid you see just because they're like your horde of niblings."

"Don't have to, no," I agree genially, "but I want to. It's fun making kids smile." I cast a glance over my shoulder and catch Justin's gaze. His cheeks turn a little pink before he is drawn back into conversation with Owen.

I wonder what their story is....

"It's not *just* the kid you want to make smile," Izzy is like a dog with a bone. "And, I hate to break it to you, bud, but the likelihood of him being into guys is slim."

"Why?" I counter, rising to the bait without thinking. "Because he's got a kid? Bisexuality is a thing. So is experimentation, and pansexuality, and—"

"Okay, *Google*," Izzy rolls his eyes, cutting me off. He wipes his mouth on his paper napkin and balls it up, tossing it onto his empty plate. "I'm just sayin', don't go gettin' your hopes up just 'cause you think he's cute."

"I just want to help the guy, is all. What were we going to do this afternoon anyway? Sit in our dorm room and drink?"

Noah scoffs. "*Pffft.* You don't drink," he tells me, sounding affronted by the very idea. "Mister 'my body is my temple'."

"I *do* drink. Just in moderation. I train too hard to waste the work on empty calories and a hangover."

"Sounds stupid to me," Marshall declares, finishing the last bites of my burger. "Izzy trains, too, and he doesn't mind the calories."

"Izzy is *supposed* to be built like a brick wall. I need to stay lean and agile."

"You calling me fat, Gabe?" Izzy asks, deadpan.

"It's not like you to come fishing for compliments, Iz," I tease back, enjoying the growl it earns me.

Before he can respond, I feel a tug on my sleeve and a cute little voice says, "'Scuse me, Mister Gabe?"

I turn my head to find Owen at my side, his chubby cheeks smeared with tomato sauce and half a piece of pizza held in his free hand. I grin. "Yes, Mister Owen? Is the pizza good?"

He giggles a little and nods. "Yup," he pops the 'p'. "But, um, Daddy said to tell you that we're gonna take our food to go 'cause you're all finished with your foods. But he says I can eat mine while we walk back 'cause it's pot...um...porable."

"Portable?" I ask as I look over towards Justin, wanting to tell him to sit down and eat his meal before he falls down, but I hold back the urge.

Owen nods. "Yeah. That." He takes another bite of his meal as if to prove his point. Then, with his mouth full, asks, "Can we get my trucks now?"

He's such a cute kid.

Nodding, I gesture to the guys. "Sure thing, bud. We're looking forward to helping you." I give my friends a pointed glare. "Right, guys?"

Despite being a grumpy asshole with us, Israel doesn't turn his moods on small children. Even he musters a smile for Owen as he mumbles his agreement.

Owen cheers, then starts tugging at my shirt sleeve again. "Come on," he urges. "Let's go!"

I look at my friends and shrug. "You heard the kid. Let's go."

Chapter Three

Justin

WE BARELY MAKE IT outside when Gabe is rushing through the door behind us.

"Where are you going?" Gabe asks.

"We're walking home?" I cock my head slightly at him, wondering why he's asking. He just stares back until it dawns on me. "Oh, yeah. I guess I should probably give you the address."

"Or..." he drags out the word and lifts a key fob to unlock a car nearby. A mini van, actually. "You can be smart and let me drive you home instead of walking through this heat again. Before you argue, I have a car seat Owen can use. Perks of having nieces and nephews."

"Oh, we can't do that." I look from Gabe to Owen. His cheeks are already red and, despite being adamant he wanted chocolate milk, he downed two kiddie cups of water in the short time we sat in the diner. Even just a couple minutes' walk back doesn't seem all that appealing.

"Daddy, please? It's hot." Owen looks between the two of us and my shoulders sag. Gabe's friends are loitering by their cars already, waiting for me to make a decision. I love Owen with every fiber of my being but having to make all the decisions and constantly weighing pros and cons is not my favorite thing in the world. I had to grow up fast at home on top of Owen being a surprise.

To be a kid again, I think.

"Sure, buddy." I give Gabe a short smile. "Only if you're sure and you have the right car seat for him."

"I have all three stages. My youngest niece is only a couple of months old and my oldest nibling is around Owen's height, so he should be able to use that one. Come on."

The blast of cool air when Gabe turns on the car is more than welcoming. The car is nice, a newer model. Definitely different from my 2010 Toyota. Not that there's anything wrong with my car. It is reliable and easy to maintain; something that's necessary when you're a single dad.

Owen is buckled up, asking a hundred questions to Gabe about whatever he can see while I point directions. It's really just two short turns and then pointing out the house with the moving truck in the driveway. My car is currently with Lauren's parents, Owen's maternal grandparents. They let me leave it at their place two weeks ago when I came out to sign for the house. Owen has never officially met his mom's parents since she passed away; outside of the job offer, knowing they would be close by seemed like another tick in the plus column for moving here.

Gabe pulls into the driveway next to the moving truck. "This place is nice. Good neighborhood too."

"Do you live around here?"

"Not too far," Gabe says. He turns the car off and climbs out, my cue to drop that line of questioning. Despite the random invitation for him to help me unload the truck, we know nothing but each other's names.

Owen is already unbuckled and waiting for me to open the back door. He hops out without my help, something that sends a small pang through me. He's growing up too fast.

Gabe's friends are parked along the road, and we all meet at the front door.

"I would offer you all a beer or something for the trouble, but I only have tap water." I was never one to host events or anything. I had friends that would come over, some with their own kids, but most would just invite me out. Half the time I had to decline because I didn't have anyone to watch Owen. They never really made the effort to do things where kids could be included, and I couldn't blame them. Your twenties are supposed to be a time to have fun and go out to meet people. Small children get in the way of that.

"Beer in this heat would mean trouble," one of the guys says as we walk into the empty house. I want to ask them to take their shoes off, but we'll be going in and out for a couple of hours at least. I'll just have to mop once everything is settled.

"Gabe! Want to see my room?" Owen takes Gabe's hand and leads him through the house before the guy can even answer. I'm grateful that Gabe stops just at the door frame and looks back at me with a nod. It relaxes my nerves a bit that I can keep my eye on him. I might be inviting these guys into my house, but I don't know them enough to let them out of sight with my kid. Gabe and his friends seem trustworthy enough, but the world can be a cruel place.

I hate that my brain goes there.

"He's great with kids," one of the others says, like they just heard my thoughts. There are three of them, and they're big. Their muscles are on full display in their short sleeve shirts and shorts. The same guy holds out his hand. "I'm Isreal. Izzy for short."

"Noah," the second guy says.

"And I'm Marshall."

"Marshall?" I hear Owen's voice behind me and can't help the smile that tugs my lips upward. I shake Marshall's hand.

"I hope you know your Paw Patrol," I warn him.

"Oh, do I ever!" Marshall turns to Owen, who is now leading Gabe back to where they're standing. Marshall squats down to Owen's eye level and points to my son's shirt. "That dalmatian right there is Marshall. Rubble. Chase. Skye. Zuma. Rocky. Then there's also Ryder and Mayor—"

"Okay, that's enough." Noah cuts Marshall off with a hand on his shoulder. "How about you save your knowledge for after we move everything in?"

"Are you also a firebiter?"

"Firefighter, Owen. Fighter." I find it endearing the way he mixes up his words sometimes, but I try to make sure he knows what the actual word is without belittling him. I grew up in a household like that and don't want Owen to feel any less than the smart kid he is.

"Fighter," he corrects himself, smiling up at me and then back to Marshall.

"I'm not, Owen."

"Doesn't stop you from roleplaying," I hear Gabe mutter under his breath next to me. I look over at him and he looks like a deer in the headlights when he realizes he said that out loud. I hide my laugh behind a cough. "How about we get to unpacking?"

"Let's get my trucks!" Owen says and rushes to the door. It's still open, letting out what cool air had filled the space while we were gone. I hang back, letting Owen have his fun while watching the four men I'm blindly trusting.

We make a game plan on how we're going to get everything out. I have to move the truck forward a bit so we can put down the ramp. Izzy and Gabe hop into the truck and hand boxes to me, Noah, and Marshall. Owen is given toys or much smaller, less breakable things to carry as well. We all joke and laugh while moving boxes. Marshall is quite funny. Noah is quieter, but he hits the mark with perfectly timed one-liners. Gabe, like he's claimed a few times, is great with Owen. I watch them interact, and there's something genuine in Gabe's expression every time Owen calls his name.

By the time we're down to just the big furniture, it's been over an hour. The boxes are sitting in each room and they will probably take at least a week to go through. Someone (me) forgot to label what exactly was in each box as I taped them up. The most they say is the generic room they'll need to go in. I watch Gabe—and the others—pick up the furniture and maneuver it inside. They are dripping with sweat, and I feel bad that I don't even know where my cups are. Labeling boxes with their actual contents didn't seem like an important step when I was packing everything. I pull out my phone as they're setting the couch in the living room to order some groceries to the house.

"Everything okay?" I recognize Gabe's voice without looking up.

"Yeah, just ordering some water and popsicles from the store a couple miles away." I don't know the store, but it's Phoenix so there are plenty of delivery services around. "Should be here in half an hour."

"I could have just driven you," Gabe says. "Save your money."

"I'm good," I say. I'm not hurting for money, and starting the job at the college soon is going to be a serious pay bump as well. "I'll be going to the grocery store tomorrow to stock the kitchen, so this is just to get us through the heat today."

"Do you have a car?" I watch the guys walk back outside to the truck. Izzy gives Gabe a knowing look, one that asks, 'why are we doing all the work?'. Owen is most likely making a mess in his room already. Marshall was commandeered to help Owen put his bed together. Last I checked on them, Owen was talking Marshall's ears off about his favorite animals. They're keeping the door open at my request.

"I do," I say. "It's at Owen's maternal grandparents' house. They live in Phoenix, which is one of the reasons we chose to move here from Virginia. They're supposed to be coming by tomorrow to meet Owen. They haven't seen him in person before."

"Oh wow, big difference in climate." We move toward the front door and walk out to look in the truck. There's really just my bedroom furniture left.

We stop that conversation when Izzy and Noah hand off the headboard of my bed frame. It takes a bit of maneuvering, but we get it through the front door and down the hall. Owen runs out when I call for him, holding a beloved toy truck in each hand. I sigh, knowing that it's going to be next to impossible to organize his room. "Can you open the bathroom door, buddy?"

"You're putting your bed in the bathroom?" He tilts his head, but does as I ask.

Gabe is the one to answer that question since he's closer to Owen. "We have to open the door so we have more room to turn sideways and get this into Daddy's room."

I don't know what the feeling is that shoots through my mind and body when I hear Gabe say the word *daddy*. I refer to myself as that all the time and Owen exclusively calls me that for the time being. Hearing a grown man, a younger-than-me grown man, calling me daddy is... different. I know my face shows the uncomfortable feeling welling up in me, but I hide it and smile before he looks back up.

It isn't wrong for him to refer to me as Daddy when talking to Owen, but it still feels...*off*. I push those thoughts away and we set the headboard against one wall. The bedrooms both have closets that are side-by-side, separated by a wall between them. Mine is on the right side of the room, where Owen's is on the left.

Owen has already gone into his bedroom, and I peek in to see Marshall is at the final stages of putting his bed together. The room is not as messy as I imagined. My earlier concerns about the guys being out of my sight with my kid have mostly evaporated.

I turn back to walk with Gabe through the house. Izzy and Noah are bringing in the footboard.

"Is Owen's mom in the picture?" Gabe asks the question when we're alone outside. He sounds hesitant to ask, but not like he's prying.

"No, she passed away when Owen was a baby."

"Oh, I'm sorry." Gabe looks nervous and I shake my head.

"No, don't worry about it. It's a logical question. She was nice and would have been a great mom. Owen was a surprise, but she loved him. She passed in a car accident a couple of months after he was born."

"And you've been raising him on your own?"

"Yeah." I grunt as I try to lift the mattress. Gabe is right beside me and he reaches at the same time that I readjust my grip. His hand lands on top of mine and we both freeze for a second, looking at each other.

"Sorry," he says and pulls his hand away.

"I appreciate all the work you guys have done. You really didn't have to do this."

"Are you kidding?" Gabe fixes me with a stare, and I don't know if I want to apologize or melt into his eyes. I have no idea what is wrong with me. This guy has to be at least five years younger than me, probably still in school. He's gorgeous, as are his friends, which seems unfair for all the gay, pan, and bisexual men in this city —myself included— and he has this *air* about him. It's confident, not cocky. Or maybe it's just been way too fucking long since I've been laid. Being a single dad in your twenties will do that to you.

I'm blaming the heat.

We're halfway through the living room with the mattress when Noah —I think— calls out that there's a delivery. At the mere mention of popsicles, Owen goes barreling down the hallway. Gabe and I both laugh when Marshall calls for Owen to finish helping him organize his toys. We take a short break and down water and eat a popsicle each. I sigh when Owen comes back from exploring around the yard with Gabe and he has blue all down the front of his shirt.

"I tried my best," Gabe says regretfully.

"Daddy," Owen cuts in before I can answer. "Did you know that we could wake up with a scor-pon in our beds?"

I look from Owen to Gabe. Where Owen's face is red from being in the sun for the last ten minutes, Gabe's is one of almost embarrassment. "Scorpion, Owen, and I didn't say it would be in your bed. I just said you had to look out for them in the house."

"Thanks for terrorizing my kid," I say jokingly. "I will now need your number if he starts crying in the middle of the night."

I realize what I said right after the words come out of my mouth. Another moment and I chance looking up at him. He's smiling, just barely. He shrugs and pulls out his phone. "Only if you give me yours too."

I text myself from his phone and hand it back. Neither of us say anything else about it the rest of the time they're helping.

***

Waking up the next morning in my own bed feels like a miracle. I am beyond grateful for Gabe and his friends. What would have taken me nearly the whole day, and maybe some money if I hired movers, took only a couple of hours to bring it all in and set it up. After I gave Gabe my number, we went inside and put the bed together. Owen didn't want any of the guys to leave, which was cute at first, but when they actually left it turned into a near meltdown. He kept repeating he wanted his friends to stay.

After Owen cried himself to sleep, I texted Gabe and we set up a tentative thank you dinner for a couple of days' time. He told me he would ask the other guys if they were available.

Thinking about it again now, I know Owen would like that a lot, too.

Our morning is slow. I order us breakfast and start going through some boxes while we wait for Owen's grandparents to arrive with the car. He is going to be spending the night with them. The beauty of video calls kept them close, even though they hadn't met yet. Owen seems excited that he'll have two rooms, one here at the house and one with them. When they arrive around eleven, I let Owen open the door.

"Oh. look at you!" His grandmother, Karen, coos immediately. "You are getting so tall, Owen. Oh gosh, Harold, look at him. He looks just like his mama when she was little."

"You're growing up fast," Harold says, giving Owen a half-hug. It is more like an arm wrapped around the back of Owen's head. Harold is only fifty-nine, but he looks closer to his late sixties, presumably from a life of hard labor.

"Do I get to go see my room now?"

"Owen," I say, cutting him off. "How about you say hi first. Maybe show them the house?"

"Oh, it's fine, Justin." Karen barely looks at me when she says it. "We're good to go if Owen is. We're just as excited to show him his room too."

"Well, okay." I wasn't expecting to have an empty house so soon, but it gives me a couple more hours to unpack than I thought. "Owen, give me a hug bye and you be good for your grandparents, okay? I love you and I'll see you tomorrow."

"I love you too," he replies, smushed against my chest. Standing back up, I hand over the backpack I organized for him this morning.

"He hasn't had lunch yet," I say before they promise to feed him well —something I'm sure we'll have to discuss— and leave. I gave them the extra car seat I had, so I know he's safe.

I spend the day running errands. I return the moving truck, taking an Uber back to the house. Then I turn around and go right back out to get groceries. I make sure to get extra veggies and healthier snacks to make up for the last three days of traveling.

I get the kitchen unpacked and somewhat organized. Then the bathroom. By the time I make it to my room, it is well after normal dinner time, and I am...hungry. I've been picturing Gabe moving my furniture, helping carry boxes, taking over putting together my own bed. It doesn't help that the first box I open in my room happens to be *that box* and my mind immediately supplies me with the image of Gabe opening it and looking at the dildo hidden under a shirt. I debate on taking advantage of a quiet house, but decide I should go out, instead.

There was a club I went to on occasion back in Virginia. Being bisexual, I didn't have a preference for the kind of club, either. After Lauren's accident, I found myself exploring both gay and predominantly straight clubs equally. Not that it happened often.

But tonight, after thinking about Gabe all day, I have specific itches that need to be scratched.

I pull out my phone and search for clubs nearby. The first several results are not what I'm looking for, but then I see it. Club Kik. It looks promising, and I tell myself it can't hurt to at least check the place out.

I change into my favorite jeans and a green shirt that I've been told brings out the green in my mostly hazel eyes. It's gotten me laid before, in all honesty, even with the Batman logo.

The drive there is uneventful, but the change of scenery is nice. Closer to the heart of the city, where the club is located, traffic picks up and I end up having to park a block away. The building my GPS tells me is Club Kik is unassuming. There's no line, but then again, it is only nine and the sun is still setting. Maybe they aren't even open yet. I try the door and smile to myself when I step inside without issue.

There's a small foyer where I show the receptionist my ID and receive a stamp on the inside of my wrist, and then I open the next door to the main club space where thumping base, strobe lighting, and writhing bodies await me.

Let's see how this goes.

Chapter Four

CLUB KIK IS *EXACTLY* where I need to be tonight. I've been wired since meeting Justin yesterday, to the point where Izzy basically told me that if I don't get my ass out of our dorm room and get laid, he might actually strangle me with his meaty bear paws. Those weren't his actual words, but they're close enough.

Anyway, after texting back and forth with the cute single dad who I am *almost* certain was flirting with me last night, I have to admit that I'm keyed up and in desperate need of some kind of release. I have to get my head (yes, the one on top of my shoulders) back on straight before my Senior year of college starts up.

I'm attending Claremont College on a hockey scholarship, and not only do I need to perform well on the team, but I need to keep my grades up, too. There's no way I'll be able to do that if I'm fixated on some random guy.

Some random super cute guy.

Some random super cute guy whose eyes practically screamed 'help me, Daddy Gabe' last night.

I mean, okay, he's more than likely straight, and I didn't *actually* get any kinky vibes from him —and it's entirely possible that I imagined the flirty tones to his perfectly normal conversation— but that's what I saw. (Probably because it's what I wanted to see.)

Iz is right. I need to get laid.

I step through the front door of the club and into the main space. It's dark in here, aided by the dark purple walls really only lit by the flashing strobe lights, and loud. The bass pumps hard, and the bodies on the dance floor writhe. But the dance space is not where I need to be tonight, even if the idea of grinding up against someone until we both come is appealing.

But I need more than just a sexual release.

Last night sparked my need to Daddy someone again. It was so difficult not stepping in and making Justin's decisions for him when I could tell he was getting tired and stressed out. I doubt he would have appreciated me doing so, for one thing, and for another...well, I like to negotiate limits with a partner before I go into Daddy mode. We didn't really have time for that, and pushing myself (and my friends) into his house to make sure he wasn't unpacking on his own and building furniture late into the night was probably enough line-crossing.

So I skirt around the edge of the main club space and make my way to the stairs along the side. The upper levels contain the kink-friendly spaces where I can let go and indulge in my deepest desires.

I just hope there's a Boy here in need of Daddy's help.

Now, I know what you're thinking. I'm only twenty-two; how could I possibly be anyone's Daddy?

Part of it is what Iz calls my hero complex, sure. But the rest? Well, let's say I was an early bloomer. I come from a big family, and I'm the third youngest of six kids. By the time I hit my teens and had proven myself to not be a troublemaker, my parents kind of just left me to my own devices. I was getting good grades, I wasn't getting into fights or doing drugs or even excessively partying, so they didn't worry too much about what I was getting up to.

And what was I getting up to? Mostly porn.

Not performing it, but watching it. Reading erotic stories. Discovering that the things that really turned me on —outside of naked men in general— were...not exactly vanilla.

I found Daddy kink first. Through fanfiction, of all things, and then I started watching the porn...and that led me to age play. I was enthralled. Fascinated by these men who dressed adorably and seemed so sweet and innocent (until they did amazingly, perfectly filthy things with the men they called 'Daddy').

As I got older, I started wanting to experience that myself. I wanted to *be* Daddy.

I already knew I had a caregiver streak —I always enjoyed taking care of my younger siblings and my older siblings' kids— and I just knew that if I had a partner, I'd want to take care of them, too. Maybe even more than I liked taking care of family, because sex would add a whole new level to the enjoyment of looking after someone, right?

It turned out I was right. I got myself a fake over 21 ID when I started college, Googled for kink clubs, and never looked back.

I don't need the fake ID anymore, but I still visit Club Kik for the kink fulfillment.

There are three levels to this club. There is an elevator out the back, but I prefer to take the stairs. The second level is where the Doms and Subs who like pain and restraints tend to hang out. The far wall is lined with shackles and St Andrews crosses, and there are a couple of ceiling hooks and sex swings suspended from above, too. In the center of the room, there are paddling benches, and the closest wall, which backs onto the stairs, houses a *huge* collection of toys and implements. The rule is, once you've used one, you need to drop it into the tub beside the shelves so it can be taken away and sanitized. And, if you're using the dildos and vibrators, you *must* cover it with one of the house-provided condoms. There are bowls of the little foil packets stationed all over the club. On top of that, many of the Doms bring their own toys with them.

Like downstairs, the walls here are painted a dark color —this time a deep crimson red— and the lights are kept dim for the atmosphere. The leather couches positioned strategically around the room are all black. (They also get sanitized frequently.)

I like level two as a voyeur, but I'm in the mood to actually partake in my flavor of kink tonight, so I turn on the landing and continue up to level three.

Stepping through the door into the room up here might have you believing you're in a completely different place. This space is brightly lit. The walls are decorated in an inviting mural of sky blue, fluffy white clouds, and brightly colored air balloons. The thumping bass from downstairs is almost completely silenced by soundproofing barriers and, instead, the music playing here is soft and instrumental. Uplifting, but kept to a gentle background level.

This is Little Heaven.

There are giant teddy bears, an epic train set, blocks and a coloring station, as well as two private change rooms which I know are fully equipped with adult-sized changing tables and toilets that look like oversized training potties, along with all the supplies you could possibly need for changing time. One of the doors is currently closed, which means it's in use, but the other door is open.

It's not the largest or most opulent age play room I've heard of, but it's the best I've found in the local area, and it still gets its fair share of use from Littles and Pups alike. It's a welcoming space to come and hang out with like-minded people, and I smile and nod at a few familiar faces as I step further into the room and survey tonight's gathering.

"Hi Gabe," Taylor, a Little I've played with on and off, waves at me from where he's pushing a car down a plastic track. He has a pacifier clipped to his coveralls, and he looks particularly adorable with his curls all messed up tonight.

I wave back and head towards him, greeting, "Hey, Tay-Tay, having fun tonight?"

Smiling and nodding, he sends the car hurtling down the track and makes a 'vroom vroom' sound as he watches it go. "Yep," he answers cheerily. "I'm playin' with a new Daddy."

I'm not surprised. Taylor, who is in his thirties and is a lawyer by day, is a catch. I look around, wondering which Daddy has the honor of playing with him tonight, just as a sinfully attractive older man steps forward with a sippy cup outstretched. He hands it to Taylor and then turns his attention to me.

I smile warmly at the new Daddy and his salt and pepper beard moves with his returning grin. We exchange short, but friendly 'hey's in greeting, but I can tell I'd be outstaying my welcome if I hung around with them for too long, so I continue my slow exploration of the space.

It seems like mostly couples tonight, and while I wouldn't be opposed to joining as a couple's third, I really just want to be someone's sole focus for a couple of hours and have them be mine.

Sadly, it's a quiet night and it seems as if my plan may not pan out, so I decide to head back down to the main club space and see if maybe anyone dancing down there might be interested in playing with me tonight.

I'm three songs in when a familiar face catches my attention under the flash of a strobe light, and my heart skips a beat.

No way.

What are the chances?

With my hips moving to the beat of the current song and excitement simmering under my skin, I move in on my prey.

His back is turned as I slide up behind him, and I enjoy how much taller I am. I'm six foot one, and he can barely be five eight, if I had to guess, and I love that I can lean down and murmur in his ear, "Hello, stranger."

Justin just about leaps out of his skin. He spins to face me, his hand at his throat, and I almost feel guilty for startling him, but then he starts to laugh. "Wow," he says, "this is a coincidence."

I'll say.

I thought he was vanilla.

I look him over, enjoying the way his jeans are practically molded to his legs and perfect bubble butt, and I smile a little at the faded green t-shirt with a vintage Batman motif. "Do you know where you are right now?" I find myself asking him.

His cheeks color. It's visible even in the near-darkness of the dance space. But he raises his chin defiantly. "I'm not straight," he declares. "I'm bi. So, yes, I know I'm in a gay club."

Given the number of same-sex couples writhing around us, he could be forgiven for the assumption. But he's wrong.

"Kik isn't a gay club, sweetheart," I tell him, stepping into his personal bubble with renewed confidence now that I know I've got an actual chance with him after all. "Though it is obviously one of the more popular LGBTQ+ hangouts." I gesture around us with a wave of my hand. "But take a closer look."

Most of the couples here start on the dancefloor and then move to the rooms upstairs, and many are dressed for their kinks of choice. There's a bevy of skin on display, plus leather and chains and various masks. Then there are the few Littles, a couple in onesies, one Girl even wearing a cute bonnet and frilly knee socks as she dances with a Mommy in a power suit.

My lips curl in appreciation before I turn back to Justin. "What do you see?"

He takes a step even closer to me, pressing his chest against mine as if seeking the comfort of someone he knows. "I...I don't..."

"It's a kink club," I lean down to tell him, then pull back, adding, "BDSM of all kinds."

His eyes are wide and he swallows. "Oh." Taking another look around, I watch as his gaze settles on a couple of Littles grinding up against each other, their butts rounded by the obvious padding of diapers beneath the rompers they're wearing. He bites his lip and his throat works again. "*Oh.*" After another beat spent watching the Littles, he looks back at me. "That...that's a real thing? Not BDSM, but...the...the..."

"Age play?" I suggest, and he nods.

"Yeah, that. It's...I mean, I thought that was just a porn thing. Not something people do in real life."

"Oh, I assure you, plenty of people enjoy it in real life."

I watch as the realization that I'm in this club and I'm comfortable here hits him. His mouth forms an adorable 'o' of surprise. "D-do you..." He stops and blinks, then shakes his head. "Wait. That's rude. I can't just ask you that."

He's too cute.

"You can ask me anything you want, Justin," I tell him, pushing just a little bit of my Daddy tone into my words.

He sucks in a breath, his gaze flitting around again before landing back on me. "Which kinks are you here for?"

Taking a step out of his personal space, I extend my hand. "Can I show you?"

After a moment of hesitation, Justin places his palm in mine. I lead him out of the main club space and towards the stairs.

"Are we allowed up there?" The worry in his voice is so sweet. I imagine he'd struggle to be a brat. He'd want to be someone's good boy. He'd want praise, not punishment.

Pausing to adjust myself, because those thoughts are taking me down a dangerous path, I nod. "We are. I'll show you the two other club rooms, okay? And, before you worry, the first one is not the one where I usually play."

I've been known to pick up a paddle or use a spanking bench a time or two, but I prefer caretaking more than Domming. I'll happily explain that to him if he asks.

I hope he asks.

Sure enough, when I show him into the first room, he squeezes my hand and tucks himself into my side, shyly peeking around me to catch a glimpse of one of the Doms lashing a sub on the farthest St Andrew's cross. "You said you don't usually play in this room?"

"No. I don't mind indulging in some basic impact play and sometimes restraints, but...I don't love inflicting pain."

Justin heaves a sigh of relief. "Good." Then he catches himself as I start leading him up the next set of stairs and he hurriedly adds, "Not that there's anything wrong with enjoying that. As long as you're safe. But I don't like pain." Then he groans. "Shit. That makes it sound like I want to do things with you." I pause to look over my shoulder, raising an eyebrow at him. His face is bright pink. "Not that I *don't* want to—I should just shut up."

Fuck, he could be perfect.

Showing him Little Heaven will be the true test on that, though.

When we get to the door at the top of the stairs, I open it and step through first. The room is busier than when I left it, with a cacophony of laughter coming from various spots inside. There's a group of Littles building a giant structure out of blocks at the far end of the room, and it's teetering with every new block they add. They squeal and laugh as they push the limits, and it's really cute to see.

Closer to the doorway, some Middles are playing Mario Kart on the TVs mounted on the wall, and it sounds like they might be betting on who is going to win. In the middle of the room, a Pup in a leather hooded mask is having his belly rubbed by one very cute bear of a Daddy.

I relax as I take it all in. This is my happy space.

"*Whoa*," Justin murmurs beside me. He's still clutching my hand, but he curls his free hand around the inside of my bicep. "Is...is this your kink?"

I grin down at him and nod. "Yeah, it is."

"Are...are you...Little?"

My answering guffaw makes him jump and I immediately draw him in for a placating hug. "Sorry," I apologize, "but...no. I'm the opposite of Little. I'm a Daddy."

Drawing back, he looks at me incredulously. "But you're so young."

"Daddy is a mindset, not an age," I repeat the mantra I've been living by since I realized how into the kink I am. "Just like you can be a Boy, or a Little, at any age, too."

"Gabe!" Taylor comes bounding over to me, and his Daddy trails after him. "You're back!"

"I just went downstairs for a bit, Tay-Tay. And, oh, meet my friend, Justin. Justin, this is my friend, Taylor."

Justin blushes and tucks himself behind me, once again peeking out from behind my arm. While he might not know anything about regression play, I am growing more certain by the minute that he would be a perfect Little.

"Don't be shy, Jussy," Taylor says, then moves to my side to help pry Justin forward. "This is a fun, friendly place. Oh! Come meet my new Daddy! His name is Edward, and he plays with toys *all day*."

"Justin might need a moment to get used to all the noise and stuff, bunny," Edward says, and shoots me an apologetic glance as he tries to draw Taylor back to his side. "And I don't play with toys all day. I'm the head of marketing for Rombold's Toy Manufacturing."

Taylor rolls his eyes. "Same thing."

"It's really not."

I snort. Now I remember why playing with Taylor was only ever a casual thing. He's a bit too bratty and high energy for me. If I find myself a forever Boy, he'll be snuggly and sweet. Maybe a bit shy. Someone who is happy to let go and hand over the reins when life gets too much for him. Not someone who will brat and sass at me at every turn.

Good luck with that one, Eddie.

"Do you want to sit on the couch over here with me and watch for a little while?" I ask Justin, ignoring the argument Taylor is starting with his Daddy. "I'm sure you have questions, and I'm happy to answer them."

"Then maybe you can come play with me after," Taylor cuts back in.

"Maybe," I respond on Justin's behalf, then lead him over to the couch set against the far wall anyway. "This is a lot to take in, I know."

We sit in silence for a few extended moments as Justin surveys the room again. "I, uh, I guess I can see the appeal in...regressing? Is that what it's called?" His eyes are glued to where one of the Littles is sitting in his Daddy's lap on an oversized armchair, his thumb in his mouth and fingers curled over the tip of his nose, and his Daddy is reading to him as they rock gently in the chair. It's a sight I also find extremely appealing. Sweet and tender. Justin turns his head my way. "But what do you get out of being a...a Daddy?"

"Joy," I blurt without even having to think about it. "Satisfaction at making my partner —or scene partner— happy and relaxed. It's not always about sex or even being overly kinky. It's...well, I like taking care of people. It makes me happy to watch my Boys relax and let go of their stress and adult worries." He nods, and I can't help adding, "But I do like being called Daddy, too. That part *is* about the kink for me. It revs my engine."

Justin bobs his head and mouths the word 'Daddy' to himself. His cheeks go pink, and he looks at his lap, where he's fidgeting with his hands. "Do you have a preference for, um, how little your...your Boys get? Because, like, those guys" —he points to the Middles playing video games— "aren't anywhere near as regressed as that one." Justin gestures to the sleepy Boy in his Daddy's lap. He can't seem to tear his gaze away from the couple.

"Nope, no preference," I answer softly. "Every Boy is unique and brings something different to Daddy/Boy interactions. I'm just as cool with changing wet diapers as I am with helping build a model car. Whatever the Boy I'm with needs, I get pleasure out of being able to look after them and provide it."

He's silent for another long moment, still watching the couple on the big, comfy, rocking armchair. "This...wasn't what I expected when I walked into the club tonight," he admits. "I was looking to get laid, maybe, but..."

Something inside me deflates a little. I knew I was reading too much into his behavior. I knew I was getting my hopes too high. I knew—

"Would it be weird if I tried it?" His quiet question makes my heart flip.

Remaining calm, I ask, "What do you want to try?"

"I..." Justin's cheeks go even more pink than before. "I think...maybe...maybe I'd like to try coloring?"

A wide grin tugs at my lips. "Sweetheart," I start, allowing the thrum of anticipation to wash over me, "you can try whatever you want."

Chapter Five

Justin

SITTING AT THE COLORING table is... different.

After a few minutes and Gabe prodding me to choose the colors I want, I find myself relaxing into the rhythmic movement of my hand. I haven't colored in a long time, not even with Owen. He's more into playing with cars and trucks. I don't know if this is what the regression side of it is supposed to feel like or not. I glance up at Gabe every now and then. He's always smiling and when I do lock eyes with him, his hand travels to my back and rubs up and down. It's comforting.

Taylor, the one I met when Gabe and I walked in, walks up slowly with his hand in his Daddy's and asks if they can join. Taylor is... adorable. He's wearing coveralls and has a paci clipped to his clothes. His hair is a mess of curls, reminding me a bit of Owen when he first wakes up in the morning. The thought of my own kid makes me sigh and I look back down at my lap. I'm definitely not dressed for this room. Gabe's finger is under my chin, and he tilts my head until I'm looking right at him. "Justin, don't be rude, please. Is it okay if Tay-Tay sits with us?"

"Sorry." The word is out of my mouth immediately and although his words were completely calm and he's smiling, I don't like the feeling of doing something wrong or rude. I'd rather be praised next time. That is, if this is something I do again after tonight. I don't know how I feel about it. I turn to Taylor and his Daddy. "Yes, you can sit with us."

He plops down without hesitation and the older man joins him, sitting between Taylor and Gabe. If I didn't understand the dynamic already, that they are both Daddies, I'd be jealous of how good they look next to each other. I study the way Taylor and his Daddy interact for a long minute. Edward, as he introduces himself, gives Taylor three choices in the coloring pages and then helps pick out the crayons he wants to use. I avert my gaze to Gabe when the two of them share a quick peck of lips.

I can see Gabe studying me. I know the look. Usually, I enjoy that look from other men because it means I have a chance of getting laid, but his eyes hold an extra depth to them. "Sweetheart? Are you okay?"

Sweetheart.

My dick jumps at the sound of it. It's such an innocent name and I can't deny that I love it. I lean into the side of his body, unable to express the swirling thoughts in my mind. Am I okay? I'm enjoying myself, certainly, but this is all so... different. I have a kid; I can't be into this kind of thing, can I? His hand glides into my hair and scratches at my scalp. It sends a shiver through my body but I don't pull back.

"It's just a lot," I mumble against his chest.

"Did I make him sad?" I hear Taylor's voice and finally look up. He's looking between Edward and Gabe. His eyes are wide, and I watch him reach for the paci.

"No." I say the word before either of the two can answer. "I'm just...really new to this. Like tonight is my first night ever experiencing being, um, Little."

43

Taylor's eyes light up and he smiles at me. "Playing here is so much fun," he says. "It's safe and warm."

"And most importantly," Edward adds. He looks from Taylor to me. He's very attractive, with his beard and soft eyes. He has to be in his late forties or close to it, but he doesn't have the typical dad bod. He has muscles and is showcasing them in the tight shirt across his chest. "It's a place with no judgement. You can explore and see what you do and don't like. There is nothing wrong with anything that feels right to you and your partner."

"This is a lot to take in," Gabe whispers in my ear, "but you're doing great, sweetheart. We can stop whenever you want, or we can try another spot in the room. Tonight is all for you to explore."

I look up at him once again. His eyes are a beautiful brown, and his hair is pulled back in a bun. Parts of it are sticking out and I want to reach up to tuck them behind his ears. I'm so used to doing that to Owen. Instead, I turn to look around at the rest of the room.

The room seems popular, with more bodies than I can count from my spot. There's a dress-up station, the video games, and the oversized rocking chair which is now empty. I briefly wonder where the couple went since the last time I looked, the Little was practically asleep in his Daddy's lap. It reminds me of the rocking chair I used to have and the thought of the gentle movements lulling me to sleep is appealing.

"Justin, would you like to try something else?" Gabe's voice brings me back to the spot we're sitting. I see his eyes glance toward the rocking chair and small bookshelf. "We can go read some books."

"I... Can we? I think I'd like to try that." It's a new thing, but out of everything else in Little Heaven, it doesn't require me to interact with other Littles or Middles. The longer I'm in here, observing and listening to the conversations and giggles, the terms come easier to me.

Gabe stands and holds out his hand to help me up. He turns back to Taylor and Edward. "We'll see you both around, I'm sure. Have fun with the little stinker."

Taylor pokes his tongue out at Gabe and I hide a smile. He is adorable. I don't know if I would look that cute. Gabe waits a few steps to talk lowly to me, "Are you okay with all of this? If you want to go, we can go back to the dancefloor or even leave. I know this can be a lot at once."

"I'm okay," I squeeze his hand, realizing neither of us dropped them once I stood. "I feel a little overdressed though."

Gabe's hand lets go of mine and slides across the top of my butt. "I quite like the jeans you're wearing, Justin."

I nibble at my bottom lip the rest of the way across the room to the chairs and book corner. There's only one other couple in this area. The others seem to be playing in groups. I recognize the couple as the Mommy wearing the suit and the girl with the bonnet from earlier on the dancefloor. Gabe gives them a nod before directing me to pick out a book. I watch him sit in one of the chairs. They're clearly fitted for two grown adults to sit on. Gabe taps his thigh, a signal he's waiting for me.

I glance over the books. They're basic kid's books and some I even have at home. I pick one at random, something about a dinosaur looking for new friends. It seems fitting, actually. Gabe holds out his hand for the book and then opens his arms for me to sit on his lap. I hesitate for a moment but he's patient. It's strange sitting on a younger man's lap and I adjust my bottom a bit before I'm mostly comfortable. My jeans aren't meant for cuddling like this and they dig a little bit into my lower stomach. I shift once more and hear Gabe let out a low noise.

"Sweetheart, I'm going to need you to stop squirming in my lap or I'm going to have a mess to clean up." His tone tells me what his words don't.

"Oh, sorry. It's just... My jeans aren't very comfortable in this position."

"Do you want to get up?" His hand is back to brushing up and down my back. It's been a while since I was with anyone, even longer since someone held me like this. I don't want to leave just yet and shake my head in response. Gabe seems to be thinking for a solution. "Would it help if you unbuttoned your jeans? The rules over on the wall say no silly business in the main room, but that should be okay."

"Silly business?" I tilt my head in question.

He smiles and sets the book down on my lap. It's perfectly balanced over where my shirt meets my jeans and I feel his hand snake underneath. Within a second, the button on my jeans is popped open and he's bringing his hand back to rest on the book. It's an immediate relief and I relax that much more. "Thank you. That really helped. Also, how did you get so good at that?"

"Lots of practice," Gabe says with a playful wink.

I feel a giggle bubbling up from my chest, but I tamp it down.

Not right now.

"Let's read, shall we?"

I nod and settle my head against Gabe's chest. I hear a mix of his words and his heartbeat and before I know it, my eyes are getting heavy.

When I open them next, the book is gone and I'm moving back and forth. I'm still pressed against Gabe's body, being held by one arm while the other is stroking up and down my outer thigh. I sit up in Gabe's lap and open my mouth to apologize but he beats me to it.

"You were out pretty quick," he says with a soft smile. His hand rubs up and down my arm soothingly before moving to cup my face. His six-foot-one frame doesn't compare to my five-foot-seven, but sitting in his lap, I meet his eyes evenly. I noticed the size difference yesterday, of course, and felt small, but now it's just comforting.

"I'm sorry," I apologize quickly. "I guess I was a little more tired than I thought. You make a great pillow."

Gabe smiles and this time we both share a quiet laugh. "I don't mind it, sweetheart. You weren't out but for a couple of minutes anyway. Is there anything else you want to do tonight?"

I shift to look at the rest of the room. When I do, I can feel the bulge in his pants. I pause and his hands go to my waist.

"I'm sor-"

"Don't apologize." His hands move to button up my jeans before he motions for me to stand. I watch Gabe subtly adjust himself and I'm aware of my own dick twitching. I also need to use the bathroom.

"Um, is there a bathroom in here?" I look around and the only doors I see are the main door and then the two that Gabe said were the changing rooms.

"The changing rooms have them," Gabe says. "But the toilets are essentially built like oversized potty training toilets. There are the main bathrooms in the—"

"No, that will be fine." I widen my eyes as another warning from my bladder hits me. Gabe seems to get the memo and we walk across the room. A few of the Mommies and Daddies wave at him or say hello, but he doesn't stop.

"Do you need me to come in with you or...?" He leaves the question hanging and I debate it for just a second. No one is paying us any attention and I nod. I don't need him to help me with using the bathroom, but I do like that we can close the door and have some privacy to talk.

The changing room is...something. There's an outfitted changing table that could hold me or any other adult. Baskets sit underneath the table. I know from experience that there are most likely wipes, creams, and possibly even diapers in them. The toilet is exactly what Gabe said. It's an actual toilet, but there is a plastic contraption built around it that makes it resemble a blue training potty. I note the stepping stool off to the side as well. I pull my jeans and briefs down to mid-thigh, knowing that I'm exposing my ass to Gabe right now, but I don't care. The relief when I'm finally able to stop holding back has me letting out a small moan and I drop my head back.

"Shit, Justin." I look over my shoulder and see Gabe palming himself through his pants. "Do you have any idea how hot you are?"

I shake my dick a few times but don't bother pulling up my pants. The cool air brushes over my bare ass as I waddle back toward him. I did come here to get laid tonight. While we might have taken a detour, there's nothing stopping us from getting each other off.

I can't read Gabe's expression when I step closer to him, invading his personal space. I take one of his hands and wrap it around me to land on my ass cheek. His fingers immediately start kneading my flesh and my dick perks right up. I look down briefly and then back up into Gabe's eyes. He's almost a whole head taller than me standing up and looks every bit a Daddy with his long hair, big muscles, and blazing eyes.

"I'm so horny, Daddy."

The word slips out as naturally as I hope. I'm fully in my usual headspace right now, but I can't deny that even letting go the little bit I did was enough to affect me physically. It doesn't hurt that I find Gabe ridiculously sexy. His eyes widen at the word, but then his other hand cups my ass as well before he pulls me flush against him. He's a good six inches taller than me, so I tilt my head up to look at him. His smile is wide, and I return it easily.

"Daddy, huh?" His voice is deep. It sends goosebumps over my whole body. "Did you like your first experience?"

Gabe moves one hand and caresses his finger along my bare hip. I close my eyes briefly. "I did."

"You were a good boy out there." Gabe's voice is a whisper, but the words have me biting my bottom lip to keep from making an embarrassing noise.

Good boy.

"But good boys wash their hands after using the bathroom." Gabe's hands disappear from my body, and I catch myself about to sulk. He steps away and I half-waddle over to the sink and wash my hands. I decide to just let my jeans and underwear fall before I walk back to him, grinning and holding my hands up.

"The best boy," Gabe says and pulls me flush against him once more. My dick presses against his inner thigh.

"Fuck," I whisper at the contact.

"Ah, ah." Gabe dips his head and nips lightly at my neck. "I don't like my boys to curse when they're Little. Such a pretty mouth shouldn't be saying dirty words, should it?"

Gabe pulls back and the spot he nipped and licked is cool when the air hits it. I'm on pins and needles right now. My dick is pressed firmly against his thigh. There's no way he doesn't feel it. I might be super new to the age play scene, but I've had sex with men before and I'm so close to blowing my load handsfree.

"I'm sorry." I look up at Gabe through my lashes and use the most innocent voice I can muster. "I'll be good for you."

Gabe grunts and spins us so I'm pinned between him and the closest wall. I let my head rest against the wall and arch my back to rub against him. His hands land on my hips and I try to get his jeans undone to do the same, but he's kissing me now and I'm losing my focus. And my breath.

After a few seconds, his hands knock mine away and soon we're rutting against each other, pants and briefs long gone. It's quick and hot but there's something else about it. Another layer that is making my dick leak pre-cum like crazy.

I let out a long moan when Gabe's hand wraps around my shaft. His thumb glides over my leaking slit, using it to make his glide easier. I'm panting hard, but he seals our lips together once again. Moving my hand to wrap around his cock, I note that he's larger than my five inches. I glide my fingers up the underside of his length, exploring blindly as Gabe continues to jerk me quickly. With the way I'm angled, my thighs are trembling.

His cock must be at least seven, maybe eight inches fully hard. He's not the thickest I've ever been with, but with his length, I know he would stretch my hole so good.

"Come for me, sweetheart." Gabe's words whispered hotly in my ear mixed with the visual of being fucked has me shooting my load over his hand. Some of it lands on my stomach. I'm shaking through it, pleasure coursing through my whole body until I'm dropping down to my knees and looking up at him. I waste no time sucking the head of his cock into my mouth.

It's been a while since I've given head, and I make sure to not rush in my eagerness to get him off.

"Oh, shi— Justin. Sweetheart, your mouth is so good." Hollowing my cheeks, I suck hard, swirling my tongue. I reach up and grip his balls lightly, teasing, tugging just slightly. "I'm coming, Justin. Shit. I'm coming."

His orgasm fills my mouth. I do my best to swallow it all, but I can feel a couple drops drip from the corner of my lips. I wait for him to pull back. We gather our clothes and adjust them rightly.

"So..." I say, unsure of how to proceed.

His clean hand moves to cup the side of my face and I lean into it. He gives me a small smile and kisses the tip of my nose. "You are incredible. Do you want to go get something to eat and talk?"

Chapter Six

GLIDING ACROSS THE RINK, I relish the familiar, rhythmic *snick* of ice beneath my skates and the cold air on my face. The arena is empty, and I love mornings like this. It's early, but that's exactly why I'm here. The silence calms me. Being alone allows me to focus on my movements and nothing else. Every stride, every turn, and every pivot are reminders of why I love skating. Of why I play hockey.

I've been on this ice countless times but today feels different. There's a mix of excitement and nervousness coursing through me as the new season approaches. It's my senior year, and my mind whirs with anticipation and even a touch of mild dread for the year ahead, and for the uncertainty of what comes *after*.

Once I've skated a few laps, I grab my stick and my puck. Swinging my stick back, I connect with the little rubber disc and send it flying towards the goal. Unfortunately, the sharp clink of the puck rebounding off the post echoes around the empty arena.

The sound frustrates me. Retrieving the puck, I line up another shot, determined to perfect my accuracy. I mean, I'm alone on the ice. There's no goalie, no opposing team bearing down on me, no audience at all. Missing the net seems nearly impossible, and yet I managed to do it.

Get your head in the game, Nagy.

It feels like my entire future is riding on the success of this year. No pressure or anything.

Lost in my thoughts, I almost don't hear the voice calling out to me. "Gabe! What are you doing out here?" Turning, I see Coach Overton standing at the edge of the rink, his hands on his hips and a curious look on his face.

Dan Overton is a former NHL player. He's only in his early forties, but his pro career was cut short by an injury. Even though he'd probably earned enough to retire and live comfortably ever after, he didn't want to leave his beloved sport entirely, and when he found out the NCAA and Claremont College were working together to bring Phoenix back into the college hockey circuit, he threw his hat in the ring to coach.

He's been the coach of our team since its inception. Sometimes, I'm convinced that he loves our team more than he loves his own kids.

I'll admit that I startled a little at the sound of his voice. College doesn't start up for another week, and I was pretty sure the building would be empty when I let myself in this morning. I should have realized Coach would be in his office. He's *always* in his office. I'm convinced he's got a bed hidden in there somewhere.

"Just sneaking in some extra practice, Coach," I reply, skating over to him. "Making sure I'm ready for the season."

It's not like I can tell him that I've had extra energy thrumming through my veins since I hooked up in a kink club bathroom a few days ago. The only thing known to calm me down when I get like this is skating.

Well, skating and sex.

But, seeing as I haven't heard from Justin since I left him to process everything we'd done and spoken about, sex is off the table right now. At least until I know where I stand with him.

Coach nods, a small smile playing on his lips. "I admire your dedication, Gabe. But don't forget to rest. You'll need your energy when the season starts."

I appreciate his concern. "I know, Coach. But this is my senior year. There are no second chances anymore."

The words feel forced as they leave my lips. Unlike most of my team, I'm not sure that I want to play hockey professionally. I'm not entirely sure that I don't either, but the more I think about it, the more confused I feel.

He claps a hand on my shoulder. "That's the spirit, but try to keep some balance in your life, too. You're still young: you won't get your college years back." There's a surprising hint of melancholy in his tone before he gives his head a shake and then smiles. "Anyway, how about you finish up here and come to my office after you've showered and changed? I'd like to discuss something with you while I've got you here."

I nod. "Sure thing, Coach. Be right there." As I skate back to center ice for one last lap, I let my gaze wander around the entire arena. It's eerie seeing it so quiet, so devoid of life.

My family often joke that people only attend the games because they want an excuse to avoid the Arizona heat. But over the past few years, our team has slowly grown a following. Serious fans who want to see us succeed, and who let us (or, rather, our social media accounts) know when we've disappointed them.

Even though I'm not sure about my future after I finish college this year, I do enjoy being a part of this circus. I get swept up in the excitement, my heart pumping with the cheers of our fans even when I'm on the bench, waiting to jump the boards and do my best to make them proud. The adrenaline of it all is addictive.

After taking my lap, I retrieve my puck and head back to the locker room for a quick shower. Then, with my hair still damp, I make my way to Coach's office. His door is wide open, but I still tap my knuckles on the doorframe and wait for his permission to enter.

He grins at me and gestures to the seats in front of his big, cluttered desk. "Take a seat, Gabe."

Doing as he asks, I watch as he steeples his fingers and then regards me in silence for a moment before he says, "I know you're not captain, but I'm counting on you to take the freshmen under your wing this year," he follows this up by shooting me a smile that almost feels knowing. "I've watched you with the new players over the past couple of years. You're good with 'em. You've got a real...*nurturing* kind of vibe."

His Texan drawl is kind of hot and, not for the first time, I wonder how a southern boy like him ended up being a pro-hockey player. Texas seems about as far removed from icy sports as Arizona. Then I blink rapidly to focus on the conversation at hand, because thinking of my coach as anything other than just Coach seems kind of weird and inappropriate.

I blame Justin for the desperate buzz beneath my skin. It's really all his fault. Justin, with his sweet smile and his 'help me' eyes. Justin, with his earnest interest in dipping his toe into age play at Club Kik. Justin with his hand —and then his mouth on my dick.

Gah! Do not *get hard in Coach's office, you moron.*

Clearing my throat, I focus on replying, "You're not the first to accuse me of that," I joke. "I guess it comes from being a middle child in a big family."

"Well, it's a great quality to have. Makes you a natural team player if you're lookin' out for others as well as yourself." He tilts his head to the side and scratches fingers through stubble that seems to be turning a little salt-and-peppery, even if the hair on his head is still dark as night. "Using the same logic, you'd make a good coach or assistant coach, too. Even for a junior league. Weren't you studying medicine or somethin'?"

"Sports medicine," I acknowledge with a nod of my head. "Yeah."

He whistles, low and impressed. "Brains and brawn. But, more than that, it's the kind of degree which ought to set you up in a career in hockey even if you don't get drafted. But I think you've got as much a chance of that as Burns or Weston."

I blink at him. "Really?" It's no secret that Vincent Burns and Zach Weston are our best players and the two most determined to make it to the NHL. Zach's even our captain this year.

Coach hums. "Really. But now's the time to start thinkin' about where you see yourself ending up if the NHL doesn't come a-calling. It seems to me that you might enjoy working on the sidelines anyway." He cocks his head. "Did you want me to see if our med team would mind talking to you about your options with your degree? They might even have some ideas about puttin' you to work behind the scenes."

It's not a bad idea, and I am not dumb enough to turn down any offers from Coach, so I readily agree. "I'd like that," I answer. "It might even help earn me some extra credit for some of my classes." Even if it doesn't, any kind of practical experience is better than none, especially when my future is so up in the air.

"You're mature for your age," Coach grins. "It's not a bad quality, either...which takes me back to why I asked you in here. You okay with helping the newbies get settled?"

It speaks to my Daddy traits, so I bob my head enthusiastically. "Of course. Not that the rest of the team doesn't do what they can to help the freshmen settle in."

"I know, but there are a couple of you who go above and beyond. I'll be honest, it's gonna be quite the loss for these guys when you've graduated. On and off the ice."

It's nice to be appreciated, and I tell him so as I push to my feet, feeling the natural end of the conversation drawing near. I shake his hand and add that I'll see him for our first team meeting, before I grab my duffel and make my way through the halls and to the exit of the arena.

***

Me

> Hey, just checking in, wondering how you're doing.

The second I send the text, I want to take it back. *Unsend*, I think frantically at my phone, even as the little 'read' text pops up underneath the blue box, *Unsend!*

The bubbling ellipsis appears on the left of my screen, then stops. Then start again. Then stops.

Finally, a reply comes through.

Justin

> I'm good, thanks. I think we've finally unpacked the last of the boxes.

More ellipsis bubbles appear, then three more messages follow in rapid succession.

Justin

> Thank you for the other night, too. I've been thinking about it.

> A lot.

> And I know you answered a lot of my questions after we played at the club, but I have more.

My heart thumps in my chest and I start to compose a reply telling him that I'd be happy to answer any questions he has, when another message appears.

Justin

> I swear I haven't been ghosting you. I've mostly just been thinking.

"Aww," I murmur out loud, smiling to myself as I delete my message draft and start again.

Me

> I completely understand. You left your comfort zone and tried something new and kinky when you weren't expecting to. Whether you liked it or not, it can take a while to process those feelings. But I am happy to answer any new questions you have, too.

I sprawl out on the couch in the apartment I share with Izzy on campus. He's out with some of his football buddies, so I have the place to myself. It means I can relax and focus on this conversation, which suddenly has my complete attention. Even more so when he texts again.

Justin

Can I call you?

I can't reply fast enough.

Me

Yes, of course.

I stare at my phone after the message sends, willing him to read it and act on the invitation. Then I curse myself because *I'm* the Daddy here. I should be taking the indecision out of his hands, whether he's a Little or not.

So, not overthinking it, I bring up his contact page on my phone screen and press the green handset icon.

"Gabe, hi," he answers after three rings, sounding a little breathless. Even though it's not a sex sound, it makes my cock twitch with sudden interest. "Sorry, I...I was going to call, but I..."

"Got nervous?"

"Yeah," Justin sighs. "Sorry. I'm just...well, this is all new to me."

"Just the kink?" I ask him, careful to keep my tone neutral. "Or having a guy express interest in more than just hook-ups?"

After our impromptu scenes in the club, and the resulting orgasms, I took him to the old twenty-four seven diner in town. There, we had coffees (or, rather, he had a hot chocolate and I had a coffee), and he peppered me with questions about the age play, my rules for my Littles, how I had gotten into it, and how long I had been a Daddy.

I'd answered everything honestly, and then I had asked him to think about whether he had enjoyed his Little time while also gently asserting that I'd be interested in more —in taking him out on dates— whether he wanted to continue exploring the kink or not.

He'd asked for time to think it all over, and I'd agreed to let him. Until today, apparently, because after not hearing from him in almost a week, I couldn't take it any longer. I sent that first message because I just needed to know he was okay, but now my Daddy instincts are telling me that I need to be a little more assertive with him if there's any hope of us becoming more than just friends or a one-time hook-up.

"...All of it," he answers quietly. Then he clears his throat. "I mean, I've known I was bi since I was in my teens, and I'm not...I mean, I have experience with guys. But, yeah, that's all been very...casual. Grindr and club stuff."

I nod even though he can't see me. I'd assumed as much. "And there's nothing wrong with that," I assure him. "If you'd prefer that—"

"No!" His interruption is loud and vehement. I smile and imagine him blushing as he stammers a much quieter, "N-no. I think I want..."

Oh, God, I wish he would finish his sentence.

"You think you want...?"

"More." Justin's confession is soft and sounds vulnerable. "I...I really liked what we did the other night. Not just jerking off and blow jobs...but...I liked being held. Feeling cared for. Being able to just relax completely without having to be the person in charge. And, um, when you said you'd like to...to maybe date me...well, I really like the thought of that, too."

I pump my fist into the air and barely refrain from crowing in delight. The smile on my face grows wider, stretching my cheeks until they ache. "Yeah? Can I take you out tonight?"

"Oh," the regret in that single word, has my smile slipping, "I'm sorry, but I have Owen and no sitter. I—"

"What if I come to your place? I can cook for you both, and after we —*you*— put him to bed, you and I can hang out." I wince over my slip up, and I hope he doesn't think I'm moving too fast or insinuating myself where I don't belong. I'm just really good with kids, and I've got night time routines down pat.

Plus, I feel like, since his ex died, he hasn't had much of a support system when it comes to his kid, and being a single dad at his age —close to my age— can't be easy. In fact, I assume that's why he's moved all this way, so Owen's maternal grandparents can help out and spend more time with their grandson. Even so, I like the idea of helping him myself. It ticks all of my boxes and then some.

"I don't think I'll be comfortable, y'know..."

"Oh, sweetheart, I'm not inviting myself over for sex."

His laughter bubbles over the phone line. "Good to know," he tells me, then says, "but I meant the...*Little* stuff." The last two words are whispered. Before I can react, he rushes to explain, "It's not that I don't want to explore more, because I do, but...not with Owen around, you know?"

"Hey, that's totally fair," I assure him. "To be honest, I've never dated a Little with a kid before. Not that they don't exist. I'm sure they do. But—"

"Most guys in our age bracket don't have kids," he finishes easily. "Or, if they do, they're usually in relationships. I mean, I would probably still be with Lauren, so..." Justin trails off, then snorts. "Shit, sorry. It's probably not great dating etiquette to mention my ex-girlfriend, right?"

"She's your son's mother and she passed away. I totally get you talking about her." My grin sneaks back onto my face again. "So...dating etiquette, huh? Does this mean we're dating? Like...officially?"

"Well, you haven't actually given me a proper date yet," he teases, pausing for only a moment before adding, "Daddy."

I groan, my dick even more interested now. "Sweetheart, that's cruel."

He laughs and I want to record the sound and set it as the alert tone for his messages...and *wow*, that escalated fast. I need to reel myself in a bit before I scare him off with my creepy stalker vibes.

Then Justin asks "So...what are you making us for dinner tonight?" and my plan to maintain my chill flies right out the window.

"Do you and Owen like spaghetti and meatballs?"

Chapter Seven

Justin

I DON'T KNOW HOW to react to how easily Gabe fits into our new lives.

Owen gives him a whole ten seconds to say hi and hand over the ingredients for dinner before taking his hand and pulling him to show off his room. Owen is talking plenty loud enough and Gabe answers with the same enthusiasm that I don't bother following. I smile when I hear Gabe asking specific questions about some of the toys. He really is good with kids. I can see the whole Daddy thing and how it works for him.

Thoughts flash through my mind of our time at the club last week. I'm no stranger to a hook up, but what we did was something completely different. It felt different. Still feels different. Finding someone I'm attracted to is the last thing on my to-do list.

Actually, it wasn't even on the list.

After unpacking, the whole list went as follows: make sure my paperwork for work is in order, get Owen signed up for kindergarten and ready for the orientation next week. That's it. That's the list. And it's a lot.

Also, I am not ready for Owen to start school; he's growing up too fast.

"What do you think you're doing?" Gabe's voice pulls me out of my thoughts and I look up. I know I look like a deer stuck in headlights. Gabe's smile is slightly lopsided, and I drop the noodles into the water.

"Cooking?" I say the word slowly and raise the end of it like a question. "Was I not supposed to? You handed me the bag, so I just assumed."

"I handed you the bag because Owen was pulling me away." Gabe crosses the open space and stands inches away from me. A warm hand encases my hip. My glance shoots towards the living room and hallway, confirming that Owen isn't in sight. "I didn't come over here for you to cook, sweetheart. I'm doing all the heavy lifting tonight." His fingers trail slowly up under the hem of my shirt. It's a small touch but shivers rush through my body. "Why don't you get out of these jeans and find a movie for all of us to watch?"

"Okay." My voice is barely above a whisper, but my dick is definitely making some noise. Well, if dicks made noise.

Gabe's hand drops and he winks at me before turning toward the stove and hip checking me to move out of the way.

I walk past my bedroom door and peek into Owen's room. His head is hidden in a shirt and I'm pretty sure his pajama pants are on backward. The sight is adorable. I lean against the doorframe with my arms crossed and watch the struggle to get his head through the correct hole. He gives me a bright smile when he sees me.

"Gabe said we're going to have spaghetti with balls tonight!" Owen says excitedly. I feel my cheeks immediately redden with embarrassment.

I hear Gabe cough in the kitchen and lean back to look at him across the house. I love that it's a clear line of sight from one end to the other. His expression is one of holding back laughter. I turn back to my son.

"It's called spaghetti and *meat*balls," I correct Owen.

His little head bobs, but he ploughs on with the conversation. "Gabe says we're going to watch a movie too. Is he staying with us?"

I brush away the mental image of the three of us living together. It is much too soon for even a thought like that. We don't know each other's middle names yet! But after calling him Daddy, some part of me has run far, far ahead of any kind of rational thought.

"He's going to be here for a little bit today," I answer, moving into his room and shutting the door behind me. This conversation is something I'd prefer Gabe not overhear. I squat down in front of Owen, lifting my arm to fix his mess of curls. "Are you okay with him being here? He's Daddy's friend, but this is your house too, buddy."

"I like him here," Owen says. "He asked me about all my toys and he tells jokes about dads."

I am somewhat of a Master in Owen-ese. 'Jokes about dads' means Dad Jokes. I can't imagine what Gabe told him, but my son's laughter is a good sign.

I stand back up with the weight of that off my shoulders. "I'm going to change into my pajamas too, then we can pick out a movie together, okay?"

"Happy Feet!" Owen jumps up and down, giving a little dance move in excitement. "Penguins, please."

We've watched Happy Feet three times this week alone. I don't mind it, though, because I love the movie just as much as he does. Sometimes, I've even watched it without him.

"You can go out and ask Gabe if he wants to watch it, but fix your pants first, buddy. They're backwards. Remember how I told you that the little tag goes on your bottom?"

***

The house smells like garlic when I walk out of my own bedroom in a pair of gray sweats and a white t-shirt. I don't own any real sets of pajamas. Heat courses through me when I catch Gabe giving me an up-and-down onceover.

Owen is sitting at the island holding a slice of bread. It's the basic sandwich slice type and it's cut in half. Owen is truly glowing as he chews with his mouth wide open. "Daddy! Gabe gave me garlic bread! It's so yummy!"

"I cut it in half," Gabe says quickly. "He said he never had it and I don't know if that's true or not. Figured he could have the other half with his spaghetti...which will be ready in just a minute. I hope you don't mind I used your air fryer for the meatballs. I cleaned it already."

"The air fryer is a lifesaver," I say. "And it's okay with the bread. I don't think I've given it to him before, but he doesn't have any allergies. I would have told you if he did. On sandwich bread, though?"

I sit at the island next to Owen. I stifle a laugh when Owen takes an exaggerated bite, making a chomping noise as he bites into the bread.

"It's how my mom made it when I was growing up," Gabe says. I look back at him, admiring the way he steps around the kitchen area with ease. "Impromptu garlic bread when it would take too long to make *langos*." The word rolls off his tongue in a wholly different accent. Something European. I want to ask him about it, but he continues, "Toast the bread, spread some butter, and sprinkle garlic salt. It was a last second decision."

"If I don't have to cook, I don't care what you do in this kitchen."

"Daddy, Gabe says we can watch the penguins." Owen interrupts. "He showed me pictures of a big penguin dancing."

"He did?" I keep my voice light, like it's the coolest thing Owen has ever told me.

"Alright, you two," Gabe interrupts us, "I hope you're hungry."

***

I wake up on Tuesday morning to Owen's alarm in his room. He's only five, but he fell in love with the duck light that doubles as an alarm clock. It quacks to wake him up. I want to throw it every morning, but I can hear him imitating the noise after he turns it off. A few seconds later, my door cracks open and he climbs into my bed.

"Daddy, wake up!" I pretend to still be asleep. I can feel Owen climb on top of me, his little hands pressed to my chest. "Wake up! We go to school today!"

He has two weeks before he starts school, but they're doing an orientation for the new class grade today. They will be showing the parents around the school and the kids where everything is in their classroom.

Owen bounces right on my bladder and I let out an involuntary grunt. He finds this hilarious.

We get our day started by brushing our teeth together. I put him in a bath and, afterward, attempt to style his hair a bit. It's an 'A for effort' situation. I dress in a pair of slacks and a button up short sleeve. I want to make a good impression. Owen, on the other hand, decides to go full Paw-Patrol with his shirt and shoes. We compromise on the blue shorts to match Chase.

"Do you want to see where Daddy's going to be working?" I ask once we're buckled in the car. The sun is still rising, but the temperature is already in the high seventies and getting hotter by the minute. I crank the AC in the car.

"Yes!"

It isn't a terrible drive through Phoenix to get to my new workplace. I imagine the traffic will be thicker when schools start back up, but today it only takes twenty minutes to navigate around neighborhoods and businesses. I pull over to the side of the road when we get to the large, rectangular building. It has a dome-like top and there's a fence erected around the whole thing.

"I'll be working here, buddy."

"That is huge!" Owen exclaims from the backseat. I look over my shoulder and laugh at the gaped expression his mouth is left in. "Can I come to work with you one day?"

"Maybe, buddy. Let's get you to your school."

My thoughts travel back to Friday night when Gabe came over. We did end up watching Happy Feet. Owen fell asleep between us, his head in my lap and feet in Gabe's. I carried him to bed and tucked him in while the credits rolled.

After that, Gabe and I spent two hours talking, sharing small touches, and possibly a quiet make-out session at some point between. He answered each of my questions, and I had a lot. We talked about scenes versus lifestyle Littles, specific things that Gabe likes or doesn't like to do from his experience, and aspects I may have Googled and found interesting. Gabe even showed me a website where you can buy clothing and other items to fully indulge in age play. On it, there are all sorts of things, from stuffies and train sets, to bottles and blocks aimed at a younger regression.

There are also diapers, which I don't think I'd enjoy. The training pants and underwear are kind of cute, though.

I push my thoughts to the back of my mind when I pull into the lot at Owen's school. Park Elementary. It's a decent-sized school, with two floors and several hallways that give the building an R-shape. There are two playgrounds to the side of the school, one clearly for smaller kids.

We check in and are directed down a hallway and to the right. Other families are mingling about, talking to teachers or each other. I feel Owen squeezing my hand a little tighter. I get it. This feels overwhelming to me, so I can't imagine how it feels to him.

"This is your classroom," I announce once we finally get through the crowd. The door is the next to last in the hall. "Your teacher's name is Miss Riley."

"Well, well," a familiar voice says behind us, "if it isn't Mister Owen!"

I turn around to find Gabe waving from two doors down. He's surrounded by three kids, all looking from him to us. Owen drops my hand without a second thought —which, *ouch*, dude— and runs to Gabe. Gabe, the wonderful guy he is, scoops Owen in his arms and hugs him tight. My heart does a happy dance at the sight.

"Is Owen in Miss Riley's class?" Gabe asks when he gets closer.

"He is," I answer. Gabe's smile widens.

"That's awesome!" He shifts Owen around to prop him on his hip. Owen is almost too tall to carry like that, for me at least, but Gabe is taller than me by a good several inches. "Brian is around here somewhere, but he'll be in the same class. He's one of my nephews."

A woman walks up, not disguising her curiosity as her gaze shifts between me and Gabe. "Mandy," Gabe begins. "This is Justin. He's..."

I realize that we never discussed what we would tell others. I didn't think I'd have anyone to tell or be introduced to so soon. I lick my lips, making brief eye contact with Gabe.

"Justin is going on a date with me tonight," Gabe says with a half-smirk. I'm sure the shock on Mandy's face mirrors my own. "I mean, if you can, that is."

"My little bro," Mandy says. "Always talking before thinking. It's nice to meet you, Justin. Is this your kid?"

I nod. "This is Owen." Gabe sets him down on the carpeted hallway. Owen shifts to hide partly behind me and wraps his arms around my leg. "We just moved here last week."

We make polite small talk until the door is opened and two women and a little boy walk out. The teacher, Miss Riley, waves us in. She is petite, with ash blonde hair and green eyes. She's the same height as me in her short heels. At least she's not taller.

"Welcome to the classroom," Miss Riley says. Her voice is as kind as her face. "We have a whole bunch to go over. If the kids want to look around or play on the carpet, that's fine. This shouldn't take more than ten minutes."

***

Six hours later, I'm on the phone to Gabe. "His grandparents will be here in half an hour. I'll be ready any time after that."

"Sounds good," Gabe replies on the other end of the line. "I'm going to hop in a shower and then head that way."

After the orientation, Gabe texted to double check if I can go out tonight. He apologized for springing the question out of the blue, but joked that I did say he needs to take me on a date before we call it official. We've been texting non-stop all day. Owen's grandparents were more than happy to take him for another sleepover tonight. I didn't tell them the real reason, using the excuse of Owen starting school soon and wanting him to get as much time with them as he can.

Owen gives me a big hug and kiss on the cheek before he leaves with his backpack on and toy dog in his hand. I stand at the door and watch them back out of the driveway and drive down the road. Gabe's car comes into view exactly five minutes later.

I grab my house key and wallet before locking the front door and meeting him at the car. He greets me with a quick kiss right on the lips. I smile when he pulls back. "Where are you taking me tonight?"

"I thought we could go get dinner at a semi-casual restaurant I like and then head to Dave and Busters. How does that sound?"

"I haven't been to a Dave and Busters in years," I clap my hands together with mounting excitement. "I'm in."

The restaurant is sit-in style with dim lighting, but we don't stand out in our jeans and tees. I let Gabe order for me and am pleasantly surprised at the taste of the garlic shrimp pasta. For himself, he orders a grilled chicken salad in a bowl the size of his head. As we eat, we talk, moving from one topic to another with ease. I probably ramble a bit too much about Owen and how sad I am to see him growing up. Gabe suggests that we plan a playdate for him and Brian soon.

The arcade business is only a ten-minute walk away so, once we finish our meal, we leave the car and opt to walk hand-in-hand down the street. The weather is cooling slightly as the sun sets, making the journey less miserable than the last time I chose to walk around Phoenix in summer.

Dave and Busters is an adult's playground, and Gabe spoils me. It's nice having someone else paying and indulging me for once. It's been a long time since I last experienced anything like this. I can feel myself easily letting the worries of Owen starting school, my new job, and other adult thoughts slip away. I don't totally lose myself, but I do let loose and have fun.

We start at the game machines until our cards run out of credit. Then we join a team of two other guys for laser tag. My favorite experience, though, is the tiny bowling alley they have in the back. It's only three lanes wide, but Gabe reserved a spot for us for the last hour. I'm not good at it, but Gabe doesn't make fun of me. Instead, he stands behind me, pressing up close to guide me through the motions to roll the ball in a straight line. I cheer when I knock over half the pins.

"Are you having fun?" Gabe asks when he comes back with a refill on our drinks. He made me stick with water since I had a soda with dinner. I tried to argue, but that look —that *Daddy* look— he gave me shut me right up.

How did I never know that kind of thing was such a turn on before?

"I am. Seriously, this has been amazing tonight. Thank you for everything."

"Of course, sweetheart." Gabe leans down and steals a kiss. I get butterflies knowing that anyone can see us. He's younger than me by five years, but he definitely gives off the more dominant vibes in this dynamic.

I whisper against his lips, low enough that only he can hear it. "Thank you, Daddy."

Chapter Eight

"DUDE, ARE YOU GOING to be able to concentrate on your classes?" Izzy teases me the night before our Senior year of college is set to officially begin. He tilts his chin towards my phone, where I'm texting with Justin. "Or is the new boyfriend going to be a distraction?"

"Shut up," I reply lazily, eyes on my screen. "I've dated, studied, and practiced for the team before. I know how to balance stuff—*shit*." I backspace on my screen where I have typed the word 'balance' in the middle of my sentence.

Izzy snorts. "Uh huh."

After sending my message, I look over to where he's sprawled on the couch and I roll my eyes. "You wanna find someone else to dom, man? Because I've got my life under control."

And I do, honestly. Dating Justin, however new our relationship is, has settled the itch under my skin. We kind of just click, with an underlying compatibility that honestly kind of surprises me. I know we're in different places in our lives, that even though our age gap is small, it's enough that he's working full time and has a kid while I'm still a college student. Still, even though we are at fundamentally different places in life, I feel like Justin gets me. On top of that, he certainly seems to enjoy dipping his toes into the

Daddy/Boy dynamic, too. I can't help feeling like I've lucked out in meeting him. We just have to keep it relatively low-key, what with my studies and his kid needing to take priority and all. A real relationship, but nothing too intense. Having fun together, or whatever.

"Except you never really dated anyone did you? Like, you had a couple of flings with some of the guys from Kik, but this" —Israel waves his hand over my phone— "level of attachment is new for you."

"I didn't know you'd switched majors to psych," I taunt him, ignoring the fact that he's not exactly wrong.

Before now, I've played with the Boys at the club, even taken a few on some dates (and playdates), but they've never felt like actual relationships. I've never been invested. I never *allowed* myself to be invested. I had too much going on between my large family, my studies, hockey, and my social life. Adding in a real relationship seemed like too much work.

Until now.

I don't know what it is about Justin that makes me want to put in the effort, but there's *something*. I felt it from the moment we met — that lightning bolt to my soul which demanded that I give him the time and attention he deserves.

I'll admit it: that is definitely part of the *something,* the fact that he deserves to be someone's priority. For a guy who is only in his late twenties, he's been through a lot. Is *still* going through a lot. Yes, that speaks to my savior complex, as Iz calls it, but I wanted to help him even before I knew his story.

So, no; Israel isn't wrong. But that doesn't mean I can't balance everything. I can have a real relationship on top of everything else.

I just need to make sure Justin and I are on the same page. Dating, but taking our time.

"I'm just saying, man," Izzy holds his hands up in surrender, but he has a cocky little grin on his face which speaks volumes on its own, "something's gotta give at some point. This year isn't exactly going to be a walk in the park for us."

"All the more reason to extend my support system, then." I smirk right back at him.

Surprisingly, my roommate considers my rebuttal with a serious nod. "Yeah, okay, I'll give you that. Plus, sex on tap will also keep you from getting all...*grrr*."

"Grrr?" I repeat, trying not to laugh at him.

"You get all wound up and you're hell to deal with, and you know it."

I toss a cushion at him as I laugh, "You know, every time you say that, I think it's pretty rich coming from you. When's the last time you got laid?"

"None of your damn business is when."

"Which means too long ago," I shrug, ducking as the cushion hurtles my way again. It hits the wall behind me with a muted *thump*. "*And* your whole personality is basically the grumpy bear stereotype on crack. Ergo, *you* need to get some."

Izzy gapes at me for a long moment. "Did you just say 'ergo'?"

"That's what you're taking from my epic argument?"

He snorts, and I cheer internally at cracking his cranky façade. "You're an idiot."

"Seriously, though," I tell him after I've finished chuckling, "you should get out there and let off some steam. Channel that Daddy Dom energy you've got going on because trying to dominate me isn't working."

"Ugh, I don't have the patience for brats like you."

"Then find a sweet, pliant sub." My thoughts flit briefly to Marshall, but I am not going to be dumb enough to stir up our group of friends if my suspicions aren't one-hundred-percent on the money. "All I'm saying is maybe you've finally hit your abstinence limit, too."

He grumbles under his breath, but the fact that he doesn't completely dismiss my observations is a surprise. I'm half a breath away from calling him on it when my phone alerts me to a new message. It's from Justin.

Justin

Are you alone?

My lips curl upwards and I push myself out of the armchair I've been lazing in. "Well," I tell my roommate distractedly as I type out my reply, "I'm about to take care of my lack of abstinence right now."

"Dude, come on," he protests as I press send.

Me:

I'm about to be. Heading into my bedroom now, baby. Is there something you need?

Justin's bubbling ellipses appear and disappear as I watch. Shutting my bedroom door, I cross the small space to my twin bed and settle myself against the headboard.

After a few more seconds without a reply, I decide to take charge and I call him via Facetime. His cute face fills my screen almost immediately, and I drink in the sight of him, even though I saw him only yesterday.

"Hey, sweetheart," I practically croon, watching the already-present blush darken his pale cheeks. "Talk to me. Tell me how I can help."

"It's silly," Justin's teeth sink into his plump lower lip. "So much is happening tomorrow, and I need to get to sleep early, but I..."

"Can't make your brain stop whirring?"

His hazel-green eyes widen, and he seems almost dazed as he looks at the camera. "Exactly! So, um, I...*gah*, it's so dumb."

"Nothing is dumb if it actually helps, baby." I cock my head. "Did you try to take the edge off? Rub one out to make yourself sleepy?"

His pink tongue sneaks out to wet his gnawed-on lip. The sight of it takes me from half-mast to almost fully hard with zero effort, but I don't give in to the temptation to reach down and ease the sudden ache just yet.

"I..." he starts, then swallows. "I thought..."

Realization dawns on me. "Oh, would you like Daddy to help?"

We've fooled around a bit since we started dating, but it has obviously been limited by his schedule with Owen, and around my family commitments, too. So I am *very* on board with this idea, if it's the path he'd like to go down.

"Please?" he asks plaintively.

How can I deny this sweet Boy anything?

"Just double checking that you're in bed? Door closed?" He nods, chewing on his lower lip again. "Good. Now, put the phone on your nightstand, okay? Prop it up and shuffle back so I can see all of you — yes, that's it. Perfect. I'm gonna do the same."

Setting my phone on my desk, I make sure to angle it so the camera can see most of my bed, but so I can still see the screen. Then, after snatching the lube from my drawer on my way back, I stretch out on top of my sheets and palm my cock over my boxer shorts. Justin moans, but he doesn't reach for his own dick.

"Good boy for waiting without being told to," I practically purr, and he nods, flashing me a bashful smile.

From this distance and the small size of the screen, I can't see nearly enough detail of his features, but that's okay. This is just a teaser for what we can do together. Besides, it's not about me — it's about helping him. I know he's starting his new job tomorrow, and it's Owen's first day at school. I'm surprised he's not more frazzled. But if helping him orgasm means that he will get the rush of sleepy neurochemicals, it's a cross I'm happy to bear.

"Pull down your pjs, sweetheart, I wanna see you."

He does as he's told and his cock practically springs free. Even lying on his side, it strains towards the soft curve of his stomach, seemingly unaffected by gravity.

"Do you want to touch yourself, baby?" I ask him, absently rubbing over my own aching erection.

Biting his lip some more, he nods, and I'm pretty sure he's blushing.

"I need words, sweetheart."

"Yes," he practically whimpers. "Yes, Daddy. Please."

Oh, God, he's perfect.

Releasing my own dick, I pop the cap on the bottle of lube, drizzling some into my palm. "Stroke yourself for me."

He also seems to prefer using lube to jerk off, because he produces a bottle from just outside the camera's view, pouring a bit into his own hand before recapping it and tossing it aside. Then his hand is on his cock, and he shuts his eyes as he starts to stroke. I mirror his actions, imagining his hand stroking me instead.

I wish I was there with him or that I at least had a bigger screen to take the show in properly. To see his long lashes fluttering on his cheeks, to hear his breathing shift into gentle pants, to see the mattress wobble with the increasing thrusts of his hips...

"Imagine that's my hand, baby," I instruct, my voice deeper and slightly raspier with lust. "Do you feel me slowly stroking you? Squeezing a little bit at the base and running my thumb over your slit when I get to the head?"

His lips part. I watch his chest rise and fall a little more rapidly as he nods and recreates my promised actions with his hand. "F-feels good, Daddy."

Hearing him call me Daddy, especially during sex, is *everything*. I have to tighten my hold on the base of my cock to fend off the near-orgasm his sweet, sexy words try to pull from me.

"Mmm," I hum, knowing that I'd be pressing kisses to his neck and sucking hickeys into the skin if I was there with him, "do you feel me picking up the pace? Jerking you faster, twisting my wrist and rubbing the head of your perfect, leaking cock on every upstroke?"

"D-Daddy..." Even through the small screen, I can see his hips thrusting forward, picking up speed to match the faster shuttling of his fist.

In my own bed, I speed up my stroking, too. "That's it, baby. Show me what feels good. Come for me. Let Daddy watch you fall apart."

"Oh, *ohhhh*," he whimpers, then bites down on his lip. It's a shame that he's silencing himself, but I understand that he has a sleeping kid sharing a wall with his room.

Meanwhile, I couldn't care less if Izzy hears me rubbing one out. It might encourage him to finally get his shit together and get laid.

"That's it, baby. Daddy's watching. You're being so good."

"Oh, fuck, Daddy!" he whisper-shouts, arching his back as his cock erupts, coating his hand and the sheets with spurts of cum. "*Nnngh.*"

"Yes, baby, just like that." Watching him takes me to the edge and it only takes a couple more short, sharp jerks of my fist before I follow him over the precipice with a loudly groaned "Fuck" of my own.

Once I catch my breath and my brain re-engages, I reach for my nearby supply of wet wipes and tissues, cleaning up my mess.

"Thank you, sweetheart," I say, glancing up at my phone again with a soft, sappy smile. "That was…" Trailing off, I realize that he's half-asleep already, a wad of tissues discarded to the side of his mattress. My heart gives a funny little flip at the sight. "Sleep, Justin. We'll talk tomorrow."

"Mmm," he agrees, but I don't think he actually heard me. "Night, Daddy. Lo—" the word is cut off with a huge yawn, but my heart is hammering, even though he doesn't finish it, ending with a sleepy "*Hmmm*" instead.

Heart in my throat, I can't deny that maybe Izzy had a point after all. I've never had a serious relationship before, and this one is suddenly feeling very serious when I was only just thinking how slowly we should try to take things.

But that's still not a bad thing, is it? As long as I can maintain a balance between school, my relationship, my family, and hockey, it's all going to be okay. After all, that's all my life revolves around. If I stick to that, I can't imagine any other curveballs will be thrown my way…or whatever the equivalent hockey metaphor is.

(Shut up, I think I broke my brain when I came.)

Chapter Nine

Justin

"Iᴛ's sᴄʜᴏᴏʟ ᴅᴀʏ!" I say excitedly as I twist the handle on Owen's door. He's spread out on his tiny bed, face smushed into the pillow. I gave up trying to break him of that habit long ago. I worried myself for a solid year, checking on him every hour throughout the night to make sure he was still breathing. I'd move his head to the side, but by the next time I checked on him, he was face down in the pillow again.

Owen gives no indication that he's awake. I walk quietly into his room, careful to not step on the toys he left scattered around. I wouldn't be surprised if his toys actually came to life at night and scattered themselves. At least, I'm telling myself that, since I definitely remember asking him to clean up his room before he went to bed.

"Owen, buddy, it's time to wake up." It's six in the morning. School starts at seven-thirty, and I have to be at the college by nine. We'll be having a team meeting with the Penguins to kick things off. I'm only needed for a while today, so I'll be able to slip out and pick Owen up from school and spend the afternoon with him. He'll be going between an afterschool program run by a few teachers and his grandparents throughout the school year, but I wanted to be there for his first day. I hate that I won't be able to pick him up from school most days, but I do like that we have our mornings together, at least.

Owen peeks one eye open and immediately closes it, clearly hoping I didn't see.

I play along for a few seconds. "Hmm, I guess I'll just have to eat all the French toast in the kitchen by myself. And drink all the orange juice. Maybe I'll even eat all the snacks in Owen's bag." I can see his little body squirming under the blanket. He's laughing, still thinking he's fooling me. I walk towards the door. "I wonder if the school will let me have Owen's ice cream today, too."

"Ice cream?!" Owen nearly leaps out of his bed and runs into the hallway, flying past me. I'm surprised he doesn't trip over his own feet. He's well past the bathroom when I clear my throat.

"You know the drill," I point a finger toward the bathroom he ran right past.

I spent four months trying every trick under the sun and moon to potty train Owen when he turned three. He flat-out refused for the first month. Then he consistently wet his pants the second month. He did well in familiar places after that but, in new places, he would regress back and have accidents. I made it a point for us to walk into every bathroom we could when we were out, no matter what we were doing. I wanted him to get comfortable using the restroom. Even now, I make sure the bathroom is the first place he goes in the mornings to reduce any accidents.

I busy myself with grabbing his clothes for the day while he's doing his business. He left the door wide open, so I can hear him talking to himself. Another thing I taught him. I saw a video once of a mom having her kids repeat a positive mantra, and I thought it was a good idea. That's something I'm always worried about for him; he's a great kid, my whole world, but I know he's at the age where he's going to really start questioning where his mom is. I've discussed it with his grandparents briefly, laying down boundaries on what I do and don't want them to share.

I shake my thoughts away when Owen calls out that he's done washing his hands. I won't dare get him dressed until after the sticky syrup has been consumed. Instead, I lay his clothes out on his bed and make sure his shoes are on the floor next to it.

I have a clear view of Owen when I step out of his room. He's climbing up onto one of the chairs at the island counter.

"Be careful, buddy." The words come out automatically. A knee-jerk reaction to make sure he's safe.

He gives me the widest smile when he's finally seated, and I plate up his breakfast. Two sticks of French toast —the microwavable kind because I know it's his favorite— with a dollop of syrup for each. I pour us each a glass of juice and lean against the other side of the counter to watch him eat.

Another flash of Lauren crosses my mind. I miss her, but it isn't a deep ache like I've heard some people describe. Owen might have been a surprise, but we always planned to raise him together. We were content, even had fun together at times. Still, I can't help but compare how I felt toward her to how I felt on my date with Gabe. It's not fair, but Gabe is just... different. I'm different when I'm with Gabe. It's like he's tapped into a part of me I had no idea existed before.

"Daddy, I'm..." I look from my empty cup to my son. His red hair and fair skin are slowly getting used to the Arizona heat. I have three bottles of sunscreen in the bathroom alone to make sure he doesn't burn. His thin brows are furrowed, and I can see a world of emotions in his eyes.

"What is it, Owen?"

"I'm scared to go to school," he mumbles. "What if they don't like me?"

"Where is that coming from?" I ask, genuinely concerned. There haven't been a lot of chances for socialization since we moved here. There's a park within a short driving distance and I've watched him play with a couple of kids the few times we went. Then there's Gabe's nephew in his class. We haven't scheduled a playdate yet, but I need to change that.

He shrugs one shoulder and puts his fork down. He still has half a stick of toast left. His green eyes meet mine and I can sense we are about ten seconds from a meltdown. I hold out my hand to take his, squeezing twice and running my thumb across his wrist.

"Owen, it's going to be okay. Daddy is scared about starting his new job, too, but we're going to get through this day together. Then we'll come home and talk about all the fun things you did and have dinner tonight. I'll let you pick the movie, too."

"What if I'm not good at school?"

I really don't know what has prompted any of these worries. He's never been worried about something like this. He's too little, innocent, pure, and kind for these types of thoughts. My heart hurts for him and I round the counter to pull him into a hug. He wraps his limbs around me, and I hold him tight.

"Buddy, you are going to be amazing today. I promise. You're going to have so much fun. Remember how much you liked the classroom when we visited? And you'll get to go outside and play on the playground, too."

I hear a sniffle, but I can feel him nodding. His chin digs into my shoulder with each bob of his head.

"How about we make a deal?" I wait until he pulls back to look me in the eyes. He scrunches his nose and huffs out a breath way too big for his little body. "You go to school, and I'll go to work. Then, when I pick you up, we'll go to Ma's for dinner instead?"

His answering smile and enthusiastic nod are a relief.

"Can I have the pizza again?"

My lips quirk. I guess Gabe has introduced Owen to new things, too.

***

Claremont College is huge. I've only been here once, back before we moved, to sign papers and officially join the Penguins as a physical therapist. I park in one of the employee spots behind the building that houses the hockey arena. The moment I step through the door and feel that rush of cold air, I sigh in relief and let the stress from this morning roll off my back.

"Let's do this," I repeat to myself. I ball my fingers up and give a pretend fist bump to the air, just like I did to Owen before watching him walk into his classroom.

"Justin!" It takes me only a second to recognize Coach Overton. "A bit early, aren't you?"

"Ah, yeah. The kid had a bit of a rough start this morning, but we got to school on time. It's kind of an awkward amount of time to go back home for half an hour."

"Well, I'm not going to complain if you're always early." His smile is infectious and settles my nerves. Dan Overton is attractive, with graying stubble and a thick head of dark hair. But, even though he's built exactly as you'd imagine a former hockey player, he's not intimidating at all. "Follow me. I know you didn't see much of the place last time you were here, but we have some time before the team arrives. It's a rowdy bunch this year. Six of them are Seniors and they're determined."

I don't really know a lot about hockey outside of movies and the few local games I went to back in Virginia. It isn't a widespread thing back home, and none of the colleges in the area I lived in have their own team. I know I'm in for a lot of work if the videos I've watched of hockey players showing off bruises and injuries like they're trophies is anything like this team.

We walk down a corridor with cement flooring and cinderblocks painted in the school colors. Splashes of purple, white, and black arranged artfully really catch the eye. There are banners announcing the hockey team's season start and a list of the players. I only catch a few names in passing. Photographs and other banners hang on the walls between the different doors, and the corridor ends at the entrance of the arena. There is no door closing it off, which is where the draft is coming from.

It's chilly and I regret not bringing a jacket or anything with me. I'll remember tomorrow. There are doors spread randomly on either side. "This is the utility closet, if you need any cleaning supplies, trash bags, and so on." Overton points from one plain door to another across the hall. I swivel my head, following his motions. "Restroom. Then there's the locker room where we'll meet the team."

Coach takes us right past the locker room door, to one more door only a few feet away from the tunnel which leads to the arena proper.

"This is your office," he says. "This is attached to the gym the guys use, and you'll share the space with one other physical therapist, Frankie. She'll be the one traveling with us to away games since you'll be here for home games."

He opens the door and steps to the side to let me look around. The space is clean. Sterile. There are white walls with a mix of motivational quotes and biology posters. A row of tables with navy mattresses sit to the right. Light exercising equipment like yoga balls and small weights are placed neatly to the left. A set of three stairs are against the back area, next to a floor-to-ceiling mirror.

"This is...Wow."

It wasn't quite so put-together last time I saw the room. They were still moving things around and getting ready for the season to start. It looks amazing.

"I'm glad you like it," Coach says. He glances at his watch. "It's about time to meet the team. Let's get going. I'd like to introduce you to one of the players specifically. He's one of our seniors this year and is getting his degree in Sports Medicine as well. I brought up the possibility of him shadowing you and Frankie from time-to-time, and he seemed enthusiastic."

"Happy to help," I smile.

He pushes the door to the locker room open and we're greeted with laughter and chatter. The volume is what you'd expect from a locker room full of college guys on the first day of a new season. The excitement is contagious.

"Hey, Coach!" someone yells and everyone follows suit. All eyes turn to us. Well, probably to Coach, but I'm standing next to him so I see a few eyes flick my way.

"Everyone, settle down!" I glance at coach and see his head moving slightly, like he's taking count of who is and isn't here. "Where's Nagy?"

The name piques my interest. Nagy. Gabe's last name. Surely, it's someone different. I know he goes to this college —kind of hoped I'd run into him once or twice— but maybe it's a cousin of his or something. He's always talking about how big his family is, but has never mentioned hockey in all the times we've talked.

"I'm here Coach!" A *very* familiar voice calls across the locker room. Instinctually, my head whips toward the sound. I watch as if in slow motion as none other than Gabe, the man who held me in a rocking chair while I slept —the man I sucked off in a restroom designed for Littles— rounds the corner in nothing but a pair of pants.

His hair is dripping, and he has a towel slung over his shoulder. His muscled chest and miles of smooth skin are on full display. I bite back the feeling of jealousy that everyone can see him like this. "Sorry, I got a bit carried away on the ice before everyone else showed up, and I have class at eleven. Couldn't exactly stay sweaty all day."

"Show off!" One of the other players says and pushes Gabe's shoulder playfully. Gabe retaliates by reaching over and smacking him on the back of the head.

"You're just jealous I'm the better player, Mason."

"Save it for the games," Coach says, stopping their chirping from escalating.

Gabe finally looks up and our eyes lock. A range of emotions show on his face: recognition, confusion, shock. His eyes dart between myself and Coach. His lips part, like he's about to say something, but Overton beats him to it. I give myself one more second before looking at the rest of the room. I start counting heads while the coach talks, introducing me and letting them know what I'll be doing for the season.

There are twenty-five men, a full roster. Some look fresh-faced while others seem a few years older and more comfortable in this room. Gabe sits down on the edge of a bench next to a guy who's about his size. There's a small elbow jab between them, which I only catch because I'm watching his every move.

"Justin, do you want to add anything?"

I didn't pay attention to what Coach said. I look at him for a second, swallow, and then face the crowd of men. I feel like I'm a new student, even though I know I'm at least five years older than any of them. Not that that matters with Gabe, my boyfriend...My Daddy.

God, what did I get myself into?

"Um." I stammer and clear my throat twice. I talked Owen through his almost-meltdown this morning, I can talk myself through my own. "I'm excited to be here and work with all of you. I'm also excited to be working in a place that doesn't involve your Arizona sun."

That gets a round of chuckles from most of them, and I sigh in relief. My eyes flick to Gabe on instinct once more. He smiles and gives me the barest of nods. His silent way of saying I did a good job. I'll take it.

"Okay, well, I'm going to get some stuff together," Overton wraps us up. "We're not gearing up today, but we are running some plays and drills. I'll see everyone out there in ten minutes."

Everyone shouts at the same time, "Yes, Coach!".

I don't know if I'm supposed to be following Coach or not, but I'm greeted by a few of the players immediately after Coach steps away. Everyone is nice and asks genuine questions to get to know me. Nothing deep, but I do let them know I have a five-year-old who started school today and that, for the most part, I won't be traveling with them for games. After five minutes, they all start heading out of the locker room. Without looking, I know that Gabe is hanging back.

When it's finally just the two of us in the room, he stops pretending to look through his locker and turns to face me. I rub my hand up and down my opposite arm. It's a nervous habit.

"So," Gabe begins. He smirks, and I can tell by his tone that whatever he says next is going to be sarcastic, "I guess we never hit the 'what do you do for work' portion of our talks."

I laugh, pushing out all the nerves. The locker room is getting cold quickly without all the bodies in here. I fold my arms across my chest. "I guess so. I'm surprised you never mentioned you were on the hockey team."

He shrugs. "I love the game, don't get me wrong, but it's not my whole life. Not like some of the guys on the team this year. I prefer to identify myself in other ways."

Daddy. He means as a Daddy.

"Um, so, what are we supposed to do?" I don't know where we go from here. This is...unexpected.

Gabe cocks his head. "What do you mean?"

I gesture around us. "I'm working for the team you play on, Da-Gabe." *Woah.* That almost slipped out way too easily.

The look on his face tells me he caught my almost slip-up. "It doesn't have to change anything. It's not like you're the team's coach."

I worry my bottom lip and cast my eyes down. This is my first big job as a physical therapist. I've worked my ass off the last several years to finish my degree and secure my license. I took this job to give Owen the best life I could give him. I can't jeopardize that.

A finger tugs at my bottom lip, pulling me out of my spiral of thoughts. I glance around, but we're still alone. Coach's office is next door. He could walk back in at any moment, though. I think Gabe senses my hesitation and drops his hand.

"We'll figure it out, okay?" He turns around and grabs a hoodie from his locker. "Here, take this. It's cold out there and I'm assuming you didn't bring your own."

Just as I'm taking the hoodie from him, Coach walks around the row of lockers. I drop my hand, still holding the fabric and we both step away from each other. I didn't even realize how close we were standing. Gabe gives me a concerned look, but Coach speaks before either of us can come up with an excuse why we're both still here alone.

"Oh, great. You two have met," Coach says with a smile. "Justin, this is Gabriel Nagy. He's the senior I was telling you about earlier."

"Come on Coach; you're going to make me blush if you keep talking about me." I laugh along with Coach, but a pang of jealousy hits me that Gabe —my Daddy— is jokingly flirting with another man in front of me.

I know he's only playing, but still. He's *my* Daddy.

Overton ignores him and looks at me. "I'd like Nagy to shadow you here and there. He's going for Sports Medicine as well, so getting some first-hand experience will be great for him. If you're okay with it."

I avoid looking at Gabe for fear that all my thoughts will show and Coach will know. Would I like an excuse to spend more time with him? Yes, it isn't even a question. Except Coach doesn't know we're dating, and I don't want to jeopardize anything if there's a rule against it.

I've uprooted my life —Owen's life— to be here. I can't let anything risk what we're building together. Not even the man who has turned my whole life upside down in barely a handful of days. Even if I really like him.

Chapter Ten

HOW THE HELL HAVE Justin and I never had the 'what do you do for work?'/'what do you do at college' conversation? My mind is blown at seeing him in my locker room and blown further still at being told that he's our new physical therapist...and also the guy I'm supposed to be tailing for my practical experience.

At least I know we get along...

The thought makes me smile as I pack up my gear and head out of the arena. We're obviously overdue a serious discussion about how life is going to work around college, as well as his job and kid, and it's more vital now than ever that we have that talk. But, even though seeing him today threw me for a loop, it excites me, too.

I mean, I kind of get to work with my boyfriend. *And* we obviously have more in common than either of us realized, too.

"What's that smile for?" Marshall asks when I drop my bag inside the doorway of the apartment Iz and I share. My friends are all lounging on the couch, a box of pizza open in front of them.

My stomach rumbles at the sight of the food, but I force myself to grab a healthier snack —a sandwich container filled with precut veggie sticks and a tiny tub of ranch dressing— and I drop into my usual armchair. The melty cheese and pepperoni are out of my reach, and I tell myself the carrots taste way better than the pizza smells. (I'm lying to myself.)

Izzy leans over from the couch and smacks my knee. "You were spoken to," he reprimands.

Crunching on a piece of celery, I chew before looking at Marshall. "Sorry, man. I was on a mission and not listening."

He smiles widely and waves my apology away with a large hand. "Nah, I was just asking why you had that goofy smile on your face when you came in."

"Oh," I chuckle, "right. Turns out the guy I've been dating...Justin?"

"The one with the kid," Noah mumbles with a mouth full of carbs and cheese.

I scrunch my nose. "Yeah, the one with a kid...a kid who has way better manners than you, by the way."

Noah shrugs.

"What about Justin?" Marshall leans forward, all wide-eyed and invested in whatever I have to say.

"It turns out he's the team's new physical therapist. Well," I frown, "maybe not exclusively for the team. He might be there for the football team, too. We didn't really get to talk about it...but he's also the guy Coach told me I should shadow for my practical credits."

"And that's not gonna be awkward for you?" Israel arches an eyebrow. "I mean, considering your dynamic..."

"He's not Daddy when they're on the ice or whatever, though," Noah answers before I can.

The guys are all aware of my kink and they're cool with it, even if Iz happens to be the only one who I know to also have less-than-vanilla interests. Still, it's a surprise that Noah seems to have done some research about it. Well, either that or a lucky guess.

"What he said," I tilt my head to Noah, who is sitting cross-legged on the floor next to Marshall's seat. "In the club or in our private lives, I'm Daddy, but I'm not one of those guys who gets all macho and offended if his sub or Little is superior to him in public."

"It's not like you've had to experience it yet, though," Izzy argues. He leans into Marshall's space so he can snag a slice of the pie before it's all gone. Before he takes a bite, he adds, "It might be an issue without you even knowing it. And if it's not for you, it might be for him."

"Oh, true," Marshall nods enthusiastically. "I read that some subs want their Dom —or their Daddy— to always be the one in control, in and out of the bedroom." He cocks his head, his nose scrunching as his face contorts into a thoughtful expression. "Justin seemed like the kind of guy who likes it when someone else takes over for him. Well, he did when we moved him into his house. And, hey," he pouts, "wasn't he going to have us over for dinner?"

"He's had a lot going on," I assure my friend. "I'm kind of responsible for a lot of his distraction. But I'll remind him." If nothing else, Justin could use more friends. Friends who aren't also his Daddy. And my friends are pretty awesome, if I do say so myself.

Marshall beams. "Please? We can do a potluck kind of thing so he doesn't have to do all the work or spend a heap of money to feed us."

"That's really thoughtful, Marsh," Izzy commends softly, taking the words right out of my mouth.

As Marshall preens under Israel's praise, Noah and I share another one of our 'when are they going to get their act together?'

looks. The thing is, I'm not even sure either one of them know that they're into men or, if not men in general, each other.

"You gonna have a slice?" Noah asks me, nudging the pizza box my way. I frown at it and dip another carrot stick into my ranch.

"Nah," I wave the dripping carrot stick in the air, "I'm good. You should go for it."

I'm not unaware of the looks that Noah and Izzy share, but they don't get it: I need to stay lean to stay fast on my skates. I'm agile, and it won't stay that way if I weigh myself down with grease and cheese.

"Your loss," Marshall tells me, oblivious to the silent conversation our friends are having. He grabs himself the second last slice and munches down happily. "Mmm, pizza."

***

"This was a great idea," Justin tells me as I help him carry a bowl of salad to the outdoor table. It's already laden with a couple other salads, scalloped potatoes, and the steaks and hot dogs hot off the grill.

Out in the tiny square patch of backyard, Owen squeals and pushes his little legs as hard as he can to outrun the college-aged guys "chasing" him for the ball in his arms. His little rounded cheeks are red from exertion, and his mop of red hair is plastered to his head from sweat, but he's wearing a huge grin.

"Yeah," I say as I watch my friends entertaining the kid, "thank you for having the guys over. They've been looking forward to it. Marshall especially."

My Boy smiles and his gaze drifts over to watch the guys entertaining his son. Marshall has switched teams and is planting himself in between the other two and Owen, dramatically yelling "Run, O! Save yourself!"

Justin snorts. "He's a big kid, too, huh?"

"Yep. He's actually studying to be a grade-school teacher."

"It suits him."

"I think so, too." Marshall is a big goofball with a heart of gold who loves kids even more than I do.

"I'm surprised you didn't have other plans for Labor Day, though," Justin adds, still watching the guys horse around. "When I was in college, it seemed like everyone always took advantage of the holiday and partied hard. I mean, not me, because I had Owen, but..."

I shrug. "We're not big on the party scene. I prefer to go to Kik if I want to dance, Noah has some social anxiety and prefers smaller gatherings, and Iz...well," I look at the big guy, my lips quirking affectionately. "He's not a people person. Not unless you're in his circle." I look back at Justin, whose own lips have turned down into an adorable frown. "Which you are now, by the way."

He blinks in surprise. "What?"

"He wouldn't have come to hang out if he didn't like you. Izzy is one of those brutally honest types, you know?"

"So...him being here means he wants to be my friend?" There's a hint of something in his voice which I would call his Little side, even if we haven't really gotten to explore much of that since that first night at Kik.

"It does," I nod, while ideas of how we can spend our night start to circle in my brain. We've prearranged for me to stay the night, with Owen's grandparents picking him up later this afternoon.

As much as I enjoy having Owen around, I'm more than excited to get Justin to myself for the night. When we were planning the evening, we discussed an array of ways we could spend tonight, including exploring our dynamic as Daddy and Boy. And, now that Justin *sounds* like he could be ready to regress, I hope that is what he wants to do tonight.

To be honest, I think he needs it. The past couple of weeks since the fall semester started, he's been getting edgy. I don't know if he's got more of an issue with working with me than he originally let on, or if there's more going on in his home life stressing him out than he has told me, but I think letting go and being Little will help ease some of that stress...assuming he wants to give it another go.

I wasn't lying when I told him that I wanted to date him either way. He's been so cute in calling me Daddy, but if he has changed his mind and that's all he wants to do, that's okay, too.

Still, that hasn't stopped me from planning just in case.

"What are you thinking about?" he asks, pulling me out of my distracted musings.

"Tonight," I answer honestly, and I love the way a pink blush spreads over his cheeks.

"I forgot what having a twenty-two-year-old libido is like."

I can't help snorting. "Uh, you're not that much older than me, baby. But, no, I wasn't thinking about sex." *Although...* Images flicker through my mind and I smother a groan, willing my cock to stay down. "But, thanks; now I am. That's your fault."

He laughs, catching the guys' attention. Marshall's eyes light on the table and he cheers, "Food!"

"Go wash up first," Justin and I say in unison, which makes Noah snort and even Iz smirks.

Owen leads the trio through the house and Justin asks, "Okay, but what were you thinking about, then?"

"I was thinking about the bag of stuff I have in my car," I shrug, "and how I can't wait to show you what I've bought you. I know you felt weird about being Little and using Owen's stuff —which, y'know, totally fair— so I've bought Little Justin some stuff. But only if you want to try being Little again. No pressure."

"Oh." He bites his lip and his blush deepens. "I think I'd like that."

I want to pull that lip out from between his teeth and kiss it, but Owen comes barreling between us, wrapping his arms around his dad's waist. "Can we eat now? I want a hot dog."

"You have to have veggies with it. Maybe some of the nice salad Gabe brought, too."

Owen scrunches his nose. "Salad?"

"It's got lots of the things you like in it," Justin tries to placate him.

I can see the little guy is not convinced, so I cut in with, "You can always try it and, if you don't like it, you don't have to eat it." I lock eyes with Justin, hoping I haven't overstepped. "If your dad says that's okay."

Justin nods. "If you don't like it, you can just have some extra carrot sticks and cucumber."

"And I'll sneak you some of my potato salad," Marshall tells him in an exaggerated hushed whisper. "It's my favorite, but I'll share if you don't tell anyone."

Owen giggles and nods. Justin helps him onto his seat and loads up his plate with a hotdog, a tiny bit of the salad I brought, and some of the veggie sticks he cut up especially for Owen. Marshall makes a show of looking left and right before 'sneaking' a small serving of potato salad onto his plate as well.

The little guy eats as we all load up our own plates, and Justin praises him for eating every last bite of his meal when he finishes.

"My tummy's full," he declares.

"Too full for pie?" Noah asks. "Izzy brought *chocolate* pie."

The kid's eyes go wide as saucers, and he looks at his dad. "Can I have a little bit?" He holds up his hand, pinching his index finger and thumb together. "Just a teeny, tiny bit? Please?"

There's a glint in Justin's eye —something mischievous and adorable— when he smiles and answers, "Just a little bit. Don't want to sugar you up *too* much for Grandpa and Grandma."

***

"Alone at last," Justin declares, flopping down on the couch beside me.

I try not to take it too personally that he ushered Owen out the front door when the kid's maternal grandparents pulled into the driveway. I get the feeling he's putting off introducing me to them, but I can understand why that would be the case. We haven't been dating very long, for one thing, and for another, they might not know that he's bi. With everything else going on in his life, I'm not going to push him to complicate it further by introducing me until he's ready.

Still, as he slumps into his seat at my side, I can feel tension radiating off him, and he looks more exhausted than he did five minutes ago.

"What would you like to do now that we've got the place to ourselves?" I ask, then quickly follow up with, "I know that part of our dynamic involves me making decisions for you, but I can tell you're on edge right now, so I'll give you three choices. One — I can go and get the Little things I bought, and we can give you some real Little time. No set scenes, just...getting used to letting yourself regress in whatever way makes you the most comfortable. Two — we can put on a movie, grab a couple of beers and just snuggle here on the couch. Three — we can go and soak in your tub together and see where that takes us." I finish with an exaggerated eyebrow waggle, and it gets me the chuckle I was hoping for.

"I..." Justin swallows and blushes. "Can...can I see what you bought me? Please, Daddy?"

My heart soars.

Less than two minutes later, we're both sitting cross-legged on the living room carpet as he unpacks the duffel bag I brought in from the car.

"Oh, this is so soft," he muses, fingering the material of the short-sleeved romper I ordered him. It is pale blue cotton and covered in a motif of cartoon penguins playing sports.

"I can help you get dressed into it later if you'd like,"

I'm addicted to his blushing and the shy smiles he gives me. This time is no exception. "I'd like that." He looks back inside the bag and the pink of his cheeks darkens as he pulls out the matching training pants. "*Oh.*"

"Is that a good 'oh' or a bad 'oh'?" I ask. "Tell me what you're thinking."

His hand moves to his crotch, and he pushes down with his palm as he answers. "Um, good. It...it's exciting." He frowns. "Is that weird?"

"Nope, totally normal." I grin. "I'm getting excited, too, sweetheart."

His gaze flickers to the bulge in my jeans and he grins, even though he's still blushing. Then he pulls out the spare pairs of training pants and the additional rompers, all in various cartoon designs. "Wow, this is a lot."

I shrug. "Between play time and accidents, little boys can get messy. I like having spares."

"Y-you want me to" —he lowers his voice and averts his gaze— "have *accidents*?"

"We haven't seen how Little you go yet," I answer honestly. "It's not so much a matter of want as being prepared. I know you're not comfortable with diapers, but I've been with Middles who have gotten so wrapped up in playing that they've forgotten to listen to their bladders."

He blinks and squirms. "Really?"

"But if you're not comfortable with that, that's okay, too. I can give you reminders to go to the potty every couple of hours, or you don't have to regress so far that you lose all sense of your Big self. It's whatever makes you happy, baby. That's what will make me happy, too."

"O-okay," he breathes shakily, then licks his lips, his thumb still gliding over the material of the first pair of training pants. "I don't...I don't want to do that tonight. But..." he shifts from side to side on his hips, "I don't hate the idea. I...I've never been one for embarrassment or humiliation before, but then, I never thought I would enjoy calling another man Daddy, so..."

"We'll just see what you feel like when you're Little. But it's good to know that it's not a hard limit. I'll be prepared either way." I smile. "I'm so proud of you for being so open to trying new things. And planned —or even unplanned— accidental wetting doesn't have to be about a humiliation kink. It also shows how deeply relaxed and regressed you are, and how much you trust your Daddy to look after you. *Or* it's about being in control of losing control, if that makes sense?"

He nods, then discovers the toys in the bag. His eyes brighten and his blush starts to fade as excitement takes over. "A coloring book!" he declares happily. "And my own crayons! Oh, and a stuffie!" He laughs when, unsurprisingly, it's a penguin...and it's wearing the team jersey. Our college sells them online as a fundraising thing for the school.

"What are you going to name him?"

He's slowly slipping into Little space, and I'm happy to guide him along as he goes.

Tilting his head to the side, he turns the stuffed toy in his hands, with a super cute look of concentration on his face. Then he nods to himself and answers, "Kelvin."

It's really difficult to contain my bewildered amusement. "Kelvin?"

"Yeah, like the old refrigerator brand."

"Ah." I chuckle. "I get it. Because of the cold."

"Yes!" Justin cheers. "Exactly!" Then he tucks Kelvin under his arm. "Let's see what else Daddy got us, hey buddy?"

Not knowing how Little he might go, nor what kind of interests he might have, I got a handful of different kinds of toys. A truck, some Matchbox cars, a wooden train, a small package of wooden blocks...and— "A sippy cup?" he looks up at me with excitement and extends it towards me, waving it from side to side. "Apple juice, please Daddy."

And so it begins.

"Let's get you into your comfy new play clothes first," I suggest. "Then I'll get you a sippy cup of juice and we can play with some of your new toys."

"Oh, yay!" he claps his hands, then stops and plucks Kelvin out from his armpit. "Sorry, Kelvy. I squished you."

My heart feels as squished as the stuffie, and I come to a sudden, startling realization.

This Boy is going to ruin me, and I'm going to enjoy every second of it.

In his bedroom, I lay out the selection of short-sleeved/short-legged rompers on his bed. I already have a feeling I know which one he'll choose, if his tight grip on Kelvin is any indication, but I still give Justin the choice of outfit.

Sure enough, he selects the penguins, and I grab the matching underwear, too.

"Let's get you out of these uncomfortable big boy clothes," I say, reaching for the waistband of his jeans. I pause before I pop the button, though. "You remember your safe words?"

Nibbling on his bottom lip he nods. I arch an eyebrow. He releases his lip and dutifully explains, "Red light for stop, yellow for pause to talk about it, green means go."

"Good boy," I kiss him on the forehead, feeling him squirm a little. "So, what color is this?"

"Green, Daddy. It's all green. I'll tell you if it's red."

I understand him not wanting to be brought out of his slow regression by being asked for his traffic light color for every new experience, so I nod. "Okay. I'm the same, baby. Just remember you can always say yellow or red at any time. Any time at all."

"Yes, Daddy, now hurry." He wriggles on the spot. "I want juice and playtime."

I give him a light swat on his still-denim-covered ass in warning, making him gasp. We've talked about rules and potential consequences, so he knows that a spanking is always on the table if he's bratty.

"We ask for things nicely, sweetheart."

His eyes glint back at me mischievously. "Yes, Daddy. Sorry." The little smirk on his face tells me that as sweet as he is, he's going to *want* a spanking at some point. Clearing his throat, he widens his eyes almost comically. "Can we *please* hurry so I can *please* have juice and playtime like you promised, Daddy?" His lips twitch. "*Please?*"

Oh, God, I've created a monster.

The sass is adorable, though, and it's going to take a lot more than that to earn himself a real spanking.

"You're being cheeky," I complain without any actual irritation. I pop the button of his jeans and squat so I can tug them and his underwear down. Thankfully, neither of us are wearing shoes, so he's able to step out of the pants easily.

It takes a lot of willpower to ignore his semi-erection before I push back up and lift his t-shirt over his head.

"Uh-uh," I waggle my index finger at him when he reaches down to touch himself. "It's not that kind of playtime. Plus," I gently grip his wrist and I know my smile is a little devilish when I declare, "little boys shouldn't play with themselves like that. That's for Daddy to touch."

Justin turns pink, but he groans in protest. "That's not fair."

"We've talked about the rules, haven't we?"

His lower lip juts out, but he nods slowly. "Sounded more fun than it is."

I snort and kiss the tip of his nose. "It makes it *much* more fun when Daddy says you *can* play with it, though."

The evidence of how much he enjoys my teasing is irrefutable. But this isn't supposed to be sexy playtime. Not yet. So, to calm us both down, I reach for his underwear and bend to help him step into each leg hole, one at a time.

His cock presses valiantly at the slightly padded, tight fabric once it is safely tucked inside, and Justin swivels his hips, likely trying to get some friction. I find that adorable as well.

"And now the penguin romper," I tell him, holding the item out. It does up with a zipper, running from the inside of his left leg and up across his belly to finish at the collar under the right side of his neck. It's a two way zip, designed to accommodate diaper changes and easier trips to the potty, and I prefer this style to the older ones with the snap clasps.

When I stand back to admire my handiwork, my heart gives another squeeze.

"How do I look?" he asks me, spreading his arms wide, with Kelvin dangling from his right hand. He does a slow spin on the spot.

"Perfect," I answer, feeling mildly choked up with emotion. I'm not sure why, but seeing him exploring his Little side like this, knowing that I'm the first man to get the privilege, is making me feel fluttery and anxious inside. Not in a bad way, but in a way that I'm not accustomed to.

Thankfully, Justin is regressed enough that he doesn't seem to notice the strange moment I'm experiencing. He grins. "Yay! It feels good, Daddy." He swivels his hips again, then bites his lip. "But...I think I shoulda gone potty first."

"I should have asked," I acknowledge, feeling like a rookie all over again. What is it about this man that throws me off my game so easily? "But that's okay. It means I can show you how to go while you're wearing your romper."

I lead him by the hand into the bathroom across the hall, and I show him the zipper and how to undo it from the leg.

"It feels funny," he giggles when his romper is exposed to his naval. But he steps up to the toilet and turns his back on me, adding, "No peeking. I can do this bit myself."

After he's done his business, I help him get the romper zipped up again and then we wash our hands and head back into the living room, making a quick stop in the bedroom to retrieve Kelvin.

"Do you want me to play with you?" I ask as I hand him his requested sippy full of juice. "Or do you want to see what it's like to play by yourself first?"

Some Littles find that it's less pressure to just explore their regression on their own, while others need Daddies or other Littles to play with them so they don't feel as on display or even as self-conscious exploring their kink. I think Justin could go either way.

"Play with me?" The request is sweet and tentative.

"I'd love to."

So we do. We spend an hour trying out the different toys I bought, and we discover that Justin loves coloring but isn't a big fan of building blocks. He liked racing the cars along the surface of the coffee table, but was otherwise not really invested in them. And, finally, he *loves* building forts.

By the time we're under a blanket fort constructed from his couch and the blanket from his bed, he has completely regressed. Without any inhibitions, he's giggly and playful and sweet, just like I thought he would be. His speech patterns are simplified but not infantile, and even though he's a little bit sassy, he's not bratty.

He's the perfect Boy for me.

When he yawns big and wide, I look around at the mess we've made, feeling a bit disappointed that we're coming to the end of his first real exploration of Little space. But he's tired, and I need to be a responsible Daddy.

"Well, tiger, I think we need to start cleaning up so we can wash up for bed."

An expression that matches the disappointment I'm feeling flickers across his face, but he nods. "Okay, Daddy," he acknowledges. "Can you read me a bedtime story?"

There goes my heart again.

"That sounds like a wonderful idea."

Chapter Eleven

Justin

"WE NEED" —I SUCK in a quick breath, my chest pressing further against the wall. My fingers curl, seeking some sort of purchase but finding nothing— "to hurry."

Gabe's tongue licks across one cheek and then the other. He doesn't seem to be taking my panted words seriously because he sure as hell isn't rushing what he's doing. My pants are down around my knees, and I know he's wearing his base layer of clothes. He should be in the locker room with the rest of his team, getting ready, pumping each other up. Instead, he's in a supply closet, on his knees, and teasing me.

He's still pumping something *up, I guess.*

I let my head fall forward and rest against the wall, sticking my ass out to meet Gabe's tongue. I can feel his breath against my bare ass when he laughs. "I'm going to take as long as I want," he says.

My words catch in my throat and instead of saying something back, a long moan fills the small space when his tongue brushes against my hole.

"Daddy." The word slips out as naturally as his name now. Despite our busy schedules, we've found time over the last month to go on dates or hang out at the house. Owen has joined us a few times, and it's in those moments that I see how easily Gabe fits in with not only me, but with my son as well.

When we've been alone, we've explored my Little side. I love getting to spend time with Gabe, but also how liberating it is to let all the worries and stress melt away and just *be*. Daddy is hands-on too, playing with me and anticipating my every move and want. He keeps my sippy cup filled with apple juice or water, helps me dress in my underwear and clothes. My most favorite time is when we cuddle at night and he reads me a book until I fall asleep against his chest.

My thoughts stop montaging the last month of our lives when his hand slips around my hip and grabs my cock. I'm close already, and the added friction of his calloused hand around me is getting me there quicker. My body can't decide between moaning and biting my lip. I know I can't be too loud. Daddy's other hand reaches up and grips my hip. His face is buried in my ass, and I *so* wish I could see what we look like.

His tongue breaches my hole slightly just as his hand tightens around the head of my cock. My whole body shivers. I am fast approaching the point of no return. His tongue flicks over my hole again and again, adding pressure and then going back to licking.

"I'm so close, Daddy. So close."

In a dizzying moment, I'm spun around and my back is pressed against the wall. I watch with a slack jaw as Gabe takes my cock into his mouth. In one movement, his nose is pressed against my skin and I can feel the tightness of his mouth, the heat that's driving me wild. I buck my hips and Gabe pulls back.

"Don't move, baby." His eyes lock with mine as he takes the head of my cock in his mouth and sucks, swirling his tongue around in a magical pattern before pulling back again. "Come for me, sweetheart. I need you to come before Daddy goes out there and plays the first game of the season." His hand is pumping me, the other fondling my balls, as he speaks. Daddy is the king of dirty talk.

It doesn't take but two more sucks before I'm coming down my Daddy's throat with a stifled shout. The wave of pleasure is overwhelming, and my knees nearly buckle, but Gabe is there to hold me up. He tucks me back into my pants and rights my clothes like nothing happened. The flush of my cheeks and heavy breathing says otherwise.

"I think we'll have to make this my pregame ritual," Daddy says softly, brushing his fingers across my cheek. "I'll see you out there, baby."

"Good luck," I say. My brain is still not fully back on track, but he just smiles and kisses me on the corner of my mouth before turning and opening the closet door.

I give myself a few seconds to regain some composure before heading into the main room, aiming for the sink in the corner to clean up. Gabe and I started in my office, actually going over different aspects of my job. But then one thing led to another, and then Gabe was asking about the products in the supply closet.

In hindsight, I should have seen the whole hook-up-in-the-closet move coming.

Rookie mistake.

It's the first game of the season tonight. There's been a buzz all week about it. I've worked with each of the guys on the team, along with Frankie, making sure they are all familiar with the stretches and what to look out for as far as strained muscles and injuries. I've seen pictures of roughed up hockey players, and I've even seen a small bruise or two on Gabe's body, and that's just during practice.

It makes me a bit worried for him, but I know he's been playing for years and that he knows what he is doing.

When I make my way out to the rink, the noise level is insane. There's music playing and people shouting. The opposing team is already on the ice, warming up. Since we have home ice advantage, we'll have a few minutes before the game starts to take to the ice. I check my watch. Still thirty minutes until the first period.

I'd probably be more nervous if I hadn't just come.

I spot Karen and Harold in the reserved seats I was heading towards. One of the perks of working for the team is that you can get free tickets. I invited them along for selfish reasons, but seeing the way Owen is beaming from ear to ear with excitement makes it worth it. He's holding a plastic tray of nachos with cheese smothering them. Dinner of champions, but I'll allow it tonight.

"Dad!" Owen shouts when he spots me. Karen looks at me for just a second before going back to her conversation with her husband.

"Hey, buddy," I ruffle his hair and smile, "how are you liking it so far?"

If we were in a cartoon, he would have sparkles in his eyes. "This is so much fun! Are you going to go on the ice?"

"No, I don't go out there. I get to sit here with you unless someone gets hurt. Then I would go back into my office and help them."

"Can I see your office?"

"After the game," I answer easily. Depending on how the game goes tonight, Gabe has said he'll either go out and celebrate with the team, or head back to his dorm. I'll have to get Owen home and in bed soon after anyway. I offered for Gabe to come over, but he has some exams coming up he needs to study for.

The announcer's voice comes over the speakers, grabbing everyone's attention. "Let's make some noise, for the first time this season, the Phoenix Penguins!"

The crowd goes wild and I hold back a smile as Owen joins them, scrambling to stand on his seat and almost spilling his food. I make sure it's set down before picking him up so he can see the guys come up the tunnel.

Each player grabs their gear before hitting the ice and making a few laps around. Some wave and smile at people they recognize as they pass, which makes everyone cheer louder. Not once does the crowd lose momentum until the announcer starts up again, calling out numbers and names to announce the lineup for this year. Owen squeals in excitement when he hears Gabe's name, and it makes my heart soar for so many reasons.

"Can we go up to the glass?" Owen asks. I can see why he's asking. We are in the third row and the stands are elevated, but he's only five and is surrounded by adults.

"Maybe for a bit when the game starts," I answer.

He finishes his nachos, kicking his feet with excitement the entire time. I eye the guys on the ice, slipping back into work mode to watch each of them. No one needs to know that my eyes keep drifting back to jersey number twenty-six. My initial fears about our personal and work lives mingling have mostly been settled. There's still a small bit of uneasiness I feel when I'm directing the whole team to do certain stretches during practice, or when Coach thanks me for taking Gabe 'under my wing'.

The game is intense from the puck drop.

I've had to brush up on my hockey knowledge now that I'm dating a hockey player. I knew the basics, enough to get this job, but the way Gabe talks about the game, I couldn't keep up with the different positions and rules. I'm still learning, but I know enough to truly enjoy the game. I explain as much as I can to Owen, but he doesn't seem interested in anything past when the guys get smashed against the glass.

Gabe plays Left Winger, which is unfortunate for us as he's playing on the other side of the ice from where we're sitting, but he does get pushed against the wall a few times. During the second intermission, when the guys are catching their breath and regrouping, the score is 3 to 1, with us in the red. It doesn't look good, but we still have one more period left, and I've learned that teams have beaten greater odds than that in the final minutes of a game.

"Dad, what's that?" Owen catches my attention and points to the Zamboni on the ice.

"It's cleaning the ice so that when the players come back, the rink will be clear like in the beginning of the game. Too much ice being scratched away can cause buildup and it can slow the players down or cause them to fall."

"I like when they fall," Owen says happily and so, so innocently. I roll my eyes and laugh.

"It was a little bit funny when Wallace fell, wasn't it?"

Wallace is one of our team players and I do need to go make sure that everything is okay. "How would you like to go meet the team real quick? I bet they could use some high fives from you."

"Yes! Yes!" Owen jumps up, completely ignoring his grandparents. They haven't said much during the game, but it's also been so loud. They look over at us now.

"We'll be back. Would you like anything to drink or eat?"

"We're fine, Justin. Thank you." Karen gives me a quick smile and Harold holds up his half-filled beer.

I flash my badge to the security guy standing by the door and he lets us through easily. Coach is giving a pep talk and giving the new plays for the last period when we walk in. Owen stands close to me, his hand firmly in mine. Half the guys are sitting, others are throwing down some fresh water and cramming energy bars. We wait quietly until Overton is finished. The guys have another ten minutes before they need to be back on the ice for the final period.

"Little man!" Gabe calls when he spots Owen. He shoots me a wink before motioning for Owen to run over to him. There is only a moment's hesitation on Owen's part before he drops my hand and goes full speed. "How are you liking the game?"

"It's awesome! I like when you bump into the wall and how everyone screams when you score." Owen's voice falters a bit when he realizes that most of the room is looking at him.

"I didn't know you had a kid, Gabe," someone says.

"He's not mine," Gabe says. "He's Justin's. We're just really good friends, aren't we, Owen?"

"Yes!" Owen nods excitedly.

I watch as Gabe introduces most of the team. Owen is not going to remember any of their names, but it's worth a shot. He ends up giving everyone a high five before we have to head back out. I check on the players, make sure no one needs anything from me. Frankie and I will be splitting the team for about half an hour after the game as they all get out of their uniforms, but nothing has happened to cause any injuries.

Knock on wood, I think.

We're back in our seats just in time for the last period to start. The crowd is more amped up than they've been the whole game. We score pretty quickly into the period, which seems to give the guys the motivation to push harder, skate faster, be even more aggressive. One of the guys on the other team gets thrown into the penalty box for trying to start a fight, which gives us a power play and the advantage we need to score once more.

With five minutes left in the game, we're tied.

I look from the ice to Owen. His eyes are tired, I can tell, but he's fighting it. They're glued to the ice, darting this way and that. I don't know how much he understands, but I can see a future obsessed with hockey. I'll have to look into skating lessons for him. He's never been on ice before, but I recognize that glint of excitement in his eyes.

The game goes into overtime until we finally score the winning goal. Drinks and popcorn mix all around us. I hold Owen in my arms, protecting him more than celebrating. Someone has one of those handheld horns, which I've been told are banned, and others are shouting in celebration. I catch more than a few curse words.

I follow the team and Coach back to the locker room once more. Frankie and I go to the physical therapy room, and I set Owen down in an empty chair. He's about to topple over with sleep. The excitement is leaving his body quickly. Gabe is the first to come in, along with Paul and Barry. Gabe immediately goes to Owen and scoops him up into his arms.

By the time Gabe moves to sit in the chair, Owen is passed out on his shoulder. "I'm good. All my muscles are loose, my head is good. Focus on the other guys. I've got him."

The guys come in two or three at a time. Gabe walks around the room with Owen in his arms. I don't see any signs of him hurting so I trust that he's telling me the truth that he's okay and that I don't need to make him do any post-game stretches or check him for injuries. I give some advice for a couple of them to take it easy, but I also know they're all about to go out and celebrate the first game and the first win.

Soon enough, it's just me, Gabe, and Owen. He's still fast asleep. I'm sure he'll sleep in a bit tomorrow.

"Good game," I whisper, standing next to him. I lay one hand on Owen's back and the other on Gabe's bicep. I give him a gentle squeeze. "I'm proud of you, Daddy."

I stand on my tippy toes to kiss his cheek and then take my son to head home.

"I'll call you tomorrow, okay?" Gabe says. "But text me so I know you made it home safely."

Chapter Twelve

"Gabriel," Mom declares as she throws the door open, then opens her arms wide, "darling, I've missed you."

I'm pulled into a tight hug before I can so much as say hello. Mom is short and plump, and she always smells like cookies or whatever sweet thing she's been baking. I inhale as best I can while having the life squeezed out of me, and I'm hit with a pang of nostalgia.

I haven't gone to a college too far from home, but with how busy life gets between classes, looking after my nieces and nephews, hockey, and now Justin and Owen, I haven't gotten to see my parents anywhere near as often as they'd like. Maybe not even as often as I would like, either.

"Come inside," Mom demands once she releases me, as if she's not the one who accosted me right at the doorway. She takes a step back and rakes her gaze over my body, her lips turning down. "You're looking far too skinny, Gabe. Do you get a chance to eat at that school of yours? That hockey team isn't working you to the bone, is it?"

"Mom," I groan, but I'm cut off as she turns on her heel and heads down the hallway towards the kitchen at the back of the house.

"I'm making your favorite," she throws over her shoulder. "*Paprikás csirke*. Your *nagymama's* recipe." She pauses and winks. "My mother's, not Dad's mom's."

I snort. My mom has always had a frosty relationship with her mother-in-law. Mom and Dad are first generation Americans, with their parents fleeing from Hungary during World War II. My parents grew up together in a small Hungarian community in Cleveland but moved to Tucson after they got married and Dad got a job out here. They've been here ever since.

My paternal grandmother has always seemed to resent my mother for taking her son so far away, even though it was Dad's job that brought him out here. So, Mom and my dad's mom have always had a rocky relationship. Even now, with my grandmother still in Cleveland, my mom has to get her little digs in.

"Don't let Dad hear you dissing her," I tease and she sighs.

"Mama's boys..." she mutters, before turning to frown at me again. "I love you, Gabe, but you don't need to follow in his footsteps like that, okay?"

"Well, I doubt you're going to be a monster-in-law to my boyfriend, so—what?"

We've made it to the kitchen and even though I tower over her, she shoves me hard onto a kitchen stool at the island and says, "Boyfriend? This is the first I'm hearing of a boyfriend."

"I mean," I try to backpedal, "I was kind of talking in a hypothetical sense."

She plants her hands on her soft hips and scowls. "Gabriel Tomas Nagy, I know all your tells when you're not being truthful. Now, when were you going to introduce us to this boy?"

"Man," I shift in place, uncomfortable with her coming so close to our kink roles, even though her comment was purely innocent.

"And...soon. Ish. I guess." To be honest, I have been enjoying having Justin to myself for the most part.

"You guess?"

"It's still new," I explain. "And our family is pretty big and loud. He's not used to that."

Since we've been dating, I've learned bits and pieces of Justin's life. His own parents thought he was throwing his life away when he had his son, and Owen's maternal grandparents seem more interested in looking after Owen than in Justin's well-being. I'm not entirely sure what the dynamic there is all about: he's been a bit vague on the details, and I haven't wanted to push. As long as it's working for him, I'm not going to be too nosy.

But, all-in-all, Justin is clearly used to a more solitary existence. I think bombarding him with my family would be cruel, even if he has met one of my sisters at Owen's school.

"Who's not used to what?" Dad's voice cuts into our conversation and I smile in greeting as he strides up beside Mom and wraps his arm around her shoulders.

At 5'10", he's taller than her, but not as tall as me. I've inherited his more olive-toned skin, Mom's darker hair and Dad's brown eyes. I do look more like Dad than I do Mom, but, like my mother, my dad is...cuddly. I guess a lifetime of being fed Mom's rich cooking would do that to anyone.

But because my entire family equates food with love —a mentality passed down from generation to generation— I try to be a little more careful about how much I eat when I'm home. I can't afford to lose my edge on the ice and therefore my scholarship so close to the end of my degree, simply because my mom's cooking is too tempting to pass up.

"Gabriel has a boyfriend," Mom answers my dad while I'm mourning all the delicious food I can't allow myself to eat right now, "and he has kept him a secret because he's afraid we'll be too much for him." She raises a pointed eyebrow my way.

I laugh and shake my head at her dramatics. "I didn't put it quite like that…" Turning to Dad, I explain, "We haven't been together long, and he's…shy."

Memories of his first few experiences in Little headspace filter through my mind. He's always sweet, but there's something tentative in the way he tries new things; cautious and almost skittish. And I know my boisterous family can be overwhelming even without having the pressure of being one of the first guys I've dated long enough to introduce them.

"Invite him over," Mom insists. "We want to meet him."

"I haven't told you anything about him yet," I chuckle with a hint of incredulity.

"He has the good sense to date you," Dad shrugs, then winks conspiratorially. "He already gets points for that."

Mom nods, adding, "But we *want* to know about him. What's his name? Does he go to the same school as you? What is he studying? How did you meet?"

"Actually, we met before the semester began. At Ma's diner. Justin —that's his name— was trying to calm his son down and I stepped in to help."

"Son?" Dad blinks. I can tell that it surprises him, and I wonder how many conclusions he's jumping to. But instead of voicing any of them, he asks, "How old is his son?"

"Oh, wait," Mom interrupts before I can answer. She bounces her index finger in the air as she muses aloud, "Mandy said something about you seeming interested in a dad at Brian's school.

I just thought she was trying to tease me about you or get you in trouble."

I snort. "I mean, she *would* do both those things, but...yeah. Owen's five. He's in Bry's class." I can't help but smile when I think of the little boy. "He's a really cute kid, actually. And Justin's twenty-seven. He's been raising Owen alone ever since Owen's mom died."

My mother's eyes go wide with compassion. "Oh, the poor thing. Now you *have to* bring him around. We'll get your sisters and brother here and they can bring their kids, so you know Owen will be entertained and Justin can have a break."

My lips quirk. "A break while you interrogate him?"

Mom waves me off. "I am nothing like my mother-in-law."

"Of course not. You're a cool mom." I tease playfully.

She picks up a dishtowel and whips it in the air in my direction. "You watch your tone, Gabriel, or I might just push you in front of a bus."

Dad clears his throat before I can offer another movie-themed rebuttal. "So, if not a college student, what does Justin do for a living?"

Even though I know we're not *really* doing anything wrong (ignoring the sex on company time, anyway), I bite my lip. "Funny story..."

***

"Hey, baby," I grin, leaning against Justin's doorframe.

His lips curl into a welcoming smile and he takes a step back to let me in. "Hi, Daddy."

After spending yesterday with some of my family at my parents' house, it's nice to come back to the comparative peace and quiet of Justin's place. "Is Owen in his room?"

He nods. "He's playing with his trucks as usual."

I grin. "Good. That means I can do this." I swoop in for a searing kiss, pressing *my* Boy up against the nearest wall, and he returns the kiss eagerly, his tongue twirling around mine. I have to remind myself to stop at just the kiss. To not rut my swelling cock into his softer tummy.

It's hard to have willpower around him. I don't think he realizes just how wrapped around his little finger I am already.

"Mmm," he murmurs as the kiss tapers to an end, "not that I'm complaining, but what was that for?"

"I just missed you," I answer honestly, and he laughs.

"We see each other practically every day."

It's true. On the days where I'm not at hockey practice, I'm trailing him and Frankie around their jobs, trying to get some practical experience for my degree.

A couple of the guys from the team are being monitored for muscle strains and other minor injuries, so I get to sit in on their appointments and even help out with some of their treatments, too. The paperwork side of it all is much more boring, but watching the pink tip of Justin's tongue peeking out from between his lips when he concentrates makes even that part of the whole experience entertaining. However, it's all still work, *and* I have to keep my hands to myself.

"But that's not the same," I answer blithely. "I don't get to do all the things I want to with you."

Justin scoffs. I love the way his nose crinkles adorably when he does. "Like you didn't blow me in a storage closet just last week."

"My Boy is my good luck charm," I shrug. "The orgasms make it easier to focus on the game."

"My orgasm made it easier for you to focus?" He arches an eyebrow and his lip quirks. "I don't understand how that works."

"Who says I didn't also come, sweetheart?"

"You did *not* play an entire game of hockey while wearing cum-soaked underwear." Now he squirms, probably thinking about how uncomfortable that would have felt under my hockey gear.

"No, I didn't. I cleaned up in the bathroom before I made it back to the locker room." It really would have been too uncomfortable putting my protective cup into a jizz-coated jockstrap. "I think things through, baby, I swear."

"Uh huh." He shakes his head, and it's only now that I notice the dark circles under his eyes. Concern immediately takes over and my amusement —and arousal— vanishes instantly.

"Are you okay?" I ask, reaching to cup his jaw. I smooth my thumb over the dark skin beneath his left eye. "You look tired. Stressed, even."

He sighs and steps out of my reach, running his hand through his hair. "Yeah, yeah, I'm fine. Just had a little argument with Lauren's parents. It's nothing."

Hmm.

I still haven't met Owen's grandparents, but I know they have been helping pick Owen up after school and stuff. I can only assume it has been a huge adjustment for Justin, uprooting his entire life so Owen could spend more time with his grandparents. Going from being the sole carer of a kid to practically sharing custody with his former in-laws must be a stressful experience.

"I think maybe you need some Little time," I eventually reply, letting the thoughts filter through a pros and cons list in my head before voicing the idea out loud. Before he can protest and tell me it would be too weird with Owen in the house, or something to that effect, I add, "After Owen's in bed, we'll lock ourselves in your room and try to get you to let go for a bit. Nothing too intense. And, if he wakes up and calls out, I can help him, okay?"

Justin thinks about it for a long moment. The green in his hazel eyes looks more pronounced when he finally awards me with a slow nod. "Okay. I think...I think that would be good."

***

Over dinner, where Owen happily catches me up on the things he has been doing at school, I consider what kind of activities might help Justin tonight. I'd love to give him a bubble bath, but with only one bathroom in the house, that's probably something better left for a night when Owen is at his grandparents' place.

It's only after Justin slips into Owen's bedroom to tuck him in for the night that I decide mirroring the experience is the best option. I want tonight to be about relaxation for my Boy; I don't want him getting all excited and fired up with silly games or invigorating play.

I choose his outfit from the bag stuffed in the back of his closet, and I pull Kelvin out from his hiding place as well. Then I arrange a sippy cup of milk and wait for Justin in his bedroom. I've linked my phone to the little speaker he keeps on his nightstand, and I've got soothing instrumental music playing in the background. When he finally joins me, Justin pauses inside the doorway.

"Oh," he murmurs quietly, taking in the scene I'm setting. The lamp on the nightstand is lit and emitting a soft, warm glow. The bedcovers are pulled back, and I have a selection of picture books sitting next to his sippy cup. Kelvin is propped up against his pillow.

"Have you gone potty and brushed your teeth?" I ask, and he bites his lip, shaking his head.

"Would you like Daddy to help you do that?" I ask, hoping that it might help guide him towards his Little headspace. It's been happening a lot more easily for him the more regression time he gets to indulge in, but with how on edge he seemed tonight, I think it might help to give him a nudge.

He nibbles his lip and blushes. "Yes please, Daddy."

"Good boy," I praise, crossing the room to take his hand. "Let's go."

We make our way inside the bathroom quietly, and I help him pull down his shorts and underwear, then press up behind him as he stands in front of the toilet. My hand wraps around the back of his and I help him aim into the bowl, then I let him go as he gives himself a couple of shakes, before offering him a few squares of toilet paper. It's a far cry from the first couple of times, where Little Justin insisted he could potty by himself.

We wash our hands together in a very similar fashion, and he giggles quietly when I rub the soap into a bubbly lather over his hands and then my own. The sound is music to my ears.

Making funny faces in the mirror as we brush our teeth in tandem, it's almost like watching a switch get flipped in his head as he finally starts to let himself go towards his Little headspace.

"You brushed your teeth very well, sweetheart," I say after we've rinsed and spat and wiped our faces clean and dry. "Daddy's proud of you."

His cheeks still turn a little bit pink at the praise, but he smiles widely. "Thank you, Daddy. You did a good job, too."

Oh, my heart.

It's innocuous little moments like these that really seem to hit me in the solar plexus, like I've been body checked by emotion. And they still scare me a bit, because it's too soon to name the emotion itself. I'm not even sure my interpretation of it is correct, because I've never felt like this before.

I've thought Boys were adorable before. I've even felt flutters of affection and excitement for them. But this breath-stealing, almost-physical ache in my gut is wholly new and daunting.

It's only been a couple of months —a handful of weeks, even— since we started dating. I know that I'm Justin's first ever serious relationship outside of the one he had with Owen's mom, and the fact that I'm his first ever serious relationship with a guy *shouldn't* make a difference...but in my head it still kind of does.

What if he's not as invested as I am? He wasn't looking for anything serious, so what if he decides it's not actually what he wants after all?

And, yeah, I wasn't looking for anything serious, either, but here I am, falling head over skates in lo—

Nope. I'm *not* jinxing this.

Getting Justin back into his room, I smile, playfully teasing and tickling him as I get him out of his grown-up clothes and into his penguin onesie. It's his favorite, and I want to give him every possible opportunity to regress properly tonight.

Then I guide him into his bed, ignoring yet another one of those pangs when he cuddles Kelvin close to his chest and looks up at me like I hung the moon, and I slide under the covers beside him.

I'm still wearing my casual outfit of gray sweats and a soft cotton t-shirt with the team's logo on the front, but the clothes are comfortable enough that I could sleep in them if I choose to. With Justin snuggling up against me like a warm, cuddly limpet, I just might do that.

Wrapping one arm around him, I hand him his sippy cup (ignoring the futility of having brushed his teeth only minutes earlier) and I grab the top book from the pile of choices.

These books are all for Justin only. I bought them for him, and we keep them separate from any which he might read with Owen. We've found that keeping his interests and toys completely separate helps with his regression, and with not second-guessing or getting anxious about his kink and his personal life crossing over.

So, the books might be a bit unconventional for most Daddies, but they work for us.

"Go the fuck to sleep," I read the title page of the first book from the pile, and Justin chuckles.

"That's a naughty word, Daddy."

"Sleep is *not* a naughty word."

He giggles again.

And so we continue on.

***

"Thank you for last night," Justin says the next morning when we're getting dressed for school and work. "I feel so much better today."

I'm proud of myself for getting him to relax and enjoy himself. "Anytime, baby," I bend to press a sweet kiss to his lips. "I love being your Daddy." The admission skirts dangerously close to naming the feeling that makes my heart pound in my chest. I clear my throat. "But, uh, I have a favor to ask. And you can say no."

"Okay..." He gives me a look not unlike the kind that he gives Owen when he's expecting an explanation for some of the kid's cheekier behavior.

At times like this, I'm reminded that he is actually the more adultier-adult in our relationship.

"My, uh, my family want to meet you. And Owen. And I know that's asking a lot, because there are like a million of them, but...I would actually really like to introduce you to them, too."

The look on his face gentles into understanding before he smiles. "Sure," he shrugs. "When would they like us to visit?"

And there's that feeling again.

Oh, I am in big trouble, I think to myself. But, strangely, I'm feeling good about it.

Chapter Thirteen

Justin

"Justin?"

I tilt my head back and roll my eyes to look at Daddy sitting on the couch behind me. I'm sitting on the floor, between his open knees, coloring. We have a TV show on, but I haven't been paying enough attention to it for the last three episodes. I want to make Daddy the perfect picture to take with him on the road.

"Yes, Daddy?" He smiles and, although his face is upside down for me, that expression is obvious, and I want to commit it to memory.

I've had so much fun with Daddy today. He came over for breakfast this morning with me and Owen, but then Owen went to his grandparents' place, and we spent all of lunch and through dinner as Daddy and Boy.

It's been amazing.

"It's almost ten o'clock. Are you getting sleepy?"

I start getting a bit dizzy from the position and turn my body around to sit on my knees, my hands on his thighs. I notice the way Daddy's eyes are slightly hooded, like he's getting sleepy himself. He didn't eat a lot for dinner, and I know he had practice this morning. Plus, he's going away for a game tomorrow. He needs to sleep as much as I do.

And, anyway, I'll never say no to cuddles with Daddy.

"I go potty first," I say without argument. Daddy Gabe smiles at me and leans forward to kiss me. It's a quick kiss and I wish I could make it longer, but I can get more kisses once we're asleep. Or in bed. Not asleep, because people can't kiss when they're asleep. Or can they?

"What is going on in that brain of yours?" Daddy pokes the side of my head playfully and I turn my face to try and bite his finger. He snorts and it makes me laugh.

"I was just thinking about getting more kisses once we're in bed," I say with a grin.

"I guess we should get moving then."

I'm on my feet in a second, pulling on Daddy's hand. I'm wearing a green shirt with two penguins on it and a rainbow behind them. When Daddy was dressing me, he had the matching shorts laid out on the bed, but I decided to go with just the training pants tonight. I love the way they feel when I wear them. Daddy surprised me with more pairs last weekend and this is the first chance I'm getting to wear them. They are a matching green to my shirt around the edges and have different leaf shape designs on the front and back. Being able to play around in just the shirt and training pants helped me slip right into Littlespace today.

I stop outside of the bathroom and turn to face Daddy. He's wearing a pair of sweats that leave too much to my imagination and a white tee. I can feel my cock gaining interest the longer we stand there and look at each other. Then, for no reason, I start to giggle. I don't know what makes me start, but Daddy joins in and I can't stop. I'm just really, really happy and I want to show Daddy that. Show him how comfortable I am with everything we've been doing and also that I've been doing my own research.

"What has gotten into you tonight, baby?" Daddy puts his hands on my hips, which stills me, but doesn't stop the growing inside my pants. I can feel myself coming out of Little space slowly, but I'm still incredibly happy and confident with what I'm about to ask. I want to give myself a few minutes to get the words right, though, so I stand up on my tiptoes and give him a kiss before walking into the bathroom.

As I use the bathroom, watching from the corner of my eye as Gabe fixes his stare on my every movement, I think about how to phrase what I want to say. My thoughts circle back to our first conversation about it, when Gabe answered all of my questions and we looked up information online together. Then I consider the things I found when I did my own research, looking further into some of the aspects of regression that interested me.

One in particular is playing on my mind. Wetting. I'm not into the idea of diapers, but I like it when Daddy helps me go potty, and the thought of him cleaning me up is raising interest in more than just my brain.

"Okay, Justin, I think you've washed your hands long enough. I can tell when you're stalling. What's going on?"

I smile and, by his tone of voice, I know he can tell I'm out of my Little headspace. He returns the smile and we face each other, both leaning against the sink. "Can we discuss doing a scene together?"

"A scene? Is what we're doing too much for you?" His tone isn't judging or worried, just questioning. He's also so understanding that it makes me extra sure about what I want. I would never feel this comfortable and safe with anyone else to ask this. Or, at least, I can't imagine feeling this way with anyone else.

"I love what we're doing," I say matter-of-factly. "I mean discussing a specific scene, something that I don't know if I'll enjoy, but I've been thinking about it, and I'd like to try it at least once."

"Okay," Gabe takes my hand, his expression open and encouraging. "What is it?"

"I'd like to try a scene where I have an accident," I start. "I like it when you help me use the bathroom, and I've been thinking about what it would be like to have you clean me up. If that's something you'd be interested in."

"Do you mean like an accident in your underwear?" He asks without missing a beat. "I don't mind cleaning you up if you pee and make a mess, but my red light is poop."

How is this not an awkward conversation? I feel completely at ease with Gabe while we discuss this. I've never had a relationship, even with Owen's mom, where we were this comfortable and close with each other. I smile and nod.

"That would be a red light for me too. I can definitely do that part on my own." We both laugh at the joke and I'm aware that we're slowly moving closer to each other. "But what do you think?"

"I think it would be special to experience that with you," Gabe answers earnestly. I can see excitement hidden behind his eyes. "Do you have anything specific in mind?"

"Not really." I shrug. "I figured once we talked about it, I'd just let it happen naturally?"

"It takes a lot for your brain to let your bladder let go like that," Gabe says. "We'll plan a day where I make sure that you drink plenty of water and we have a good couple of hours on our own, okay?"

"Okay."

I'm not sure who closes the rest of the distance, but soon Daddy is kissing me again and I part my lips easily to give him the lead. Our tongues tangle in a frenzy of want and my hands find their way to Gabe's long hair. It's almost always pulled back into a man bun, which I find insanely attractive, but on rare nights like this, he leaves it loose around his shoulders.

His hands wrap around my back and pull me against him in a quick motion. His lips swallow my moan as my erection is trapped against the soft padding of the training pants.

I need all our clothes off now.

"Gabe." I whisper his name on an exhale and lock eyes with him. The lust in his eyes reflects how I'm feeling.

"What do you need, Justin?"

I smile. He's always pulling out that low, sexy Daddy voice. It's like he knows exactly what it does to me.

"I need you to fuck me," I say confidently. His eyebrows raise, either in surprise or at my tone. "Please?"

"I'm going to let the naughty word slide just once," he says, raising a finger between us. That same finger falls back to my waist and dips just inside the pants I'm wearing. My whole body shivers at the simple contact. "Because I want to fuck you so much, baby. Get in the bedroom. I'll be right there."

I waste no time and hear Gabe snicker behind me. I save even more time by stripping out of my shirt before he comes in.

When he does come in, he's also shirtless, all smooth golden skin and lean muscle. I want to get on my knees and pull down his pants. He holds up a hand and stops me from doing just that, though. "Take off your pants and lay on the bed, okay?"

Despite wanting to worship him, I nod and do as he asks. I wrap my hand around my shaft and stroke up, letting my jaw go slack at the feeling. Gabe slips out of his sweats, revealing the thin briefs underneath which definitely leave nothing to the imagination. I swear I can see the veins in his cock with how pressed against the fabric it is.

"Are you sure?" he asks, hesitating for only a second before climbing onto the bed and straddling my waist when I give him a single nod.

"Um—" I do hesitate for just a second and Gabe stops moving altogether. I continue before he can ask what's on my mind. We've spoken about this before, but I still want to ask. I want to be his good boy. "Can I have permission to cuss while we're having sex? Because I will probably forget in the moment either way."

Gabe's laugh fills the room, and he leans forward, covering my body with his. "Permission granted, baby. Thank you for asking first. You're such a good boy."

"I love when you call me that." I tangle my hands back in his hair and pull him down to seal our lips together.

Gabe's hands roam my body as we kiss and kiss some more. I can feel my dick leaking, trapped between our bodies. When I'm sure I can't take it anymore, I move my hands to his briefs and tug on them, a hint to get things moving.

"You're impatient, you know that?" Gabe whispers the words against my mouth, but he still shimmies out of the last bit of clothing.

"Not my fault when you are perfect in every sense of the word."

He's holding himself braced on his hands above me now, our legs tangled. My eyes trace down his body. Broad shoulders, wide pecs, abs for days, the deep V that leads right to his groin and the glorious cock I've had in my mouth more times than I can count on both hands.

Fuck, he's the epitome of eye-candy for *anyone*.

Our skin tones contrast where our bodies meet, too. His olive skin, which looks beautiful and natural, like he belongs in the sun, against my lighter shade which is still getting used to the Arizona UV index.

"Perfect is a bit of a stretch," Gabe says with a small shake of his head. But he doesn't give me time to refute that comment. All thoughts are lost when he scoots down the bed and takes my cock in his mouth. I'm not that big, quite average, actually, but he doesn't seem to care.

Gabe swallows around me, pressing his nose into the curls at the base in one swoop. My stomach muscles clench in both surprise and bliss. He hollows his cheeks and sucks as he pulls back, and my mind goes into overdrive.

It feels amazing. I lose myself in it, enjoying every bob of his head, swept away by the warmth and suction.

There is an audible *pop* when Gabe pulls off my cock. I smother a whine of complaint as he grins up at me, eyes raking over my body as well. "Lift your legs for me, baby."

Hooking my hands behind my knees, I bring them to my chest. My eyes close on instinct when Gabe's tongue flicks over my hole. "Your ass is amazing, Justin." He says the words, each one punctuated with a teasing touch of his tongue.

"I love that you love my ass," I reply with my eyes still closed. I tighten my grip on my knees to stave off coming too soon. His hands spread my cheeks, and I bite my bottom lip when his tongue presses into me. It's a sensation I went years without, but I crave it now with Gabe. It's addictive. My breath hitches when he adds a finger beside his tongue.

The room fills with my moans and sounds of Gabe prepping me at his own speed. It's toeing a line of too much and not enough, which doesn't make sense, but it's the only way I can describe it.

Gabe coaches me through it all, moving my legs to wrap around his waist while he pushes three fingers into my hole. He praises me and that deep, bedroom voice allows me to fully relax as he pushes his digits into me.

I'm not even sure where the lube came from, but I don't question it.

"You're doing so good, baby, opening up for me. You're almost ready to take Daddy's cock, aren't you?"

"So ready," I answer. Looking into his eyes, I know we're both feeling the same way. Kind of sweaty, bodies aching to be connected as close as possible. A feeling I'm not ready to put a name to wells up in my chest, forcing me to swallow before I let the words slip. "Please, Daddy. I want you to ruin me for anyone else."

"No one else touches what's mine, Justin." His words are sharp and his tone is beyond serious when he leans over my body and looks directly at me. "I don't share my Boys."

"I wouldn't dream of it, Daddy." I wrap my arms around his neck and pull him in for a kiss. Our height difference has his cock teasing my ass while my erection is pressed firmly against his stomach.

Gabe pulls back once more, settling on his knees. In a move that fucks with my brain and makes a bead of precum pool at the head of my cock, Gabe reaches up and ties his hair back in one, smooth movement. The corner of Gabe's lips quirk up when he notices my cock. "Was that sexy for you? I could do it in slow motion, if you want."

"Shut up," I laugh. He reaches down and pinches one of my nipples. Recoiling, I swat his hand away. That only starts a squabble between us and, within seconds, I'm happily trapped on my stomach between my Daddy's body and the mattress.

It's exactly where I want to be.

I lift my ass and spread my legs, waiting.

There are no words spoken, but I hear the rustling of the foil packet and then feel Gabe fix himself behind me.

"Push out, baby. I'm going to go slow and let you get used to it." I brace myself for the pressure I know is coming. He's true to his word when he says he'll go slow. I grip the cover on the pillow below me and breathe through it. It doesn't take long for the initial pain to fade, replaced by growing pleasure. "You're doing so good, Justin. Halfway there."

"*Halfway*?!" I turn my head, trying to glare at him over my shoulder. I'm barely successful, but the sudden movement has me pushing back against him and I wince when more of him slips in. "Fuck. Ouch."

"Sorry, sweetheart," Gabe soothes. His hands grip around my hips and hold me still. I couldn't move if I wanted to. "Are you okay?"

"I'm good. Just wasn't expecting that. That was on me, though."

"Do you need a second?" His voice is full of concern. I shake my head.

"I'm good now." I adjust myself just slightly and rest on my forearms. I can feel sweat forming on my forehead and chest already.

Gabe adjusts himself as well and pushes forward until his hips are flush against my ass. I drop my head to the pillow and close my eyes, relishing in the feeling. Everything is perfect. Gabe is perfect.

I took a huge chance moving across the country and starting a new career. I never imagined I would meet someone who would fill a piece of me that's been missing for a long time.

And filling me he is, in more ways than one.

Each thrust sends a new wave of emotion, lust, and pleasure through my body. The sound of skin on skin and Gabe's grunts with each flex of his hips is music to my ears. I move one hand to wrap around my own dick.

"Are you going to come for Daddy? Let me see how much of a mess my Boy can make."

I try to respond, but Gabe pushes into me again and my words come out as a moan. I can feel my orgasm building and I quicken my strokes, timing the movements with pushing my hips back to meet Gabe for each thrust. "Oh, oh, Justin. Fuck. You feel so good, baby."

"I'm—" My words cut off with a choked gasp and I almost lose my balance. I squeeze my ass around Gabe's cock over and over and he adds some hidden strength to his thrusts. "Fuck, yes. Like that. Please, harder, Daddy. Fuck me until I come."

I swear I hear Gabe growl before I'm being pushed into the mattress with Gabe's hands on my back, holding himself up as he rails my ass.

"Oh, fuck yes!" I scream into the pillow, but it's muffled. My cock rubs against the blanket below me, leaving a puddle of precum as Gabe gives me his all. My body is totally pliant with whatever he wants right now.

When my orgasm hits, it's quick and powerful. I lift my head and let out a mangled sound of pleasure. Not quite a moan, kind of a scream. My cock pulses, fighting to release every drop as Gabe quickens his thrusts until he stills and I know he's come.

We are sweaty and my stomach is smeared with cum, but I don't care.

Gabe is pulling out when I fully come back to reality. He helps me roll onto my back, avoiding the wet spot, and I smile up at him.

"Like I said" —I take a deep breath and reach out for his hand— "*perfect.*"

***

As much as I wish I could wake up next to Gabe and lounge around in the morning enjoying each other's company, Gabe has to leave for the away game and Owen will be home by nine. I lay in the bed, curled up and content, and watch Gabe dress. He gives me a soft morning kiss before making sure my alarm is set for eight and my phone is on the charger.

Once we cleaned up last night and changed the blanket, I called Owen to say goodnight. It was late, but I know he has fun with his cousins on the weekends, so I didn't push it. He told me briefly about his day and then asked if Gabe was still at the house.

Owen was a bit more animated talking to Gabe. I tried not to feel hurt about that.

He bends down and brushes his lips over my cheek. "I'll call you after the game, okay?"

"I miss you already," I mumble and give him another kiss. "Have a good game and a safe flight."

"I'll be back tomorrow."

As he walks out of the room, I tuck myself against the pillow he used last night. Breathing deeply, I fall asleep again to thoughts of what we did. When my alarm goes off again, I feel more awake.

I do my business in the bathroom before moving to the kitchen and grabbing the overnight oats that Gabe made last night while I was coloring. The one he'd made for himself is still in the fridge. I frown at that. He was supposed to take it with him this morning, but I assume the team will eat on the trip to the game. It's in the next state over, only a handful of hours. He'll be back tomorrow morning.

I'm sitting on the couch, scrolling through the channels, when I hear Karen's car pull up outside. I meet them at the front door and give Owen a hug before letting him pass by and go into his room. Karen stands a few steps away.

"How was he for you?"

"Good, as always. I think he'll be tired today. He didn't sleep much last night."

"We'll probably have a chill day inside then," I say. "Thank you for letting him hang out on the weekends. We haven't quite figured out a schedule with the other parents for playdates, so I know seeing his cousins is good for him."

"Of course," she replies. "We're always happy to have him around. I have to run, though. I'm picking him up from school on Monday, right?"

"Um, yeah, I think so. I have to double check my schedule since they've started away games now. A few Fridays I'll be able to pick him up."

"Just let me know."

We share a simple nod before I close the door and head across the house.

My stomach twists. Some days, I feel like I'm sharing custody of my son with Lauren's parents, but in a haphazard kind of way. Last time, Karen called at the last minute to say they weren't going to be able to watch him and it caused... some issues. Not that I let Owen know that. Gabe stayed at school, deciding to work on paper, while Owen and I ended up driving around and spent a few hours at the aquarium to beat the heat. Had I known ahead of time, we could have organized ourselves better.

Speaking of organization, Owen's bag is at the start of the hallway and I can hear him doing something in his room.

When I peek into his room, his back is to me, but he has a couple of action figures on his bed. He isn't saying anything, but I see them moving like they're all having a conversation.

He's unusually quiet this morning.

"Hey, buddy. Did you have fun yesterday?"

His shoulders move in a silent half-shrug. I step into the room and sit at the foot of his bed. He avoids my eyes. I know my son well enough to know that he's upset. And I know me well enough that I need to know what happened before I break so many laws forcing answers out of his grandparents.

"Owen, what happened at Grandma and Grandpa's?"

He flicks his eyes over to me before the first tear slips down his cheek. Suddenly, he's full on sobbing in my lap. "I don't wanna go back. They say mean things."

The twisting sensation in my stomach turns into a pit of dread.

I run my fingers through Owen's curly red locks and hold him tight. Shuffling him so he's on my lap, his tears soak into the shoulder of my shirt. "Buddy," I start softly, "I need you to tell me what you mean by that. Tell me everything that happened from the moment I dropped you off yesterday. Who said mean things?"

"They asked me about Gabe and why he's here with us sometimes. I told them that Gabe is my friend, but they didn't believe me. Grandma told Grandpa that Gabe wasn't a friend." He wipes his nose with his palm. I cringe at the snot but wipe his hand clean with my own shirt.

"Gabe is most definitely your friend, Owen. Remember how he told you goodnight last night?" Owen nods and I wipe his cheeks once more. His eyes are big and round, looking right at me. I take a deep breath, knowing it's the best time to explain what I'm assuming Karen was talking about. "I think Grandma was saying that Gabe and Daddy aren't really friends."

"You're not?"

"We *are* friends," I backtrack. "But Daddy likes Gabe." I scrunch my nose. "*I* like Gabe. A lot. We're even *more* than friends." I emphasize the word 'more' while poking Owen's tummy. He lets out a soft giggle so I do it again.

Seeing his smile is the only thing I need right now. It's different referring to myself as Daddy after a whole day of calling another man by the title, but it's still what Owen calls me.

"Daddy and Gabe both like each other. We're dating. Do you know what that means?"

Owen shakes his head in the negative. Of course he doesn't, because I've been single his entire life. It's always been just me and him. I try to figure out how to explain it.

"Dating someone is like being friends, but you get to share fun things and hold hands and even kiss them."

Owen's eyes widen in disbelief. "You kiss Gabe?"

"I do kiss Gabe." I smile and tickle Owen's sides. "Lots and lots of times."

This time, it's his nose that scrunches. "Does that mean Grandma and Grandpa are dating? I saw them kiss before."

Chapter Fourteen

THE CROWD ROARS AS we step back onto the ice for the third and final period of our game against the Las Vegas Vipers. They're not cheering for us, but I try to let it boost me up anyway.

Despite our two-goal lead, I know I'm not completely focused. Usually, being on the ice is invigorating and motivating. The *snick-snick-snick* of skates cutting through ice, the clacking of sticks, even the crashing and thumping of players being checked into the boards is enough to drive my competitive edge. Tonight, though, I'm distracted.

Justin is at home. I've known from the beginning that he can't travel to all of our games, but for some reason I'm struggling with the distance today. Maybe it's the advances we're making in our relationship and with our kink. I mean, just last night he told me he wants to try something incredibly vulnerable as part of our play together as Daddy and Boy and I can't stop thinking about how special that is. How much he must trust me.

The thought brings both a smile to my face and serves as a distraction.

That's not fair on the other guys on the ice. Not on my team, and not on the other team, either. Most of these guys are trying to make it to the big leagues. They all deserve a teammate and a competitor who is willing to work with them to make that happen.

Refocusing, I prepare for the puck drop. Chasing it down the ice, I navigate around the opposing defense and relish in the burst of adrenaline. I growl when I'm slammed into the boards unexpectedly, and the puck is taken from me by Jake Zeigenfuse, the Vipers' ruthless left defenseman, and he skates off with it while I try to get my equilibrium back.

I'm chasing him within seconds.

My skating is smooth and I'm fast as I regain my rhythm. Our captain and center, Zach Weston, has already swiped the puck back from the other team and once again we're racing in formation towards the offensive zone.

This game has been a good one for our team. We're having a pretty good season so far and Coach has been pleased with the way our rookies have integrated with us more senior players. In fact, Cody Briarson, one of the freshman players, is currently on my line, playing right winger. Even I know that he's a better player than me, especially tonight when I can't focus properly.

He's faster than me, with natural reflexes that make half the other guys jealous. Even Zach seems a little intimidated by Cody's talent, and he's the player most likely to make it to the big leagues this year.

But I'm glad to have both of them on my line tonight. Especially when Zach's shot on goal ricochets off the post. By some miracle, I'm in just the right place to intercept it and I swing my stick, sending the puck straight to Cody who shoots it directly in between their goalie's legs and into the back of the net.

The Vipers' home crowd boos, but my teammates' ensuing celebration creates infectious joy for the moment —for Cody's first goal of the season— and it's a moment I wish Justin could share in person.

Ugh, and there I go again.

As the game continues, I try to funnel the anticipation of seeing Justin soon into determination and focus. Despite the physical distance, my Boy's support is unwavering, and not only because the college employs him.

During a shift change, as I drop onto the bench and guzzle water, I hope that Justin knows that I'll support him wholeheartedly, too.

See, I got a text from him during the long-ass bus ride here, and when I opened it, it revealed a photo of him and Owen wearing matching Phoenix Penguins jerseys. The text had read:

Justin

We'll be watching you win!

I made the photo the home screen on my phone, and I will be printing it and hanging it inside my locker at the first chance I get. But that same text only made me realize that I don't like being away from him. He's my Boy.

It's beyond kink now. It's beyond simple dating, too. I think it has been since the start.

I'm not sure I'm ready to put into words how I feel, but I do know that it's *way* more serious than any relationship I imagined I'd have in college. But even if we do break up, even if he isn't my forever person, these feelings that I'm having will come up again in the future if I do pursue a career in professional hockey. Away games will *always* be a thing. I need to really think about whether that's something I want to deal with for an entire career.

"Nagy," Coach's voice pulls me out of my thoughts, and I blink up at his frowning face. "You okay, kid?"

I nod, even though my thoughts are making me a little anxious. My vision swims for a moment before I take a deep breath and force myself to focus again. "Yeah, Coach. I'm good."

He eyes me warily for a moment, then nods his acceptance. "Okay. You boys are playin' real well tonight." He glances up at the clock suspended above the rink, big, red numbers counting down to our victory.

Even though the Vipers have already scored once this period, we're still up by two points. We're all hopeful it stays that way, but anything can change in the final few minutes of a good, well-matched hockey game.

"Keep up the good work for the last shift," he demands, gesturing for us to get our asses ready to swap out with the defensemen. "We've got this."

And we do.

The final buzzer marks our victory. As a team, relief and celebratory excitement follows as we acknowledge our win. Even as we're bumping gloved fists and patting each other's helmets and shoulders, I can't stop wishing Justin was here to celebrate, too.

Especially if my Boy wants to take our kink play further.

Did I mention how horny I get after a win? It must be the endorphins and the adrenaline of a game well-played...despite the fact that I was distracted for most of it.

***

Back in my hotel room, which I'm sharing with Mason, one of our sophomore defensemen, I video call Justin. It's late now, so Owen will be in bed, and I currently have the room to myself. I can only assume Mason has gone out to party with some of the other guys, or to hook up with someone. More power to him, but I didn't want to drink, and I also didn't want to risk Coach's wrath for missing curfew or the early bus home tomorrow.

Plus, the benefit of having some privacy to call my boyfriend was too tempting to pass up.

"Hey," Justin answers the call after two rings, his mussed hair and hooded eyes telling me he was probably halfway to sleep himself. I do feel a little guilty for disturbing his schedule on a school night. Nevertheless, he smiles warmly when he sees me, "Congrats on the win, Daddy."

"Thanks, baby." Just this tiny interaction eases some of the tension of missing him. I still want to pull him into my arms and kiss him senseless, but being able to talk to him will have to be enough. "Did you have a good day? Did the football team send any fun cases your way?"

Even though he's employed to mostly be one of our team's trainers/therapists, on the days we have mid-week away games, he has made an arrangement with the college to work with the football team so he doesn't have to disrupt Owen's school routine any more than necessary. I'm glad that the college has been so willing to be flexible with him, but then again, I've seen him work. He's damn good at his job, even if he doesn't have decades of experience under his belt yet.

"Nah," he barely gets the word out before he yawns widely, then blinks. "Whoop, sorry. Owen was a bit of a handful this afternoon."

Worry lines pull at his forehead, then he gives his head a shake and smiles at me. "And I miss you."

"I miss you, too," I admit. "But I should let you go to sleep."

Even as I say the words, I push down the disappointment that we're not going to jerk off for each other via Facetime. I can rub one out on my own: Justin's rest is way more important than mutual orgasms.

He pouts, sticking out his plump lower lip. I wish I was there to nibble at it. "I don't wanna," he whines, and my heart squeezes at the hint of Little Justin in his voice.

"I know, sweetheart, but the sooner you sleep, the sooner it will be tomorrow." This reminder is as much for his benefit as my own. I muster an encouraging smile. "One sleep, then Daddy will be there to cuddle you."

He draws his lip in between his two rows of pearly white teeth and gnaws at it. "Grown-up cuddles?" he asks coyly.

My dick, already half-hard just from seeing him on my screen, twitches with interest.

"*Naked* grown-up cuddles," I promise, reaching down to adjust myself.

"Mmm," he says, squirming a little from side to side. "I can't wait, Daddy." Another jaw-cracking yawn overtakes him, making me chuckle.

"Sleep, baby. It'll be tomorrow before you know it."

He nods, then asks, "Will you stay with me 'til I fall asleep?"

The feeling I'm trying *really* hard not to name surges through me again with a vengeance. My heart thumps harder in my chest and I nod. "Prop your phone up on your nightstand...yep, like that, good." My lips curl upwards as he settles back on his pillow. "Now, go to sleep, baby. It'll be tomorrow really soon."

He closes his eyes and smiles. "Night-night, Daddy."

"Night, Justin."

***

The bus trip home takes *forever*. I'm agitated from a restless night spent tossing and turning on an uncomfortable hotel mattress, and I skipped breakfast in my bid to make it to the bus on time. I have a headache, and the rowdiness of my teammates isn't helping me.

This is going to be a long-ass year if all the away games feel like this.

After only a moment's hesitation, I pull out my phone to text my sister. Mandy and I are probably the closest of all our sibling relationships, partially because she's the closest to me in age, and also because I spend so much time babysitting her kids. She's also been super supportive of me dating Justin since the beginning, given that her son, Brian, and Owen have made fast friends at school.

Taking a deep breath, I send my message.

Me

I think I'm completely fucked. Just had an away game and I missed Justin too much to focus. What do I do?

Mandy

More like completely pucked, right?

I frown at her text, accompanied as it is by a laughing emoji.

Me

Not funny. I'm actually panicking here.

Mandy

Sorry, bro.

Are you sure it's not just new relationship shininess? You've only been dating for a couple of months, and this is your first away game. Anyway, didn't you guys win?

Me

Win or lose, it doesn't matter. Coach knows I'm off my game. What if I lose my scholarship?

After I send that, I scrub my hand over my face. Justin is worth a lot to me, but is he worth throwing my degree away this close to the final buzzer? (The answer scares me, because it's a big, resounding 'yes'.)

Mandy

That's a huge leap to make after one game. Everyone has off days, and you have a track record as a solid player.

What's this really about?

I swallow and glance out the window, watching the scenery speed by. It's all dirt and tufts of grass and...was that a tumbleweed? Who knew they actually existed?

Looking back down at my phone, I consider how to reply. Courtesy of my sleepless night, and my increasing agitation and bad mood, I've started to panic about just how serious things have gotten. I'm only twenty-two. It's my senior year of college. I'm not supposed to be getting in deep with anyone.

Except I know that's wrong. I know that there aren't any rules for when, where, or how people fall in love.

But oh god, that word alone is scary as fuck.

Me

I'm scared. It's all getting really serious.

Mandy

LOL. I mean, yeah, bro. He has a kid. You knew what you were getting into.

Me

Theoretically, sure, but now that it's happening, I'm panicking.

I have so many away games. More if we do well in the tournament. Is it always going to feel like this?

And is it fair on him to have a boyfriend who is away all the time?

Mandy

He's a big boy, Gabe. He can handle time away from you, too. If he feels the same way about you as you do him, you will make it work.

But you should talk about this with him, not me.

The first of her two messages makes me snort a little derisively. *If only she knew...* But my kink is something I keep very private from my family. They don't need to know what gets my engine revving. That would be weird. I mean, sure, if Justin slips up and calls me Daddy in front of them, they can just think it's light daddy kink and we can leave it at that. But the age regression stuff? That's just between him and me, and any of the kinky friends we make.

Still, everything else she says makes sense.

Me

I know. But I'm scared of that, too.

I'm scared that Justin will think that this is too much, too fast. That he'll want to pause everything or stop it completely.

That he won't feel the same way I do.

I'm not used to being anything other than confident and assertive in my relationships. But today, with the separation and the lack of sleep, I'm off-kilter.

Mandy

For what it's worth, I don't think you have anything to worry about. He's head over heels for you, too.

I remind myself of the call last night, of Justin asking me to stay on the phone with him as he drifted off, and of the conversation we had the night before I left. He's been thinking about trying a wetting scene, having an accident, making himself vulnerable and embarrassed and reliant on his Daddy—on me— to look after him.

He wouldn't want any of the above if he didn't feel like I do, would he?

No.

So why does the idea of telling him how I feel still freak me out?

Chapter Fifteen

Justin

"Weekend away games suck," I say as soon as I open the door. Gabe is smiling and steps into the house with his arms outstretched.

The first away game was rough. I missed him so much and I was happy when he video called me and stayed with me until I fell asleep. He's had a few away games since. Most nights, we've fallen asleep virtually, but once he went out to be the designated driver of sorts. None of them were actually driving, but he made sure everyone made it into their own hotel rooms at the end of the night. He still texted me a goodnight around one in the morning.

This time, they lost the game by two points and none of them went out.

Before I can sink into his warmth, a flash of orange smooshes itself between us and wraps arms around Gabe's leg.

"Gabe! It's sleepover party time!"

"Sleepover party?" Gabe's eyes go from Owen to me and then back to Owen.

"Daddy said we're gonna have a sleepover with the three of us. Can we play Go Fish and watch the penguin movie and—"

"Buddy, take a breath." I lay a hand on Owen's shoulder and smile down at him. "Also, you're dripping water. How about you go back outside, and I'll be there soon."

We watch Owen scurry back through the house and out the door. The pool is only a few inches deep, but it's within clear view so I can keep an eye on him. I feel an arm wrap around my waist and I'm suddenly burying my face against Gabe's neck, fighting off tears that have been threatening to spill for hours now.

"Baby, what's wrong?" Gabe's arm tightens around me. I take a deep breath. It doesn't help much, but I push through the lump in my throat to speak.

"Owen was excluded from a birthday party today. While he was in the same house."

"What?" Gabe's arm falls from around my waist, and he stares at me. "How does that even happen?"

"Apparently Karen hosted a birthday party for one of the other cousins. Cake, presents, games, the whole works. They all had a sleepover last night and, when I dropped Owen off this morning, she didn't say anything about it. The kids must have still been asleep, and she had Owen downstairs with Harold while she hosted his cousin and ten other kids once they woke up."

His face contorts with confusion, "Wait...what? Why not send him upstairs when they woke up?"

It's a valid question, but I'm not finished yet. "It gets worse." Shaking my head, I continue, "The only reason I found out at all was because the football team wrapped up early and I came to get him an hour before I said I would. He was eating a sandwich while the other kids had nachos and cake, ice cream, toys...all that kind of stuff. I could hear them from downstairs, so I know Owen did too."

"Are you fuc-" Gabe stops himself and closes his eyes. He looks like I felt. Like I still feel. "Why would they do that? Why deliberately exclude him? Did you ask her?"

"I didn't ask. I just...I didn't know what to do, you know? I just took Owen and we left. He was quiet —too quiet— and I kind of decided to just give him one of those yes days to hopefully make him feel better."

"Did he say anything?" Gabe pulls out his phone and starts typing quickly.

"What are you doing? And no, he said he didn't want to talk about it. When I asked, he said that he stayed downstairs and watched a movie." Gabe is still typing furiously. "Seriously, what are you doing?"

Gabe looks up and smiles at me. "Don't worry about it, baby. How about you go outside with Owen, and I'll be there in just a minute? I'm going to put my bag in your room."

"Daddy?"

"Sweetheart, just do as I say, please. Trust me."

I do trust him.

Nodding, I join Owen in playing superheroes, losing myself in the imaginary play just like Owen is. I'll always do what I need to for my son, but I also know that my Daddy will do the same for me. I can feel a lump in my throat again at that thought.

Our relationship was always on a fast track, with diving headfirst into the kink and spending every moment we can together. Gabe has become my rock to lean on for anything, big or small.

"Daddy?" Owen's voice pulls me out of my serious thoughts about Gabe.

"Yeah, buddy?" I splash one of the superheroes into the water and it makes us both giggle. He wipes his face clean of the water droplets before talking again.

"I don't want you to be mad at me."

I pause and look directly at my son. "I would never be mad at you, Owen. Why would you think that?"

"You looked mad when we were leaving Grandma and Grandpa's." His shoulder slump. No five-year-old should ever feel this way. Not about their family. I hate that he's experienced this.

"I wasn't mad, buddy. Not at you. I was upset that they didn't let you join the party with the other kids."

"They said I was too little. They was playing big kid games that I didn't understand."

"Did they try to let you play?"

"No. They said I could watch, but then Grandma said I could go watch a movie downstairs because there wasn't enough room at the table for everyone."

I ball my hand into a fist and try not to cry at those words. I never want to think of my son as excluded from anything, especially at his grandparents.

"Okay, good news for both of you. We are most definitely having a party." Gabe's voice reaches us before he steps out of the house and shields his eyes from the sun. "Mister Owen, Brian is coming over, along with Rachel from your class. Marshall and Izzy are coming too, and they're bringing pizza for all of us. We have exactly forty-five minutes before people show up, so why don't we go clean up and we can build the most epic blanket fort in the living room for all of us to watch movies."

I'm left sitting in the water, speechless, as Owen jumps up and runs to Gabe. "Really?"

"Yes, really. So why don't you and your Daddy go clean up? I'm going to run to my apartment and grab some supplies. I'll be back in thirty minutes. We're going to have the most awesome party ever."

Owen disappears into the house, and I hold out a hand for Gabe to help me up. "You didn't have to do this, Gabe."

"First off, hearing you call me by my name when we're alone sounds weird. I much prefer Daddy. Secondly, no one is allowed to make either of my boys feel sad. I could see how much this hurt you."

"I know that they aren't Owen's friends, but if I'd known she was hosting a party for them, I wouldn't have dropped Owen off. I would have figured something else out. I just can't help but think what if this isn't the first time? Owen's always said he's had fun, but I know the other kids have been at the house before. What if she always keeps them separate or the others tell him they don't want to play with him?"

"Baby, please calm down." Daddy rubs his hands down my arms until I can feel my muscles relaxing again. "It's going to be okay. I don't want you to worry about a thing, alright? Daddy is going to take care of everything. You just enjoy spending a fun Saturday night with your son."

I lean up and kiss him. As the seconds pass and our tongues glide together, I do as he says once again. I let the worry and stress melt away and I promise to focus on having fun.

Owen and I take turns in the shower and I'm helping him put on a clean pair of socks when the doorbell rings. Gabe knows that the door is unlocked, so it has to be someone else. I let Owen race forward —quietly hoping he doesn't slip in his socks— and open the door on his own.

"Owen!" A small voice yells and two kids rush in and surround my son in a group hug. Mandy walks in behind them with a big bag on her shoulder. She glances my way and smiles.

"Your house is amazing, Justin. That college must be paying well."

"I can't complain," I reply, feeling my mood lighten even more. I give her a brief hug before taking the bag. It looks like snack foods and toys. "You didn't have to do all this."

"I wanted to," Mandy says. "You have no idea how much Brian talks about Owen. They're best friends in school. We really should have done this sooner."

"It's been a busy couple of months getting settled and oh, Owen, not the pool again! I'm going to dump that water. How about you show your friends your room?" I turn to Mandy. "Since this is a rare time it's actually clean."

"I feel that," she laughs. "But anyway, show me where I can put this stuff. My brother said something about a blanket fort, so I brought extra sheets as well."

"Your entire family is the best. Seriously. Your mom is amazing too."

"Hold on." She sets the bag down on the counter and spins to face me, her hand on her hip and a grin on her face. "When did you meet our parents?"

"Owen and I took a trip with Gabe last Friday. We've been invited to Thanksgiving dinner and also Christmas. And New Years is going to be here at my house with everyone."

"Yeah, totally sounds like my family." We both pause at a round of laughter coming from Owen's room. It's music to my ears. "Speaking of being awesome and stuff, this is my official offer to have Owen come home with Brian after school whenever you need it. They're in the same class and I pick Bry up from school every day, so I'm there anyway."

I step forward and wrap my arms around her tightly. She lets out a startled sound but hugs me back. We're still standing like that when the door opens again.

"I leave for half an hour and you're already making moves on my man." I smile at my Daddy's voice and let his sister go.

"I can't thank you both enough for being so amazing." I look between them. Gabe is holding a new duffel bag. I'm not sure what's in it, but he excuses himself to take it to my room, so I can only imagine the contents. I hear him greet all three kids and ask what they're playing.

"He is so good with kids," Mandy says. "Always has been."

"Owen adores him," I agree. "He's been a blessing, and I don't think he realizes it."

The doorbell rings once more and the others come out of Owen's room with smiles. All three kids are barefoot and the sound of smacking feet against vinyl floors fills the house. Gabe motions for me to meet him in my bedroom. His sister gives me an eyebrow waggle, but I don't say anything.

Gabe's back is turned to me when I step into the room and close the door. The bags are sitting on my bed, and Gabe is rummaging through one of them. "I'm not sure how the evening is going to go, but I figured that we might need some reinforcements when we're alone."

I move to stand beside him and look at the items. I see bed sheets first. "These are for the epic blanket fort. I also brought clamps to secure the blankets. This, though, is for you." He holds up a pale-yellow blanket. It's small, but I lift my hand and run it between my fingers.

"It's so soft, Daddy." I slide it against my cheek slowly. "This is really just for me?"

"It is, baby. I was walking home from the bar yesterday and we stopped by the store to get some snacks and electrolytes. The blankets were on the other side of the aisle, and I couldn't resist."

"It's perfect." I sigh, still rubbing the corner against my face.

"I'm glad you like it. We'll snuggle up tonight with it and get some much-needed sleep okay?"

"You're the best, Daddy. Thank you for everything."

Wrapping my arms around him, I bury my face against his chest with a smile. We stay like that for a long minute before I hear someone call out that it's pizza time. We walk out of the room together to the sound of chatter, laughter, and the kids talking way too loudly, but I love every moment of it.

"I like the look of a full house here," I whisper to my Daddy as we walk hand-in-hand down the hallway.

***

Three movies later, it's beyond past everyone's bedtime when the super fun night officially ends.

"Go tuck Owen in bed and I'll tuck you in afterward," Daddy whispers in my ear.

The others left after the last movie with a promise to do this again. Even Marshall and Izzy agreed to join another hang out. Marshall had been one of the kids, helping to put the fort together and then playing PawPatrol and more superheroes throughout the first movie. By the second one, he was falling asleep on Izzy's shoulder on one end of the couch.

I scoop a sleeping Owen from the floor and head down the hallway. He stirs when I lay him down and looks up at me with those big, green eyes. My heart swells with love and I lean forward to kiss his forehead.

"Did you have fun tonight?" I ask quietly as I pull the blanket from under him. He nods silently. "We'll have to tell Gabe and everyone thank you tomorrow."

"Daddy?" Owen's voice is barely a whisper, and I can see that little crease in his forehead that says he's thinking way too hard for a five-year-old.

"What is it, buddy?" I finish tucking the blanket around him and hand over his stuffed teddy.

"Is Grandma mad at me?"

***

"Justin," Karen greets me at her front door. "Was I supposed to be watching Owen today?"

They live close to us, but the houses here are larger and definitely scream 'money'. Karen is dressed like she's about to attend a business meeting. Her tone doesn't indicate any bit of remorse or desire to explain yesterday.

There is so much I want to say —to yell— at her. That she should have never excluded my son *in* her house, that it was a mistake to move here so they could see their grandson in person.

The plan to tuck Owen in and get some Little time was derailed when Owen opened up about all the things he isn't allowed to do when he's with his grandparents. They feed him, but he has to ask and can't just grab anything out of the fridge even though the others can. He's not allowed to play with the toys for his cousins. Instead, there's a box of toys he's allowed to play with for little kids.

Owen's words run through my mind over and over.

"It's okay, Daddy. I don't mind playing with them. I can play with the bigger kids when I'm older. Grandma says I need to wait until I'm more 'sponsible."

The sound of my own son trying to comfort me and make excuses is something I never want to hear again.

"Justin?"

I focus on Karen's face and try to calm myself down. "Owen won't be coming over here anymore."

"What? Why?" She lays a hand on her chest and genuinely looks surprised about this turn of events.

"Why? Because I spent last night listening to him tell me how you've been treating him differently than the others and not letting him play with his own cousins. How you made him sit downstairs while you had all those kids here for a party yesterday."

"I didn't think he'd enjoy hanging out with them," Karen argues. "He's so much younger than the other boys, and he was happy watching a movie."

"He said you made him go downstairs because there wasn't enough room at the table for him."

She hesitates for a second before answering. Her facial expressions are hard to read. "The boys were playing one of those games that requires them to all have a spot. There weren't enough chairs. That's when I suggested that he—"

"You didn't suggest anything," I butt in. "And he also says that he's not allowed to grab a snack or drink without your permission?"

"I told him he needed to ask," she responds. "It's called manners, Justin. Owen could stand to learn a few."

"Owen is perfectly mannered for his age," I spit out. "He's sweet and kindhearted and has been feeling left out here. So, like I said, he isn't going to be coming here anymore. I have someone else watching him after school."

"You're overreacting, Justin. You're really going to trust a five-year-old over me?"

"I trust my son because I didn't raise him to lie."

I turn around and head back down the pathway. It's only eight in the morning and Gabe is at the house with Owen. Owen was still fast asleep when I left, but we have a day of fun planned. All planned by Gabe. I don't want to waste any more time here than I have to. I hear the door close behind me before I reach the car.

***

"Here you go, baby."

Daddy hands me my new favoritest blanket and I curl up in the bed with it. Daddy shared a shower with me, and then mutual blowjobs, before he dressed me in a pair of training pants and my favorite pajama set.

"And here's your juice. Do you want a snack or anything?"

I'm sitting in the middle of the bed with a couple of toys and stuffies, Kelvin clutched under my armpit. It's only eight in the evening, still light outside, but Owen is already in bed for school tomorrow and we're also taking advantage of some fun time before bed.

"I'm okay." I look up from the block train that Daddy bought me last week. "Do you want a snack? You didn't eat lunch with me earlier. Your belly must be so hungry."

Daddy smiles and laughs at my joke. It's only half a joke, though. Daddy really didn't eat much today. He drank lots and lots of water, though. And made me drink lots and lots of water too, which made me have to go potty three whole times.

"Daddy's okay, baby. I had all that pizza last night, and we ate dinner earlier. Daddy's belly is not a hungry, hungry hippo." He leans across the bed and pokes my tummy, making me giggle.

He climbs on the bed and settles in on his side. I run the train up and down the bed, making choo-choo noises. Daddy tries to balance one of my stuffies on the train, but it keeps falling off, which makes both of us laugh.

We continue to play around the room for another hour. Daddy sits on the floor with me and plays bumper cars with the stash that keeps growing. It's taken me a while to really get into playing with cars, but nowadays, I enjoy them a lot.

Daddy has me count how many cars I have. Twenty-one cars and four trucks. Daddy had the trucks run over all my cars and smash them, but I saved all the people by tackling Daddy to the floor.

"It's after nine now, baby. Time to get ready for bed. You have a big week ahead and need your sleep."

"Snuggles?"

"All the snuggles, just for you." Daddy helps me into the bed, and we cuddle together under the blanket. I'm already so used to Daddy sleeping next to me. Away games are stinky because I miss having Daddy pressed up against me.

"Thank you for being amazing this weekend," I say. I'm still half in my Little headspace, but definitely coming out of it as we lay together. Daddy brushes his hand up and down my back and I hook one leg to rest between his. "I don't know how I would have handled the situation if you weren't there."

"I don't mind at all," Daddy replies. "I love spending time with you and Owen."

"We love spending time with you, too," I whisper back to him with a smile.

Chapter Sixteen

"HAPPY THANKSGIVING!" MOM BEAMS as she swings the front door open. She throws her arms out wide as she accosts my boyfriend with a hug before looking down at Owen with a warm smile. "Can I hug you, too, sweetie?"

This isn't the first time she is meeting them, but I'm glad she's asking permission before hugging Justin's kid. Owen, being the sweet boy that he is, smiles and nods. "I like hugs."

"Like father like son," I murmur as an aside to Justin. Then, as Owen starts to squirm in my mom's hold, I sigh dramatically and playfully complain, "I see how it is. No warm hello for your own son. *Noooo*. Only for the cute ones."

Owen giggles and my mother releases him, only to straighten up and roll her eyes at me. "But I get to hug you all the time. These are new victims. I mean, *family*." Before Justin can protest the inclusion, she points her orange-painted manicured fingernail at him. "And you are family now, Justin. Regardless of how your relationship with Gabe goes, you're also Mandy's friend and Owen is Brian's best friend, so you're going to be stuck with us no matter what."

Justin's voice is a little strained when he says, "Thank you," and I squeeze his hand to let him know I understand his emotional response.

"Geeze, Mom," I tease, buying Justin some time to process and pull himself together, "we're not even inside yet and you're making things weird. This is becoming a habit with you."

"So sue me if I want Justin and Owen to know they're always welcome here," she plays along, but takes a step back so we can cross the threshold. "I might rescind your standing invitation if you're not careful, though."

"I should be so lucky—*ow!*" Dual smacks land on each of my biceps.

"You deserved that," Mom says, having delivered one of them.

I turn to glare at my Boy, and he just nods. "Be nice to your mom, D-*Gabe*." His cheeks turn pink at his near slip-up and I find it so adorable that all thoughts of punishment evaporate.

"Fine," I huff. "But only because it's Thanksgiving and she's feeding us."

Justin snorts. "Uh-huh. *Only* because of that."

Mom ignores us, instead taking Owen by his little hand and telling him that Brian and the other kids are all outside and can't wait for him to join them. It's a stark contrast to the way his biological cousins and grandparents have been treating him, and I know Mom is being very clear about his inclusion because of his previous experiences.

"*That's* the real reason you need to be nicer to your mom," Justin speaks softly and gestures in my mother's direction with his chin. His eyes have turned sad, but there's a gentle smile playing on his lips. "She's awesome. You're lucky to have her."

My throat feels a bit tight all of a sudden, so I clear my throat and squeeze his hand again. "*We* are."

***

Thanksgiving dinner at my parents' house is informal and raucous. Mom and Dad have dragged the inside dining table out under the back porch, lining it up end-to-end with the outdoor table so there are enough seats for everyone. The kids have their own tables and chairs in the yard.

Even though Mom organized the meal as a potluck, she also cooked a heap of stuff herself, so the kitchen bench inside is overflowing with various dishes for everyone to choose from, buffet-style.

Most years, Marshall, Noah and Izzy join me here, because they all live away from their families, but this year my only guests are Justin and Owen. The guys are off doing their own things, and that does make me a little bit sad because, this time next year, we'll be scattered to the winds as college graduates.

If I get a job in professional hockey, I might not even be able to stay local myself. The thought turns my stomach.

I'm distracted from those feelings, though, as I get drawn into conversations with my siblings and their partners. Justin is sitting beside me, digging into the casserole I spooned onto his plate, smiling and humming at whatever Mandy has said to him from across the table.

It's not hard to imagine this being our future; Justin being my partner and truly one of the family, just like my brother's wife or my sister's husband, or my other sister's girlfriend. My younger sisters are still in their late teens, with one starting college this year and the other still a junior at high school, so neither of them is settling down any time soon.

"So, Justin," my brother, Stephen, asks from the far end of the table, "Gabe says you're a physical therapist for the athletes at the college. Are you enjoying that?"

Justin casts me a sideways glance with a secretive smirk, and I know he's thinking about some of the very unprofessional things we've done in his office and the nearby janitor's closet. Under the table, I pat his thigh in acknowledgement, and his smirk morphs into a genuine smile as he answers Steve's question.

"I am. It's different to the internships I did as part of my degree. They were all in private clinics, so the cases I saw there were really quite different to sports related injuries and conditioning. I guess I'm closer to a trainer than just a physical therapist when I'm working with the athletes, but I enjoy the variety."

"I imagine there's more pressure working to keep the college's elite tiers of athletes in top form," Steve continues. He runs his hand through his hair, which is the same color as mine but kept much shorter.

At twenty-seven, there are five years between us, with Mandy in the middle, but he's always reminded me of Dad. Mature and serious. I like to joke that he was born with a calculator in one hand and a degree in finance in the other. Our eldest sibling, Alex, is just shy of eighteen months older than him, but she's a bit of a wild child. "It's impressive that you're balancing that, a five-year-old, *and* Gabe. Because, let's face it, we all know what a rodent Gabe can be."

I pick up one of the dinner rolls to lob it at him, but my Mom points her finger at me and waggles it from side-to-side. "Uh-uh-uh. Let's not give the little ones any ideas, Gabriel."

Steve shoots me a smug grin. After glancing over my shoulder to make sure the kids can't see me, I give him the finger.

"*Boys*," Mom sighs in exasperation, while Justin snorts.

"Gabe's actually more mature than I am," he tells my brother, then looks at my lifted middle finger and sighs. "Most of the time."

I love the subtle reference to our private roles. The little nod from my Boy that, yes, I'm still his Daddy, even when we can't talk about it. But I love seeing him like this, too: confident and in his Big headspace.

"*Awww*," Mandy taunts, nudging her husband, Jeff, with her elbow, "look at Gabe going all doe-eyed."

"Shut up," I respond half-heartedly.

She laughs and shakes her head. "Not a chance. Remember the shi-er-crap you gave me when I started dating Jeff? I'm repaying the favor now."

"I was in high school," I protest, more for her entertainment than anything. "I was, like, fifteen."

"You haven't grown up much since then," Steve chimes in.

"These are all big words from people who rely on me as a babysitter," I taunt back.

"*Dad*," Mandy pretends to whine, "Gabe's threatening to stop babysitting your grandchildren."

Dad laughs and holds his hands up in surrender. "I'm Switzerland." He leans forward over his half-eaten plate of food to whisper-yell at Justin, "The last time I chose a side, I wound up in the doghouse."

Justin giggles his way through the meal, seemingly content to watch all of us Nagy siblings bicker and play fight. When the attention isn't on me and Justin, I remind him to eat and then ask if he wants me to get him more from inside.

He shakes his head and pats his belly. "I'm gonna explode," he tells me, sounding almost on the edge of his Little headspace. His eyes are all droopy with post-meal sleepiness. Then he frowns at my plate. "You've only had a bit of green bean casserole and some salad," he says. "You need to eat."

"Nah," I pat my own stomach, "I'm good. But thank you for caring about me, baby."

"*Awwwww*," Mandy coos again.

I groan.

Justin giggles.

For all my fears that we've moved too fast and that my feelings have gotten too serious, in this moment, I could quite happily commit to this being our future. Of course, I still haven't mustered up the courage to tell Justin how I feel, which means that's just a fantasy.

I will tell him, though. I will. But we have time. For now, I'm just going to enjoy moments like this one, with all of my favorite people together in one place.

Chapter Seventeen

Justin

"Owen?" I rap my knuckles against his bedroom door and lean in. He's laying on his stomach on the bed, doing some sort of coloring thing for school before he goes back in two days. He's coming to work with me today, so he's already fully dressed. He looks up and smiles, scurrying to roll off the bed and stand up. I hide my laugh behind a cough.

"Is it time to go now?" he asks excitedly. I nod, watching him skip down the hallway to the living room. He came home from hanging out with Brian a couple of days ago, showing me for a solid half an hour how he learned to skip.

"It is," I answer, trailing behind him to collect the coloring book, crayons, and the few toys that I'm hoping will keep him entertained for the three hours of practice and physical therapy. The guys are getting basic checkups today, weigh-ins and attempting different stretches, to make sure they're healthy and doing okay.

"Are we seeing Gabe today?" Owen sits on the floor to put his shoes on. We're still learning how to tie the laces. As much as I want to step in and help, I know that he isn't going to learn unless he tries on his own.

"We are." I can't help the smile that pulls at my lips.

The winter break lasted for three weeks, but there were games during that time. A few of them were away games, so I didn't get to see Gabe nearly as much as I wanted to, but we did spend the holidays with his family again. Just like Thanksgiving, there was a lot of playful banter and happiness all around. I had to bury my face against Gabe's shoulder to hide my tears when Owen realized that some of the presents piled up were for him.

His own grandparents stopped by the day after to give him a few presents. It was strained between the three of us, but Owen seemed happy that they stopped by. And Gabe helped to keep the conversation going. It was the first time he properly met them and most of the conversation revolved around Owen. Hearing the way Gabe gave every compliment he could to Owen warmed my heart. They left after a simple lunch, and we haven't heard from them since.

"Daddy?"

I turn around to see Owen still sitting on the floor. He's taken up so many mannerisms from Gabe, it's almost comical. He has his feet flat on the floor and his elbows are propped up on his knees. I can't even call him my mini me anymore.

"What's up, buddy?"

"Is Gabe going to live here with us?" I zip up the bookbag I'm packing and step over to kneel in front of him.

"Do you want Gabe to live here?" I ask. I know that Gabe has been spending a lot of nights here. Unfortunately, with his game schedule and me having Owen, we can't sneak away whenever we want.

"Did you know that Lacey, a friend in my class, has two daddies? She says they all have fun and hang out. Like me, you, and Gabe."

That doesn't answer my question, but this is a big conversation, and Owen is trying to relay his thoughts the only way he knows how. "We do have a lot of fun, don't we?"

Owen moves to stand up, shoes all but forgotten. I hold a hand up to keep him from running and potentially tripping. He keeps talking while I tie his shoes.

"Lacey says that her daddies share a bedroom too, like you and Gabe. And they dated before they became daddies."

It's no secret to Owen that Gabe sleeps in bed with me. I know we had that brief conversation about dating, but I wasn't sure if that stuck. I know we did things a bit backward and fast, but everything feels so natural with us.

I straighten my back so I'm kneeling on one knee, eye level with my kid. But, before I can form the question I want to ask him, he's talking again.

"Is Gabe *my* second Daddy?"

The question takes me by surprise, and I have no idea how to answer. Of course, if we're talking long-run plans, I'd love for the three of us to be a family on paper as much as we already consider ourselves, but it's not something Gabe and I have discussed.

"I think we have a while before that happens, buddy," I say, treading lightly. "But he still loves you just as much as I do. Maybe one day he will be. Are you ready to go?" I finish tying his other shoe and he takes off toward the door.

***

When we get to the arena, Owen bounces in his car seat, brimming with excitement. This isn't his first time here and he absolutely loves coming to the PT room. Some of the team is out in the hallway when we walk in. They greet us in passing. I've come to know each of their names as the season has continued. Harry is the one that started the running tally marks of how many bruises each of them get during a game. I think Enrique has the most points right now, not that I'm encouraging them as their physical therapist.

"Daddy Gabe!" Owen shouts immediately upon us entering the room. Every head turns toward us, including Coach. Owen runs across the room and right into Gabe's arms. Of everyone in the room —all nine in total— Gabe seems the least fazed by Owen's outburst.

"Hey, little man."

"Daddy?" One of the guys repeats as I walk past them all seated on the bench. "When did you become Daddy?"

"I'm sorry," I say when I finally reach where Gabe is now standing beside Overton. "We had a conversation this morning and I thought I made it clear that we weren't going to use that word."

"But you said he loves me like you do. So he's basically my Daddy."

Apparently, my answer was not clear enough for Owen's brain. I don't think I was ever so hard-headed and decisive at his age. I haven't yet decided if I love the trait in him or not. At least he sticks to whatever decision he's made in his brain.

"I do love you, buddy," Gabe says, not helping the situation. I shoot him a look, but Overton speaks up before either of us can say anything.

"What's this about?" Coach asks, waving a finger between the two of us. "I shoulda' guessed something was up when you had that deer-in-the-headlight look when I suggested Gabe follow you around that first day."

"We met before either of us knew who the other was," Gabe explains, taking charge of the situation. I let my shoulders relax when Coach just nods and smirks. "It wasn't until the first practice that we realized. A whole month of talking and we never discussed our day-jobs or whatever. Then I guess neither one of us really wanted to say anything in case faculty dating students wasn't allowed."

Overton shrugs. "Well, I don't think there are any rules against training staff dating students. Just don't screw it up and make this awkward for everyone."

"Got it, Coach." Gabe responds, then gives me a wink. I roll my eyes and nod at Overton.

"Yes, sir."

"Alright, well, let's get to work then."

I set Owen up at my desk with his toys and coloring while I work. The guys are coming in two at a time and going through a round of tests. It's more in-depth testing and stretching from what I learned in past jobs and internships, but I get the hang of it after the first one.

They jump on a treadmill first and do a light stress test before coming to either me or Frankie. I start with them doing basic stretches, bending to touch their toes and standing on one foot, and then have them lay on the treatment table.

I make small talk with each of them during this part. Word travels fast through the team and, while I'm either pushing them to stretch their knee to their chest or doing side crunches, they're prying into my personal life. It's all in good fun, I know it is, and it's kind of nice to be able to talk about it. Gabe is right there, waiting his turn and constantly checking on Owen, joking along with them.

When it's finally Gabe's turn for his exam, I'm not sure if I should offer for Frankie to do it. I'm still worried about there being some rule against us being together. My Daddy must see the worry on my face, because he steps closer to me and presses his lips against mine softly.

Those in the room with us erupt with cheers, and I can hear footsteps in the hallway too. When Gabe pulls back, he's smiling ear-to-ear. I'm pretty sure I am too.

"Nothing to worry about, baby." He brushes a finger down the side of my face before dropping his hands from my body altogether.

"Thank you, Daddy." I whisper it low enough for no one else to hear or possibly be able to read my lips. "Let's get started, shall we? Take off your shirt."

"I'm sure he's used that line before!" Mason jokes, earning a chuckle from Gabe.

I run my fingers along Gabe's spine, frowning slightly at the way the vertebrae stick out more than anyone else's. I know his body is lean and he puts serious hours in at the gym, but I also know that I've felt his back plenty of times and this isn't how he usually feels. He stands back up and moves into the next stretch without a word.

Mason continues to speak. "I'm the unlucky guy that has to share a room with him on away games. The amount of lovey-dovey chat during those phone calls is disgusting, really."

"You're just jealous I scored the perfect guy," Gabe taunts as he lays down on the table. As much as I want to enjoy the playful chirping, my brain is focused on the job. My brain doesn't like what it sees. "*And* more points than you so far this season."

There's a chorus of 'ooh's in the room, followed by laughter. Gabe's body is laid out before me and, as much as I want to joke and the thought of playing Doctor is in the back of my mind, I pull out my clipboard and make a few notes. His chart shows that he's dropped almost ten pounds since the beginning of the season.

"Baby?" Warm fingers wrap around my wrist, and I look over the clipboard to meet Gabe's eyes.

"Sorry, I was just writing some notes so I didn't forget. Let's get this finished up." I lift his leg from the back of his knee and direct him to let me know if anything hurts. I'm careful that no one is within hearing distance when I glance up at his face. "It's not every day I get to manhandle you like this."

"Mmm." Gabe's eyes close briefly and I don't know if it's from the stretching or my words. "You know what I think?"

"What's that?" I ask, half wondering what he's about to say. I move to the other side of the table and have him stretch the other leg.

"That I know my sister is free tonight and it'd be easy to convince her to have Owen stay over."

"Why would—*oh*." The heat in his eyes tells me everything he's thinking. "We can, but only if she says yes without you making her feel guilty."

A whole night with just my Daddy, especially after a few weeks of having to limit Little time to when we're alone in the bedroom, sounds like the best idea. My body reacts equally to both thoughts of playing with my toys and having Daddy alone all night.

"I'll text her when we're done here," he says with a bright smile.

***

By the time Frankie and I finish our assessments, it's lunch time. Owen has since disappeared with a couple of Gabe's teammates to keep him entertained. I trust these guys to keep him safe. The way Gabe kind of not-so-subtly threatened them with bodily harm also ensures that not a scratch will be found on my boy. I know my Daddy well. He's going to take Owen seeing him as a second Daddy seriously.

Gabe is in and out of the room with the others as well. I keep my eye on him and notice that he's sitting down a lot more or leaning against the nearest surface. I head into Coach's office with Frankie for a brief meeting before we break for lunch.

"How are we looking?" Overton asks. "Anything we need to focus on."

"Enrique could use a looking at with that bruise he got from the last game. It's healing slower than expected. Other than that, everyone's looking pretty healthy on my end."

"Justin?"

"Everyone is good on my end too," I say. "I noticed that Gabe has lost a bit of weight since the start of the season. I don't think it's cause for concern, but we should keep an eye on that. Maybe toy with his nutrition plan seeing as he's expending more energy as the season heats up."

"Didn't you mention the other day that he looked like he was a bit out of it during the game?" Frankie asks, directing the question Overton's way. My worry increases when he nods.

"He seemed like he was having trouble focusing," he says. "We'll keep an eye on him. Any other notes?"

"I'm good," I say.

"Good," Coach shifts in his seat and sits up straighter. "Now, with the second half of the season starting and everyone ramping up for the Independence Conference and the Frozen Four, there are going to be scouts in the crowds watching our players. I've already had a few contact me about one or two of them and I'm going to get the guys to consider finding representation. I'm proud of this team and what we've accomplished so far this year."

I'm sure Gabe is one of those that the scouts are looking at. He's great at the game, dedicated, and an overall fantastic team player. He isn't cocky like some I've seen during the home games. Some people let the moment go to their heads, but Gabe isn't like that.

Owen's questions about whether Gabe is going to live with us float through my mind. I'm not sure what Gabe plans to do after he graduates. I know he's studying Sports Medicine, but that could take him anywhere. It took me almost across the country.

I bite the inside of my cheek to keep my thoughts from spiraling, focusing on the slight pain instead.

I listen to the assistant coach chime in with a few notes from one of the away games. I'm grateful that the college worked with my schedule when I accepted the job, but I still wish I could travel with the team. Not just for selfish reasons, either. I feel like I'm missing important things, like minor injuries that I should be looking out for when they get back.

Frankie does an amazing job of documenting the things that happen, and I always agree with her suggested plans for the players, but it's still not the same.

I think Owen has a long weekend in February for a holiday. Maybe we can join a game as spectators wherever they're playing.

Once our meeting wraps up, I'm the first out to go find my kid. And my Daddy.

***

When I step into the banquet room where the whole team is waiting, I feel the tension and worry drain from my body. My son, in all his red-headed adorableness, is wearing a jersey that's at least ten sizes too big for him. He's also wearing a helmet and is dragging a hockey stick taller than his own body beside him.

It's outrageous but also so adorable. Owen looks beyond happy.

"I think we have a future hockey player here!" Gabe declares. Even past the helmet, I can see Owen smiling with all his teeth on display.

"Daddy! Look at me!" He waddles over to me, nearly tripping on the jersey it's so long. "I can play hockey now!"

"I think you might need to learn how to skate first," I say. "You got those new skates for Christmas that we can use."

"Team bonding!" one of the guys shouts. I'm so beyond grateful that everyone, college players included, are going out of their way to make sure my son feels welcome. I know Owen hides it, but I can tell that not seeing his grandparents or talking to them anymore makes him sad. "Owen, do you want to go out on the ice after we eat?"

"Yes! Can I, Daddy? Please, please, please!" He drops the stick, and his hands grab onto my shirt, in a very 'give-me-my-money-or-else' style. There is pure excitement in his expression behind that faceguard.

"That's fine with me," I tell him. "As long as everyone is being careful."

Gabe trails after me and Owen when we grab our food. I try to be sneaky and watch what he puts on his plate. It's not nearly enough, and definitely not a full, balanced meal appropriate for an athlete. Still, I don't say anything to him as we find three seats for us. I know that Gabe is my Daddy, but right now I'm still in a bit of work mode.

Instead, once we're at our table, I slide our plates around, nodding at him when he stares at the food on what was my plate. It's not a lot (I might have snuck some of Owen's snacks between evaluating the guys) but it's more than a handful of grapes and the smallest portion of salad known to man, which is the meal he had chosen for himself.

"Just eat it. Please?" I watch his face, but there is nothing to read. After a long moment, he concedes and picks up the fork. I give him a soft smile, relief washing over me. "Thank you, Daddy."

Chapter Eighteen

IT'S HARD TO BE upset with Justin when he thanks me so sweetly, but I still feel a stab of irritation at the situation itself. The plate of food in front of me seems almost excessive in comparison to the meal I'd gotten myself. The carbs and calories here are going to mean extra gym time...however I *did* just promise to take Owen out on the ice. Maybe I can skate some of the extra intake off.

I mean, it's not that I don't appreciate my Boy looking out for me. I'd do the same thing for him if I didn't think he had enough food on his plate...which, seeing as he has taken mine, now he *doesn't* have enough for my liking.

Yes, I know how hypocritical that sounds, but he's not trying to stay in top shape to be fast on the ice and keep his scholarship. As soon as I've graduated, I'll go back to eating more of what I want, too. It's not like I love having to watch what I eat so vigilantly.

And I also know I haven't spoken about this with him. With everything he's had going on in his life —moving across the country, getting Owen settled in school, starting a new job and dealing with family drama of his own— he didn't need to hear about my fear of losing my edge on the ice. Especially when I'm only worried about making it to graduation and not really about making it as a professional athlete.

But maybe I do need to talk to him about it. I should definitely at least share my thoughts about what I'm going to do after I graduate. I mean, his kid is calling me Daddy Gabe now and that's...kind of huge.

Alright, there's nothing 'kind of' about it. It is huge. It's probably even more huge than me realizing that I am ass over skates in love with Justin. Because Justin is an adult who would understand it if things didn't work out...but Owen isn't.

Even if I didn't love that kid as much as I have come to, it wouldn't be fair on him if things went to shit because I've been too cowardly to broach the big, scary, life-changing concepts with Justin.

I knew that dating a single dad would mean having a kid in my life. I just didn't think it would lead to anyone other than a grown man calling me Daddy. I guess that is as much of a surprise as everything else about this relationship has been. And, while I need to make sure that Justin is okay with his son thinking of me as a parental figure, there's no going back from here. I love Justin, I love Owen, and I guess I've decided that being a dad (not a kink Daddy, but an actual *dad*) at twenty-two when I haven't even graduated college yet is something I really can embrace.

But, before I can open my mouth to tell Justin that we need to talk, Owen starts to babble excitedly about skating, and I get swept up in that conversation instead.

***

"You're not coming out on the ice?" I ask Justin as I help Owen tie up his adorably small skates.

The whole team is anxious to help introduce our small team mascot to skating for the first time, and I would have thought that Justin would want to hover nearby as well. But he sits back on the bench and shakes his head.

"It's not for me. I can kind of skate in an emergency, but I'd rather leave teaching this one" —he gestures at Owen with a wave of his hand— "to the professionals."

"You're trusting a bunch of college athletes with your son's life," I can't help teasing. "You're either brave or really negligent."

"Shut up," he scoffs, but his eyes glint with laughter. "Besides, you're *Daddy Gabe*, remember?"

I'm the only one who understands the subtext behind the gentle ribbing. I'm *his* Daddy, and he trusts me implicitly.

Nevertheless, it makes Mason go "Ooooh, *told*."

"You know," Zach muses as he slips a sweater on instead of his jersey, "it's not cool of you to go get yourself a kid and deprive us the opportunity to throw you a baby shower."

"A...baby shower?" I ask, bewildered. "He's not a baby."

"A small human shower, then," he says blithely. "We never get to celebrate stuff like that."

"That's because most of us know how to wrap it up before...uh..." Mason trails off as he remembers the little ears avidly taking in the locker room talk. My teammate's cheeks turn pink. "I mean, it's just a novel experience for one of us to have a kid, isn't it?"

Zach nods. "And, as your Captain, I think we can consider it a team bonding activity."

A baby shower. Team bonding. Who are these people?

I catch Justin's gaze and sigh dramatically. "I'm sorry for all of this."

My Boy just smiles and shakes his head. "It's fine. And, really, it's kind of my bad. I'm the one who brought the Daddy thing up again." He bites his lip. "If you're not okay with it—"

"But he's my Daddy Gabe," Owen interrupts, pouting up at his dad. "We talked about this, Daddy."

"I think we had two very different conversations," Justin grumbles lightly, making the guys around us chuckle.

"I should be asking you if you're okay with it," I tell him seriously. "I completely understand if you're not."

There's so much more I should acknowledge. Ultimately, especially with the drama he's faced with Owen's grandparents, Justin deserves to have final say on the kinds of relationships people can form with his son. If he doesn't want to co-parent, especially when we haven't been dating for that long, I wouldn't blame him.

As if reading my thoughts, Justin's expression softens. "I'm okay with it," he tells me, then smiles down at Owen. "You're amazing with him," his smile turns coy and shy as he lowers his voice, "and with me, too."

My heart squeezes and I grin. "Then I guess I'm Daddy Gabe, huh?"

***

"Whoa!" Owen wobbles on his skates.

I've been skating backwards while holding his hands to get him used to the sensation of gliding over the ice. Once I was sure he had some balance, I let his hands go.

The fact that he's staying upright makes me feel ridiculously proud. My first time on skates, I wound up on my ass within seconds.

"Look at you, buddy!" I praise him. "You're a natural."

"Get him a stick already," Mason adds as he glides past us. He casts a playful smirk over his shoulder. "He's already outskating Burns."

Vince spins and slants his skates, sending a spray of ice up at Mason for the chirp.

"Careful," I warn, "if we don't respect the rink, Coach will probably bench us."

Owen gasps. "But you have to play!" He glares at Vince and Mason. "Don't get Daddy Gabe in trouble."

Mason skates forward, offering his hand for a high-five. "You'll make a great captain, little dude."

Owen wobbles a little more as he tentatively shuffles his skates forward to meet Mason's outstretched hand, but he makes it without falling. "I'll be a penguin too," he declares. "Penguins are my favorite."

"You're already on your way," I tell him, then glance over to where Justin is leaning over the railing at the players' bench, taking photos with his phone. "He's doing so well!" I call out, and Justin grins back.

"He has great teachers!"

My stomach flutters and flips with elation and pride. I knew that Justin trusted me with our kink and with his own vulnerability but trusting me with his son's safety is still a little mind-blowing. Even though I still haven't been brave enough to tell him that I've fallen for him, this is the kind of thing that tells me he might feel the same way.

"We should totally run kids skating lessons in the off-season," Mason says. "Or start up our own pee-wee hockey team. The baby penguins!"

I snort. "I think they're called chicks or something."

"We can work on the name," Mason shrugs. "It could count as extra practice for us, and fundraising for the team."

The more I think about it, the more I think it's not actually a bad idea. There would be insurance and stuff to sort out, though, and I think we'd all need Fingerprint Clearance Cards to work with kids, but it would be fun to train up tiny hockey prodigies. Kids like Owen.

"Look, Daddies!" Owen himself interrupts my thoughts, and I turn to watch him mimicking the way Mason skates, confidently pushing off and shifting his weight from one foot to the other.

The movements are jerky, and he's stomping his blades more than he's gliding, but he is moving under his own power, and I am filled with pride all over again.

"That's it, kiddo! You're doing such a good job!" I encourage him.

Earlier, we ran through the rules about falling safely until he could recite them by rote, so I'm not too worried about him stacking it, especially not at such a slow speed. In fact, I kind of want him to experience his first fall, so he knows it's not a terrifying thing. And, sure enough, when he does hit a chunk of uneven ice and loses his balance, he topples onto his butt and, after a moment of stunned silence, giggles.

"My butt is cold!"

He's wearing thick pants and gloves, and his little cheeks are bright pink from the cold and the exertion of his movements. His joy is contagious, and I can't help but think that he's the best step-kid I could have asked for.

Which means I really do need to tell Justin how much I love him.

Mason helps him back to his feet, reminding him to keep his fingers away from the blades of his skates, and then they're off again, slowly moving together across the ice. By the end of our short lesson, Owen's fluidity is already improving, and he's become a pro at getting himself back to his feet after falling again and again.

"We're gonna have to teach Daddy how to skate, too," he tells me as we leave the ice, and Justin shakes his head, already reaching to help Owen out of his skates.

"I think skating can be a you and Daddy Gabe thing."

And *wow*.

Wow.

I'm going to have to come up with a pretty epic way to tell Justin I love him, because this? Owen and I having our own thing together? That seems pretty huge.

***

"You really don't mind—*mmph!*" Justin's question is cut off as I slam my mouth over his.

We've just finished putting Owen to bed —*together*— and I'm still buzzing from the high of the trust he has shown in me today. I'm almost lightheaded from it, and, while I'm still not sure how to tell him I love him, I'm damn well determined to show him.

He sinks into the kiss as I carefully close the door behind us and guide him to the bed, and he matches my intensity as soon as his calves bump against the edge of the frame. We tug at each other's clothes, pulling apart reluctantly to tug shirts over our heads. We're a handsy jumble of limbs as we get each other naked within record time, and then I pull him onto the bed with me, dragging his body over mine.

"Daddy," he whines, his cock rubbing into the crease between my groin and my thigh. I groan as the spot becomes slick from a dribble of his precum, and it smooths the way for more of his rocking against me. He gasps. "*Oh...*"

"That's it, baby," I grip his hips, encouraging him to fuck wantonly into me. My own cock strains towards him, little jolts of pleasure igniting every time his belly bumps and grazes the sensitive head. "Does that feel good?"

By this stage, we've explored each other's bodies in every possible way. But this is still kind of new; having him set the pace, bracing his body over mine. I'm taller and broader than him, and my role in our kinky relationship is the dominant one, but being spread out beneath him makes that feel a little topsy-turvy in the best kind of way.

Justin doesn't have the kind of gym-toned biceps that I do, but watching the muscles in his arms bunch and strain as he rocks his cock over my skin makes my heart race. Or maybe it's the way he's making me feel like the center of his universe.

He and Owen have rapidly become the center of mine.

"*Nnngh*," his reply to my question is more a sound than an answer, but it tells me everything I need to know anyway. "Fuck, yes," he adds, his breathing ragged, "*Gabe.*"

It's my turn to groan now, surprised to hear him using my name instead of 'Daddy'. It happens so rarely when we're alone that it's like a shock to my system. It's not a bad thing, especially not when he says it so desperately, and I love that he's comfortable to alternate between both.

My fingers flex on his hips and he adjusts his position, nestling more centrally between my legs and rubbing our cocks together instead. I fumble blindly around the nightstand drawer until I feel the familiar cylindrical shape of the lube bottle. After snapping open the cap, I drizzle some of the liquid into my palm and then wriggle my hand between our bodies to coat our lengths properly.

"Oh *god*," Justin fucks into my fist, spreading the lube over my cock as he does, "that feels unbelievable."

He's not wrong. I tighten my hold a little, squeezing our rock-hard shafts together while his hips move more forcefully. Bursts of intense pleasure shuttle through me with our combined movements and the slickness of the lube. His skin is warm where it's pressed against mine, and the sounds of his increasingly erratic breathing and unconscious whimpers are going directly to my balls.

"Baby," I warn him, my own voice coming out strained and breathy, "I'm getting close."

"Me too."

That's exactly what I wanted to hear. With my balls drawing up, I force my eyes open so I can grin salaciously up at my Boy. "You gonna paint me up with your cum, baby? Mark me as yours?"

"Oh, fuck," Justin swallows roughly.

"That's —*mmmm*— not an answer." I move the hand still on his hip to smack at his ass. "Daddy asked you a question."

"I...I forgot..." He sounds as though he's trying to hold off, trying to prevent the inevitable. I twist my wrist a little on his next thrust and his mouth opens in a soundless cry.

It's hard to remember myself. I'm too distracted by how gorgeous he looks as he rocks into me. After a moment, it hits me, and between panted breaths I tell him, "I asked if you're going to paint me with your cum, baby."

"Y-yes."

"Yes what?"

"Yes, D-daddy," he arches his back, and now he sounds on the verge of sobbing, but in a good way. "I'm...I'm gonna..."

"Do it," I encourage him. "Come all over me, baby. Make a mess for Daddy."

"Oh," Justin whisper-cries, throwing his head back, "*Ohhh.*" His hips convulse as warm wetness coats my belly, cock, and hand. "*Daddy...*"

Watching him ride out his orgasm and hearing him calling my name pushes me over the edge with him. We're a mess of cum and sweat as we flop together on top of his sheets, but neither one of us seems to mind while we catch our breaths.

"Thank you," he murmurs sleepily, pressing a sloppy kiss to my shoulder.

I think about how fulfilled I feel when I'm with him, and how happy my future looks when I think about having him and Owen in it, and I know that I'm the one who should be thanking him. But, when I turn my head to tell him as much, I realize he's already asleep.

I kiss his sweaty forehead anyway. "No, baby," I murmur affectionately. "Thank you."

Chapter Nineteen

Justin

"Buddy, I promise that the orca is not going to hurt the penguin." I look at my son, whose eyes are brimming with unshed tears. They've been like that since the first intermission, when the two mascots went head-to-head with each other on the ice.

I brought Owen here to get away from the drama with his grandparents, not give him emotional trauma over a penguin.

"They were just pretending to fight. That's what the mascots do for games like these. I bet you they are both in the locker room playing games together."

Owen clutches his penguin stuffie to his chest but doesn't say anything. We're close to the end of the second period now and it's looking like it's going to be a close game. I'm learning more and more about hockey as the season goes by. Gabe can go on his...*speeches*. He doesn't like me calling them rants, but I find it funny to rile him up. Sometimes it gets me some kisses and tickles or tossed onto the mattress if it's around bedtime.

I tune back into the game and try to keep up. Our team is crossing the blue line, which I believe is a good thing for us. Someone gets pushed against the glass in front of us, making me jump but Owen cheers excitedly.

"Mason!" Owen shouts. I take a second look, and it is, in fact, Mason. He lifts his hand to Owen before skating off quickly to continue playing. The other team is aggressive and has bodychecked someone on our team every play it seems. I'm surprised there hasn't been a penalty yet, because some of the checks seem unsportsmanlike. The opposing team's captain seems to be the ringleader of the aggression, which doesn't help the situation.

As if I thought it into action, there's a commotion on the other end of the rink. One of our teammates is on the ice. The other four players crowd whoever they are. I look up at the jumbotron for Gabe's number and sigh when I see he's standing. I know this is an away game, but I have the urge to walk to the bench and offer my services. If I didn't have Owen with me, I would.

The whistle blows and an announcement is made.

"Luke Hotchkiss, charging. Five-minute misconduct penalty. Power play to the Penguins."

There are equal cheers and boos within the arena. Obviously, we are cheering. Owen, for all his worry, starts bouncing in his seat and cheering with the rest of the crowd as well. The camera zooms in on Luke, the captain of the other team, shouting something. The referee looks done with the guy and appears close to issuing another penalty.

As Hotchkiss slides up to the Caldwell Orcas' penalty box, I can't help but notice the guy behind the box's glass. He looks younger and a bit timid, with his attention focused solely on Hotchkiss. He's also holding an orca stuffie, clutched to his chest like Owen has his penguin. The interaction between Hotchkiss and the guy with the stuffie is brief because someone lays a hand on the guy's shoulder and Luke sits down, a scowl on his face clear even from where I'm sitting.

I wonder what his issue is, but then I'm distracted by the game restarting.

The Phoenix Penguins take full advantage of their power play. We somehow score two goals, the guys on the ice moving in a way that seems almost synchronized. When we hit the second goal, putting us three ahead, the tension in the arena grows.

Our guys play smart. We avoid excessive body checking and the shift changes are flawless. By the time the third period starts, the win feels like a foregone conclusion.

Owen is sitting in my lap now. I wouldn't let him stand in his seat for safety reasons, and also to not block the people behind us. I can feel my phone vibrating in my pocket intermittently, but I ignore it.

This trip to Colorado for the away game was a spur-of-the-moment thing. Karen and Harold kicked up another fuss because I didn't make Owen go to their house for a family event a couple of weeks ago, and since then I've been even less inclined to send him over there.

The words Owen said to me flash across my mind over and over again.

"Daddy, do I have to go? I don't want Grandma to be mad at me again."

No one in my son's life is allowed to make him feel bad like that. When I texted Karen to let her know that Owen wouldn't be coming, she blew up my phone with messages declaring that I'm keeping him from them, that they have a right to see him, and so on. There were words in those texts that no one should use to describe another person.

Those texts have slowed down in the last week, but there are still some others in the family that are texting me. Apparently, Karen gave my number to Lauren's extended family to try and guilt trip me that they just want to get to know Owen.

"Yay!" My attention is brought back to the present when a buzzer sounds, and the Penguins supporters are all on their feet and cheering. It takes two whole seconds to react and realize we won. I stand on my feet, cheering with Owen and the other fans. "We won, Daddy! The Penguins beat the Oras!"

"Orcas, buddy." I correct him with a smile. "But yes, we did win! How about we head to the hotel and we'll meet Gabe and all of them there?"

"Yes! Yes!" Owen rocks his body back and forth with excitement in my arms. "I go swimming?"

"We'll see if the pool is still open." I know the guys will be a while before they come back to the hotel. Some will probably go out for a bit, but they have another game tomorrow so they can't afford to get drunk.

I'm looking forward to sharing a hotel room with Gabe. Having Owen means he'll get one of the beds while we'll get the other. Mason has already agreed to share a room with two of the other guys so we can have the room to ourselves.

***

"We're taking the kid!" One of the other players shouts from the doorway. Honestly, there are four of them in this room, including Mason and Vince, so I'm not sure who shouted it. They've all been around for Owen's skating lessons with Gabe, so it isn't like he's being taken by strangers. "We'll be in room ten-twenty-four watching Happy Feet! He's cool to sleep over if needed."

"I'll check in in a bit," I call back out. "Owen, listen to the guys okay?"

"Yes, Daddy!" Owen's voice calls out and I can hear the excitement in his voice at being able to hang out with the cool hockey players. It seems that most of them decided to come straight to the hotel after changing and everything else they had to do.

As such, they caught up with Owen and me in the pool. We all swam until thirty minutes past the time the pool was supposed to close, courtesy of the hotel staff. I kept my eyes on Gabe, hoping that the way he stuck to the shallow end and not being as wild as the others was just because he was tired after the game and not because he's still not eating enough.

Arms wrap around me when the door closes behind my son and his herd of unexpected babysitters. I smile, leaning my head back against Daddy's shoulder. I can smell his shampoo and take a deep breath, letting it relax me. This weekend is for me as much as it is for Owen.

"How are you?" Daddy asks. "I'm sorry I didn't get to see you before the game. We stepped right off the bus and went straight into warmups."

"It's okay." I turn in his arms and smile at him. "We're here now and we're alone. And I brought things."

"You brought *things*, huh?" Gabe's smile turns to a smirk. "What kind of things? Because I know we ditched the condoms a while ago, baby."

That we did. It was the best decision ever once I got tested. Gabe had to get tested at the beginning of the season, and I hadn't been with anyone in a while, but it had still been over a year since my last test, and we'd wanted to be sure. Plus, I used the whole thing as an excuse to put on my big boy pants and get Owen and myself set up with a Primary Care doctor in the city.

"I brought some toys," I tell him, shaking off my distracted thoughts. When I realize how that sounds, I clear my throat and continue talking. "Actual toys. Not sex toys. I thought maybe I could have a bit of time being Little? But if it's too late or you're ti-"

"You can have some Little time, baby." He presses his lips to mine softly. "We don't have to be on the team bus until ten tomorrow."

It's only eleven, so we have a good two hours before we need to go to sleep. I move to my bag and pull out the stuffie he bought me, a blanket, and then the monster truck cars.

"You really came prepared, didn't you, baby? Did you bring any clothes to change into?"

"Yes." I did come prepared. With our schedules and everything going on this week with Owen's family, I've been looking forward to our next time alone. I packed my favorite penguin shirt and a pair of sleeping shorts. I pull out the training pants as well.

"Let's get you in a quick shower, okay? I can still smell the chlorine on you." I smile and take Daddy's hand into the bathroom. He undresses me slowly, his hands exploring as each piece of clothing drops to the floor.

I did get Owen in a shower before all the guys showed up at our door, but I didn't have enough time for my own. But that's a good thing, I decide as I let Daddy guide me into the warm stream of water a minute later. I know he's already taken a shower, but he strips out of his clothes as well and joins me.

"Feels good," I say with my eyes closed. Daddy massages the shampoo into my hair. "So good, Daddy. Thank you."

"You're welcome, baby." His lips press against the back of my neck. The rest of the shower is mostly quiet, with a little giggle here and there when Daddy washes my sensitive and ticklish areas. When Daddy finishes drying me off, he turns me to face the toilet.

"Let's go potty and I'll get you dressed, okay?"

He stands behind me and helps me aim into the toilet. I love it when Daddy helps me potty. We haven't talked more about doing a wetting scene, but I know it will come with time. Life has just been too busy to do it the way we talked about.

Once I'm dressed, Daddy sits on the floor with me, and we start playing pretend. I explain to Daddy that there's a monster (my stuffie) preventing the prince from being rescued. We run the trucks into the stuffie over and over again until Daddy decides he's finally been defeated.

"Oh no, Daddy." My eyes go wide, and I look up at him. His hair is falling over his shoulders and I want so badly to pull the ends of his hair toward me and kiss him. I love tangling my fingers in Daddy's hair. It's so soft and pretty. I refrain though. "We don't have a prince to rescue now."

"How about you be the prince?" He says it quickly, like he'd been waiting for me to realize this plot hole myself. "Daddy can rescue you and make you feel all better."

"Oh, yes please!" I hold my arms out and Daddy stands up, hooking his hands under my arms and pulling me to my feet. "Daddy is the best rescuer ever!"

"And what does Daddy get for rescuing you?" He moves us to the bed. I let out a small giggle as his lips trail down my neck.

"Um…" I pretend to think really hard about what Daddy gets. "A pickle?"

Daddy pulls back and looks completely confused. It makes me laugh harder. He rolls over and cuddles up next to me, holding me tightly in his arms. "How about you tell Daddy a bedtime story? I love listening to your stories, baby."

I start with a random story, playing off our pretend play with the monsters and rescuing the prince. Daddy chimes in every minute or so to push the story forward.

I don't know when either of us fall asleep. I'm sure it was in the middle of the story. I sit up in a panic, unsure for a second why. Then I remember. I fell asleep before checking on Owen. Gabe stirs beside me, but I barely register him. My entire mind is focused on making sure my son is okay.

There's a knock on the door and I rush to tear off my clothes. I'm fully in my adult headspace and kind of panicking. My heart is racing, and blood is rushing through my ears. I throw on the first shirt and shorts I can find, keeping the training pants on because no one will see those.

I'm expecting Owen at the door with one of the players, but it's not. It's a total stranger. At least, I think it's a stranger. "Are you Justin Anderson?"

"Yes." I take a deep breath. "Is something wrong?"

"You've been served." I'm handed a stack of papers paperclipped together. The man is already walking away when I look back up. Ignoring the papers for the moment, I head down the hallway to the room the guys said they'd be in. I give three loud knocks, ensuring I wake whoever it is up. I realize then that I didn't check the time and I really hope it isn't the middle of the night.

There's a shout telling me to wait one second and then a round of laughter. When the door opens twenty seconds later, I'm greeted with a wild-haired little boy and two of the guys behind him.

"Daddy! We are watching the mouse movie!" Owen says excitedly. "And they ordered me pancakes that they brought to the room."

"That's awesome, buddy." I fold the papers under my arms and squat down to give my son a hug. "I'm so happy you had fun. Are you ready to go back and we can get ready for the game today?"

"Bye stinky face!" Owen says with a laugh, turning to wave at Vince and Mason. They're both sitting on the same bed and it looks like the other one was barely slept in.

"See you later Tater Tot."

Owen giggles and takes my hand. I wave at them, thanking them once again for keeping him overnight. We walk back down to our hotel room and knock. I didn't grab the hotel key in my panic.

Gabe opens the door, rubbing his eyes. "Sorry I rushed out. I woke up and there was someone at the door and then I went and got Owen. We fell asleep before calling to make sure he was okay."

Gabe steps aside and Owen runs into the room. I note that my clothes have been picked up after my haste to get out. "You fell asleep, baby." Gabe's voice is quiet as he pulls me in for a hug. "I made sure he was okay to stay the night before I fell asleep. I wanted you to have fun last night so I took care of everything."

"Thank you," I whisper. The ball in my stomach dissipates and I lean into my Daddy's body. The papers still under my arm crunch, and I pull back to look at them.

"What's that?" Gabe asks.

"Some guy was at the door when I woke up. He knew my name, so I'm not sure if it's something to do with the college or not."

I scan over the first page. It's a legal document, that much I'm sure of. I flip through a couple more pages before I realize what I'm looking at. My hands start to shake, and I feel like I can't breathe.

"It's a document to take Owen away from me."

Chapter Twenty

SEEING THE ANXIETY ATTACK for what it is, I act quickly to usher Owen back down the hall. I feel guilty that I can't assuage his confusion, but Justin is my main priority right now. The guys take Owen without me needing to explain anything, the look on my face enough to tell them something has gone wrong. I am incredibly grateful for them as they usher Owen back into the room, distracting him with their hijinks.

When I get back into our room, Justin is right where I left him, sitting on the edge of the mattress. Unlike when I left him, he is now hyperventilating with tears streaming down his face. Rushing to his side, I rub his back and encourage him to take deep breaths.

"I can't...I can't breathe," he wheezes, and he clutches at his chest, "it hurts, Daddy. It hurts. I can't breathe."

My heart breaks at the fear in his voice, but I remind myself to stay calm. "Yes you can, baby," I soothe. "Focus on taking slow, deep breaths for me. In...that's it," I murmur, my hand still moving in circles over the cotton of his tee, "and out. Good boy. Again. In..."

We repeat this over and over as he fights to regain control of his breathing. He calms momentarily and then, as soon as he sees the papers strewn across the bed beside him, the whole episode starts over again, with heaving breaths and heart-wrenching sobs.

Eventually, the panic attack releases its hold on him, and his crying tapers off into hitching, shaky inhalations as he slumps against me. Not wanting to risk setting him off again, I refrain from asking about the papers, waiting for him to speak first.

The team bus will be leaving soon, but the guys will bring Owen back before that becomes an issue, so I'm not too concerned about time. I'm more concerned about the papers Justin was served. About what that means for my Boy and, on some level, the small family we're forging together.

"Th-they're taking my son," Justin says, and I feel him tense up, as if his body is braced to meltdown again. "Karen and Harold. They're taking Owen."

"They can't," I reply firmly, anger at his former in-laws boiling my blood. I have zero legal knowledge or experience, but I refuse to believe that the older couple can just demand custody and take it. "They *won't*."

"You can't promise that," Justin snaps back, then bursts into tears again. This time, though, he isn't hyperventilating. "I can't afford a lawyer. I can't...It's just *me*, Gabe. How...how am I supposed to compete against a married couple who own their home and have God-only-knows how much money in savings, and—"

"It's not just you. It's *us*, and—"

"You're a college kid on a scholarship," he cuts me off with an edge of frustration, and I try not to feel the sting of insult in those words.

This is the first time he's called me a kid. The first time our differences have been raised as a problem.

I know he's not saying it out of spite or malice. I know that, on paper, being in college is not as stable as being employed full-time.

205

I also know that being all of twenty-two to his twenty-seven seems like a much bigger deal than it feels in reality.

"Plus," he continues when I don't argue with him, "you're a guy. Look me in the eye and tell me that our legal system is progressive enough to think that's just as *healthy*" —he sneers the word derisively— "for a child as a man *and* a woman. And no, you know I don't think it makes a difference, but a judge probably will. *Plus* you and I have only been dating for a few months and—"

"Breathe," I cut in, not wanting him to work himself into a state again. "I know. I know that on paper, they're 'more appropriate', or whatever, but you are his biological father *and* the only parent he's known before this year. I'm obviously not a lawyer, but I think they take stuff like that into consideration. And, like, social workers get involved and talk to the kids and stuff."

"I don't *want* a social worker coming in to scrutinize my whole life!"

"I know, baby, I know." I feel powerless right now. And angry.

Owen's grandparents are lucky that we're so far away at the moment, because I'd be sorely tempted to drive over there and...what, exactly? Make things worse for Justin by threatening them? Maybe *I'm* lucky that we're so far away.

"Where's Owen?" Justin demands, sitting up straighter, frantically searching the room with his eyes. "God, I just had a breakdown and I didn't even think about him. Maybe they're right to—"

"Don't you dare finish that sentence." I frown. "You're spiraling and I get it, but you are an amazing dad, Justin."

"Yeah, right," he scoffs, then gestures towards the bag containing his Little supplies. "Such a good dad that I regress to a freaking toddler instead of spending time with my kid."

"You indulge in kink and have date nights. Lots of parents do."

Shaking his head despondently, Justin waves towards the door. "Can you please just go get him? I just...I need to be with him right now."

That I can understand completely. I wouldn't be surprised if the threat of having Owen taken away has Justin clinging to the kid more than ever. I have the urge to do the same to reassure myself that nobody is taking him away.

Retrieving Owen from down the hall, he babbles happily at me about the card game the guys were playing with him and a fierce sense of protectiveness wells up inside of me.

There's no way Justin's former in-laws are taking this sweet, well-adjusted, *happy* kid from us.

No fucking way.

***

Life becomes a whirlwind of mounting stress after that. Once we get back to Phoenix, my parents help Justin get in touch with a lawyer friend of theirs who agrees to help us pro bono. Because I'm not legally anything to Owen, I'm more of a hindrance than a help, and I'm kind of sidelined for any of the legal discussions and negotiations. In fact, Harbir, the lawyer, suggests that I just focus on keeping my grades up because that will look best for my involvement or something.

So, that's what I do. Between hockey and studying, and Justin distracted with the legal stuff and his job, we barely get to see each other outside of the times I tail him at work. And, even then, he's not the sweet, playful guy I have been falling in love with. He's stressed, drawn, and exhausted. He desperately needs Little time, and I desperately need to step back into being his Daddy, but we just don't get the opportunity.

Away games suck even more now, because Justin outright refuses to travel, not wanting to let Owen out of his sight more than necessary, and his enthusiasm for watching our games on TV has faded away, taking a backseat to his worries over his custody battle. We still text, and he still sends sweet supportive messages, but he's distracted, and I can't even blame him. I'm distracted by it all as well.

The hockey season is well and truly heating up, but my head isn't in the game. I feel like I'm letting down my teammates, but everything happening in my life —and in Justin's life— is putting things into a different perspective for me.

The guys who want to make it to the NHL are completely focused on that, but hockey isn't as important to me as my Boy and his son. However, I need hockey to keep my scholarship, and I need my scholarship to graduate, and Justin needs me to graduate so I look better on paper...so hockey should be important to me.

God, it's all such a mess.

"Get your head out of your ass, Nagy!" Coach yells as I lose the puck to an opposing player during our game in Atlanta.

I grit my teeth and nod, speeding after the puck.

My head feels foggy, and I remind myself yet again that I need to do well in this for Justin's sake. Not only for my scholarship, but also for his job. If Coach thinks my distraction is because of him —because of our relationship— then that could cause even more problems for Justin in the long run. Problems he doesn't have the capacity to deal with right now. Problems that might negatively impact his fight for custody.

The more I focus on that, though, the dizzier I feel. My arms and legs feel leaden, and for the first time in my entire life, I feel shaky on my skates.

"Gabe, you good?" Mason asks as he passes me, and I try to blink away the weird feeling in my head so I can focus on the game.

He snags the puck as it slaps off our goalie's stick, and I glide around the back of our goal, leaning forward to race after my linemates on their way back towards the opposing net. The movement makes my head feel like my brain is swimming, and black spots dance in my vision.

Dimly, I realize I skipped both breakfast and my pre-game protein snack. And last night's meal was kind of light, too. With everything going on, I haven't been hungry, and staying lean keeps me faster on my skates, so I've never really been one to eat a lot anyway...but I might have pushed my limits on energy consumption verse expenditure just a bit too far today.

Trying to right myself and slow down is a mistake, making the lightness in my head even more overwhelming. Then the black spots turn to complete darkness and I don't even feel it when I hit the boards or crumple to the ice, the sounds of the arena disappearing into nothingness as well.

Chapter Twenty-One

Justin

THE GAME IS ON the TV too late for Owen to watch with me, so I'm curled up on the couch alone. I have my phone on the arm of the couch, but Gabe stopped texting over an hour ago. He's not supposed to have his phone turned on in the locker room or during games. His last text was a series of kissy faces and hockey sticks.

I'm glued to the TV, trying to catch every glance of my Daddy that I can. They've reached the pinnacle of the season now, the part which dictates whether they'll make it to the playoffs or end their season early, which means that they're traveling more than ever and I'm staying busy with treating "bumps and scrapes" (the guys call them that, I call them bruises and sprains) during their practices.

I know that I haven't been in the scene long, just a few months, but I already miss it when I have to go a week or so without Daddy with me. We try to make it work, but he's been more and more focused as the weeks go on, so even our phone calls are sparse.

It's partly my fault too, because I've been distracted with Karen and Harold and the fight to keep custody of my son. I've met with the lawyer a handful of times already and we finally have a date for the case in front of the judge. It's next Friday and, unfortunately, it clashes with one of the Phoenix Penguins' last games. If they win the game, they'll move on to the playoffs. If they don't, the season will be over for them. Gabe has mentioned more than once about skipping the game, but I refused to hear it.

Instead, before he had to leave for his flight, he helped me get all the papers together that the lawyer requested, and I have to settle for watching him on the TV. They're playing in Atlanta tonight, so he's way too far away for me to join him. Not that I could. I've been instructed to stay in the state, to keep Owen on his usual schedule as much as possible. Karen isn't allowed to text me directly anymore, but it hasn't stopped the extended family from sending messages.

Owen, for all it's worth, has been his usual, funny self. He's been cracking jokes and keeping me sane. There are moments, usually before bed, when he gets serious and asks me if everything is going to be okay. Each time, I reassure him that no one in this world or the next can take him away from me.

I've taken every possible step to make sure I can keep that promise. I've taken his grandparents off the approved pickup list and explained to the administration at the elementary school that he is not allowed to be picked up by anyone outside of me, Gabe, his parents, or Mandy.

"Looks like Phoenix's number twenty-six is having some trouble," the commentator brings my attention back to the screen. The camera has zoomed-in on one of the players from the other team, but it pans down the rink to the other end. All the guys are moving fast, skating around. I spot Gabe's jersey number the second that he falls to the ice, just as the commentator says, "Oh!"

There was no one around him, nothing to trip him. Gabe just...*falls*.

And he doesn't get up.

The whole arena goes quiet and the refs rush to Gabe, medics also making their way onto the ice. My heart races and the screen turns to an announcer as they speculate about what has happened. I can't hear anything that he's saying. I can feel tears in my eyes as I reach for my phone. It's already ringing, Mandy's photo on the screen.

"Are you watching the game?" she asks.

"I am," I say. "Is he okay?"

I know in the back of my mind that she isn't going to know anything more than me. I still ask, hoping that someone magically has an answer. On the TV, the medics are putting Gabe on a stretcher.

He's still out cold.

I don't realize I'm holding my breath until my lungs are screaming at me to breathe.

"He'll be okay," she says when I take a deep breath. She sounds like she's trying to convince herself as much as me.

"I need to go to him," I babble, "I need... I can't leave. I..."

"Justin, slow down." Mandy's voice does nothing to help. "Can you call the coach and see what's going on?"

"Um, yeah. Let me..." My brain isn't working, filled with all the bad things that could be happening. The ice is suddenly empty. Each team is taking a break. I glance at the timer, which has stopped with six minutes to go in the last period.

That's not usual. Not unless someone is really injured.

I feel panicky and sick.

"Justin, call your coach and then call me back, okay?"

"Okay." She hangs up and I switch over to my contacts list. I have to blink my eyes several times to see the names on the screen.

The phone rings three times and I almost hang up to try again, but Overton finally answers. I can see him answering the phone on the TV after only a two second delay. "Justin?"

"How is he?" I demand. "What happened?"

"I don't know," Coach says. It's surreal to watch his lips moving on the screen in front of me. He turns away when he realizes that he's on camera. "He's still out. They're saying he fainted, and his heart rate is weak, but he's stable otherwise."

"Is he going to be okay?" That's all I need to know.

"They're going to hook him up to an IV and take him to the hospital. I'll keep you updated." The line goes dead, and I'm left thinking the worst.

If Gabe hasn't woken up yet, that's not a good sign. Is he dehydrated? Pushing himself too hard? I know that he's worried about letting the team down and his scholarship and he wasn't eating a lot...

"He stopped doing that," I mumble to myself. I lift a hand to my eye and swipe the tears away once more. "He told me he was fine."

***

"Hey, baby." Daddy's voice is like every good thing in the world mixed together. I barely slept the last two nights, trying to get updates on him and debating if it was worth catching a red-eye flight. Now, he's standing in front of me and giving me that smile. He has bags under his eyes, but other than that he looks okay. "I'm sorry if I scared you."

"You did," I say. I can hear the mix of emotions in my voice. I'm relieved that he's okay, but I'm also still scared and a little mad. I don't want to be mad at my Daddy, but I can't help it. "You said you were okay."

"I know, baby. I will be okay, I promise."

Turning on my heel, I walk back into the house, knowing that he will follow. I sit on the couch and face him. I want nothing more than to crawl on his lap and never let him go, but I know we need to talk about this.

"What happened?" I ask. He looks sheepish. "Why did you faint?"

"I was dehydrated," Gabe answers. "I didn't eat breakfast, and then we wanted to get an extra practice in before the game and I forgot to eat. I was sweating a lot during the game and then I felt lightheaded."

"Gabriel." I'm in full work mode right now. I know that he's my Daddy and he sets the rules and everything, but I'm in charge of making sure he's good on the field. Ice. Whatever. I knew he was losing weight, and I brought it up to Coach, but I didn't follow up on it. I thought he was taking care of himself after he told me he would do better. "You can't do that, and you know it."

'I know."

"I don't think you do," I interrupt him firmly. "You are studying Sports Medicine, Gabe. You know the effects not eating has on an athlete. It's dangerous. Not only can you faint, but you put stress on your organs, and it slows down healing any bruises or other injuries. You need a minimum number of calories just to function, let alone build the muscle you need to power through games and withstand bodychecks and—"

"I know." He takes my hand. I can see tears glistening in the corners of his eyes. "And I'm sorry, baby. I really am. I was just under a lot of stress, and I thought if I could just get through this season, I'd be fine. I didn't want to let the guys down; I wanted to give them the best chance at making it pro. Especially since I decided I don't want to go that route."

"You don't?" I look into his eyes. He swipes a thumb under one of mine and nods. He takes my other hand and moves closer to me. Our knees bump together with the way we're sitting.

"I've been thinking about it since last year," Gabe says. "I love hockey, I really do. But I've realized that the traveling and constant practices aren't how I want to spend the rest of my life. I want to come home each night. Wherever home is."

This time, I do move to crawl onto Gabe's lap. I straddle his legs, and his hands cup my ass. My lips are on his before either of us can say another word. I missed him so much. I was so damn worried.

Our tongues dance together, like they've been practicing this dance forever. I run my hands through his hair, pulling the hair tie out in the process. I'm just as obsessed with his hair now as I was when we first got together. Obsessed with him. With all of him.

"You always have a home with us." I whisper the words against his lips. "Now, take me to bed. Please."

"It's only noon, baby." It's noon on a Saturday, and Owen is actually with Brian and their family. Gabe's parents made the drive when they heard the news as well. They've been staying with Mandy for the past two days. They were at the airport when Gabe landed.

"Then you better grab us two bottles of water, Daddy." I give him a smirk and tug on a strand of hair. "Because I don't have to pick Owen up until seven."

***

The courthouse is very... brown. The seats are long rows of brown wood, with a maroon, almost brown cushion. The stand that the judge sits at is brown. The dress that Karen is wearing is even some shade between tan and brown. I don't want to be judgmental, but it's not a good color for her. I'm being petty, but I don't care.

We've been going back and forth already for twenty minutes. I thought this was going to be a quick over and done with thing, but their lawyer is bringing up everything from my past. Not that there is anything that would even remotely affect Owen. I never brought exes or hookups to the apartments. I've never done drugs. The only time I drank alcohol was during nights out, when Owen was in the care of a trusted friend or adult. All of this is explained to the judge.

I hate that I have to justify my perfectly normal existence this way.

Then the moment that I've been dreading arrives when the judge asks Owen to come up and answer a few questions. Owen looks nervous, but I give him a hug when he passes by, and I tell him to just be honest with the judge and any question he's asked. He nods.

To give credit to the judge, he lets Owen sit on his lap and smack the gavel a few times. I relax only when Owen starts giggling.

"Daddy! Look at me! I'm a judge!" He waves and I wave back, a smile spreading across my face.

"This is perfect," my lawyer whispers next to me. I ignore it. It's not like I've trained my kid to be so adorable: this is just who he is.

"Alright, Owen. I have just a few questions for you, okay?" Owen nods and glances at me once before looking up at the judge. "Can you point to your dad for me?"

Owen points at me and then turns back to the judge. It's cute how excited he is now.

"And do you like living with your dad?" Owen nods again, a toothy grin splitting his face.

"Daddy's the best. We have a big house and we play a lot and he lets me help pour the cereal in my bowl. He also bought a pool, but I gotta wear sun... sun..." He looks at me and tilts his head in the most adorable way. I can see the bailiff standing to the side trying to hide a smile. "Daddy, what's that stuff called?"

I wait for the judge to nod before I answer him. Owen might be having fun without understanding how serious this is, but I know better. I can't afford to get comfortable and then have the other shoe drop.

"Sunscreen," I say simply.

"Sunscreen," Owen repeats, turning to the judge. His red curls bounce a bit when he moves. The judge smiles at him.

"So, you and your daddy have fun?"

"Yes. I have friends here too. Me and Brian was over at my house and Daddy let us run around and pretend to be bad guys while him and Gabe chased us. We were put in jail when they caught us."

"In jail?" The judge feigns shock and I'm so happy that he's taking care of my son, even though I'm standing right here. I glance over at Karen, who is glaring at me. I don't give her any sort of reaction and turn back to watch Owen.

"It wasn't real jail," he says with a laugh. "We was just sitting on the couch and had to count to twenty before we could run away again. We put Daddy and Daddy Gabe in jail, but they had to count to fifty."

"And who is Daddy Gabe?" The judge asks, his eyes scanning the room.

Gabe has been mentioned before, brought up by Karen and her lawyer. I hold my breath, knowing that this is going to be a pivotal answer. I'm not worried. Nothing bad has ever happened with Gabe, or any of his friends or anyone on the hockey team for that matter.

I don't hear what Owen whispers, but the judge laughs and pats Owen's back before dismissing him off his lap. "He's good to sit with Justin," the judge announces. "For the court record, I will repeat what Owen told me. Gabe is Daddy's boyfriend because they kiss a lot."

Everyone but Karen has some sort of positive reaction to that. I wish that Gabe was here for this. Court cases were running long today, and he had to go for the midday game. It's a home game and potentially their last depending on if they win or lose tonight, so we'll see him tonight. I hug Owen tight to my chest, kissing the top of his head as he wraps his arms around me.

"Well, I think I have my verdict," the judge declares. He shuffles some papers before looking at me and then Karen. "I've heard from the parties present, and from Owen himself. I've reviewed the witness statements and the home visit from the social worker. There is no evidence that Justin is not a fit father, nothing to warrant issuing split custody between him and Mr. and Mrs. Green. Custody will remain the same, and Owen will remain fully in the care of his father, Justin Anderson."

I can feel tears falling down my cheeks. The stress of the last couple of weeks melts away and I hug Owen tighter until he complains that I'm squishing him. I loosen my grip, but no way am I letting him go right now.

"I want to commend you, Justin, for raising such a wonderful young one. I know that being a single parent isn't easy, but you're doing great work."

I manage to choke out a relieved, "Thank you, sir."

The judge smacks the gavel and Owen claps, unaware of what that sound means. I stand and hold him with one arm while shaking the hand of our lawyer with the other. "Thank you so much," I say earnestly.

"It was my pleasure," he replies. Owen gives him a high five. "And you, Mister Owen, were fantastic answering all those questions. Good job."

Owen smiles and turns his attention to me. "Can we go to the hockey game now?"

I look at the clock on the wall. The game will definitely be over by now. "I think we missed it, buddy. But we can go home, and Gabe will meet us there."

"Okay." Owen bounces in my arms before wrapping his arms around my neck and hugging me. "I love you, Daddy."

"I love you too, Owen." After a moment, I have him stand beside me as I gather my stuff. I don't have a lot. Just a couple of papers that I shove into a folder and stick into my bag. I glance across the aisle and see that Karen, Harold and their lawyer are already gone. It's going to take a while before I'm ready to face them again, if at all. "Let's go home, buddy."

***

When we walk out of the double doors and down the hall, we're greeted with a lobby full of people. Not just people, but people we know. It looks like half the hockey team, Izzy and Marshall, and even Overton are all standing around the room.

"Owen!" I don't know who shouts it, but Owen lets go of my hand and runs for the person standing in front of the whole crowd.

My son runs full force into the waiting arms of the one man who shook up my whole world in the best possible way.

"Daddy Gabe!"

I'm watching the way Gabe spins Owen around in a tight hug when I feel a hand on my shoulder. I turn my head to see none other than Judge Willis beside me.

"I meant it," he says quietly enough only I can hear him. "I know firsthand how hard being a single dad is. I've spent my whole life creating a safe and loving space for my kid. You are doing a great job with Owen."

I thank him and turn back to the scene before me, warmth and contentment settling over me.

I don't feel like a single dad anymore. Gabe completes every missing puzzle piece in my life. He's my Daddy when I need him and my partner, my equal, when Owen needs us both.

I meant it when I told him that he'll always have a home with us. I just hope he knows that wherever he is home for me, too.

Chapter Twenty-Two

"I'M SORRY YOU LOST the game," Justin says, leaning into my side as half the team chases Owen around the small backyard.

I shrug. "It's fine. The other team played better. And, no," I give him a little squeeze, pre-empting his concerns, "it wasn't because I was distracted by wanting to be at the courthouse with you."

I mean, I did want to be there, but I knew things would be fine.

"I hope not," he sighs. "It's nice that the team cares so much, though. I can't believe so many of you turned up."

"Yeah, well, I was kind of anxious, and because they're still hung up on the idea of having a 'small human shower' for the kid I've accidentally procured" —I can't help chuckling at how hung up on the idea they still are— "they wanted to celebrate you winning the custody thing."

"But...how could you be so sure I was going to win?"

Smiling, I tell him, "For one, your lawyer was super confident. And secondly, I knew that any judge with half a brain would be able to see what an awesome dad you are."

Justin hums softly. "Hmm. I wasn't as sure that would happen."

"I know. It was scary. And stressful. But it's over now."

"Thank God," he slumps against me, as if he needed to hear the finality spoken out loud. "No. Actually," he tilts his head up to look at me with wet eyes that tug at my heartstrings, "thank *you*, Daddy. I couldn't have gotten through all of this without you. And you turning up to the courthouse today...it really means a lot to me."

"Baby..."

"No, no, I need to say this. I...I know that in the past couple of months we haven't had much of a chance to" —he lowers his voice— "*play*. And I know this all got so serious really quickly, and you're only twenty-two, and I know how scary it is when things get serious at that age."

"Justin..."

His glance drifts to Owen. He was my age when he was born and changed his whole world. "And there's no expectation that you should saddle yourself with all of this—"

"I love you."

Justin inhales sharply and the moisture in his eyes wells over.

Before he can say anything, I gently tug him inside the house so we can share the moment in private. "I love you," I repeat softly, allowing the once terrifying emotion to fill me up and warm my insides. "I turned up to the courthouse because I love you. I will *always* turn up for you. And for Owen. I love him too, baby. So much. You are a package deal, and this is me signing up for a lifetime subscription."

Justin lets out a watery bubble of laughter. "Dork." The amusement on his gorgeous face softens into a reflection of everything I am feeling for him. "Gabe..." he starts, then stops and licks his lips, giving his head a little shake. "I love you, too, Daddy."

I smile, so happy to hear those words returned. Then we're kissing, and I'm backing him up against the nearest wall, and the sounds of raucous laughter from outside fade away. With our 'I love you's still on the tips of our tongues, the kisses almost feel different again. New. Renewed with excitement and the relief of Justin winning the custody dispute.

The past few months have been rough, and I know that we still have the realities of me finishing out my final year of college and working out what the actual fuck I'm going to do afterwards ahead of us, but I am giddy with excitement for everything that we can build together after I graduate.

"Whoa," Mason's voice sounds out behind me, filled with amusement and a hint of cheek, "there are little eyes here, guys."

"Daddy and Daddy Gabe *always* kiss," Owen's little chipmunk voice replies with the kind of exasperation only a five-year-old can project. "That's what I told the judge man."

Justin is shaking and I pull back a little, concerned that he might be upset at Owen's reminder of what they went through, but I'm glad to see that he's just trying to contain his laughter. Pressing a kiss to his forehead, I release him from the wall and turn around to face my teammate and his grinning co-conspirator.

"We kiss all the time because we love each other," I tell them, a grin stretching my lips at how good it feels to say it openly. I don't know why the concept scared me so much before. There's nothing more wonderful than knowing Justin loves me. I want to shout it from the rooftops. Then I look down at Justin's redheaded miniature and make grabby hands in his direction. "And I love you, too, kiddo."

He squeals with delight, already catching on to my plan. "You can't kiss me if you can't catch me!" he cries as he takes off running outside again.

"You'll slow down at some point!" I yell right after him, earning another laugh from Justin.

As we head back out to join the others, I think about how much has changed for me in such a small time and how happy I am now.

***

My wonderful, amazing, superior, intelligent, super thoughtful sister takes Owen to her house for a sleepover playdate on Saturday. She winks at me when she picks him up, telling me to enjoy reconnecting with my man.

She is definitely my favorite of all my siblings.

Even though Justin has spent the past few months stressing about letting Owen out of his sight, even he seems grateful for the break we've been offered. A big part of that is probably because, aside from nighttime stories and short scenes in his bedroom, he hasn't had much of a chance to be Little. With all the stress he's gone through, I know he could use some proper regression time to really let go.

"What do you want to do today, baby?" I ask him after Mandy's car has reversed out of his driveway. "Or do you want Daddy to plan a day of all your favorite Little things?"

"I'd like that," he says, but then his teeth sink into his lip and I frown.

"But...?"

His cheeks turn pink. "I, um, can we...I mean, I know we briefly mentioned it a while ago, but..."

Closing the front door, I take him by the hand and gently push him to sit down on the couch in his living room. Sitting beside him, I encourage, "You want to try something new?"

He nods, swallowing roughly. His fingers tangle in the hem of his t-shirt as he fidgets. "I...I want to, um...can we...can we try an accidental wetting scene?"

A thrill of anticipation shoots through my body. He's right: we did talk about it a long time ago but never got a chance to explore it further with everything that happened. And yet it was his trust and vulnerability the first time he asked which made me realize how serious my own feelings had become, and now that we've exchanged declarations of love...well, I can't think of a more perfect time for this, really.

"I'd love that," I answer him honestly, watching him relax with my easy answer. "How do you see it playing out?"

We talk through his options, and eventually he decides that going with my original idea of regressing as usual and enjoying all of his favorite Little activities will feel the most natural. I'll get him extra drinks while we play, and I won't remind him to go to the potty. Whatever happens from there is up to how deeply regressed and comfortable he feels: we're not going to force the scene to go any particular way.

"I'll probably feel really embarrassed," he says as we talk about comfort levels and re-confirm safe words. "But...I'm kind of excited about it, too. Is that weird?"

"Not at all," I assure him. "There's something really liberating in giving up complete control. It's why so many people who like wearing diapers use them when they're regressed. I know you're not interested in that," I add, smiling, "but we'll see how you feel after today. You might really like the idea of trying potty training play or pushing the limits of your bladder and seeing if you can make it to the potty in time, that kind of thing. Because you know that, no matter what, your Daddy won't be angry or annoyed, and I will really enjoy getting you all cleaned up again."

He squirms, his cheeks pink again. "Can I wear my training pants today, Daddy? I'm a big boy."

I'm not surprised that he's already sinking into his headspace. He's been anxious to do so ever since Mandy texted to say she was kidnapping Owen to give us some much-needed grownup time.

If only she knew.

"No pull-up?" I ask him indulgently. "Just in case?"

He gives me one of his sassy little eyerolls. "I'm a big boy. I don't need a pull-up." Even as he says it, he blushes again. We both know that he's lying about that today.

I lead him into his room and let him pick his outfit. Surprising me, he chooses puppies instead of penguins. Then I realize that he's leaving me the option to dress him in his penguins later.

Normally, I would tell him to go potty before we start playing, but today I stick to the plan we've discussed. As I help him into his training pants, I ask him one more time about his safe words, and he responds with a sweet, "Still green, Daddy."

We start by playing cars in the living room, and he guzzles a sippy cup of apple juice happily. It gets refilled with water, and he drinks that more slowly when we switch to playing with a train set I bought for him during an away game not too long ago.

"Toot toot!" he cheers, watching the battery-operated train chugging around the plastic track. "Look, Daddy, it's going under the bridge!"

"You did a very good job building that bridge," I tell him, having enjoyed watching him construct it with his small collection of blocks, his tongue peeking out of the side of his mouth as he concentrated.

He wriggles a bit, and I watch him carefully, though he hasn't had that much to drink yet, and we've barely begun playing. I guess I'm as excited for this new experience as he is, especially when it could happen at any time. A pleasant sense of anticipation bubbles away in my gut.

"Daddy's going to start making us some lunch," I tell him, and unlike his Big self, Little Justin doesn't take the opportunity to remind me to make a proper meal for myself, too. He just beams at me and asks, "Dino nuggets?"

"And tater tots and carrot sticks," I confirm. "Maybe some cucumber, too."

He sits up straighter, the train forgotten for a moment. "Can I have a chocolate milk, too?" The far-too-innocent question is posed with widened eyes and batted lashes.

He's so damn adorable.

"If you eat all your veggies."

Heading into the kitchen, I throw the tots and nuggets into the trusty air fryer, chopping up some veggie sticks while the machine hums on the kitchen counter. I can hear Justin making train noises in the living room, intermittently talking to Kelvin, his co-conductor.

I sit with him while I wait for lunch to finish cooking, just enjoying seeing him regress so completely.

I love seeing Justin so comfortable with being Little. I love watching him so relaxed and free. It's even more rewarding to hear the lightness in his voice now, after so many weeks of strain and worry.

We pack away the train set and blocks together just as the timer for the air fryer chimes. I take Justin into the bathroom to wash his hands, and I note that he doesn't even glance at the toilet.

I wonder how much of that is pure Little distraction, and how much is because he is completely confident with the experience we agreed to try.

My thoughts are interrupted by my Boy racing into the kitchen, telling me his tummy is growling, and I hurry after him with a laugh.

We talk about playing some card games after lunch, the promised chocolate milk little more than a memory and a faint moustache over his upper lip, and I'm not oblivious to him wiggling in his seat.

The not-so-subtle potty dance makes me smile.

Oblivious to my thoughts, though, Justin chatters about playing Go Fish. Moments later, his chair clatters to the ground as he stands up suddenly. "Uh oh!"

"What's wrong?" I ask, though I think I can guess.

My guess, it turns out, is wrong.

"Kelvin!" he cries, running into the living room to retrieve the abandoned stuffie. The penguin is held out like baby Simba as he is heralded into the room. "Daddy, he didn't get any lunch!"

"Oh no," I play along, "he can get some of the fish when we play Go Fish."

"There's no fish in Go Fish!"

"Then why is it called Go Fish?"

"'Cause you're fishing for the cards you need. Silly Daddy."

I snort, finding him too cute for words.

"Maybe he can have a cookie?" Justin asks slyly.

"Oh, *Kelvin* wants a cookie for lunch? Does that sound like a healthy choice?"

He sits down and wiggles again. "I ate—uh, I mean, *Kelvin* ate lots of veggies. Um. For breakfast. 'Cause he missed-ed lunch."

"I guess Kelvin is getting a cookie, then. You wouldn't also want a cookie, would you?"

His eyes widen at the prospect of *two* cookies, his hair flopping into his eyes as he nods quickly. "Please, Daddy?"

I am such a pushover for this Boy.

Once he's got his cookies, we settle back into our card game. I'm not paying a whole lot of attention to it, though, much more interested in the increased squirming happening in the seat across the table. I don't know if Justin is even aware of his movement, not with the way he is staring at the cards in his hand, the pink tip of his tongue once again poking out of the corner of his mouth.

"Do you have any fives?" he asks me, then splays his hand out wide to demonstrate the number.

I hand him a five of spades. "Card shark," I accuse playfully.

He giggles and pairs his fives up. The game continues and we go back and forth a few more times, and I become so used to his unconscious potty dance that I forget all about it, sinking into my competitive mindset for the card game instead.

"Do you have—" I start, then stop as he gasps, his back going ramrod straight.

"*Uhoh.*" This time the words are a whimper, and Justin's face is bright red. He looks down, his lower lip quivering. "Daddy..." He sounds so much *Littler* in that moment, his voice wobbly and uncertain.

"What's wrong, baby?"

"I...I'm...I'm going potty," his voice cracks, "*in my big boy pants.* I can't hold it."

"Shh," I round the table and reach his side, hearing the telltale hiss and patter of his accident as he makes a puddle on the chair and floor. I crouch beside him, not caring about the mess on the vinyl, or the ammonia scent. "It's okay, baby. Accidents happen. Let yourself finish. We got too caught up in playing, didn't we? And you had a lot to drink today."

He hangs his head. "I'm sowwy, Daddy."

My heart clenches at the sniffles and quiet sobs that overtake him. Neither of us anticipated his embarrassment to escalate to shame and sadness, but I probably should have. With all the stress he's been through lately, the deep regression and release —if you'll pardon the pun— of something like this was likely to bring out an intense emotional reaction. It gives him a trigger to really break down and cry and let go of everything he's held on to for the past few months.

"Everybody has accidents sometimes," I assure him, rubbing his back. "Are you all done?"

He nods, still crying, and I help him up carefully. I pull him in for a hug, heedless of the moisture clinging to his skin, or the wet fabric of his shorts pressing into my thigh. I'm not squeamish, and we're going to get cleaned up anyway.

I hold him until his tears subside, then I help him out of his shorts and underwear right there in the dining area, because I'd rather not leave a trail of drips on our way to the bathroom. I leave his shorts in the puddle on the chair, deciding to clean that up later, once Justin is settled again.

"Let's go have a nice warm bath," I tell him. "We can play with the duckies *and* the boats."

He's subdued as I guide him into the bathroom, letting me strip off his shirt and run the water without any of his usual chatter. I put in extra bubble liquid and make sure the temperature is just the way he likes it before helping him into the tub. It's a tight squeeze for us both, but with his unexpected emotions, I want to cuddle him in the warmth, so I take off my own clothes and slide in behind him.

With the washcloth I brought with me, I wash his back, then his chest. He practically melts into me at that point, which makes me smile. I wash his thighs and then his cock, which stirs to life at the touch.

"Feeling better, baby?" I ask lowly, my voice still sounding loud in the stillness of the little tiled room.

"Mmmhmm," he rubs his cheek against my jaw. "Thank you, Daddy."

"Do you want to play with your toys?"

"Hmm," the sound is contemplative. "Not today." He skims a hand over my thigh.

I chuckle, starting to understand. "Do you want grownup touches?"

I can feel the stretch of his cheek against my skin, and I hear the coy smile in his voice as he answers, "*Maybe.*"

I turn my head towards him, and he meets my mouth with his eager lips, dragging me in for a sloppy, somewhat uncoordinated kiss. He grabs for my hand, splashing water over the edge of the bath, but neither of us pays it any attention as he puts my hand directly over his cock. His very hard cock, bobbing under the water.

I wrap my fingers around him, relishing in the way he moans and arches into the touch. His movement and the warm, firm weight of him in my hand has my dick hardening almost instantly, too, rubbing against the small of his back.

We resume our kissing, heedless of the awkward angle or of the waves we're making as we undulate beneath the surface of the warm water. Justin whimpers and mewls into my mouth, panting

"Yes" and "More" and "Please, Daddy" every time he pulls out of the kiss for air.

"You're such a good boy for me," I tell him, fisting his cock, relishing in the feel of his flesh in my hand, the water not doing much for lubrication at all. Not that he seems to care, not with the increased bucking of his hips or the way his body is strung tight with pleasure. "You gonna come in my hand, sweetheart? Make another pretty mess for Daddy to clean up?"

"*Oh*," he gasps, rocking almost violently as he chases his orgasm. My cock slides against his back, but it's the sounds he's making and the bliss on his face which are really revving me up. "Oh, Daddy, *ohhhh*."

Bingo.

"You like that, don't you baby? You like making messes with your perfect cock. You're Daddy's messy little boy, aren't you?"

"*Nnngh,*" he whines, practically non-verbal. He rests his sweat-dampened hair on my shoulder and writhes. His cheeks are flushed, and his skin shines with sweat, most likely from the warmth of the water, while his dark lashes rest on the tops of his rounded cheeks. With his pink, pouty lips parted in bliss, he is the picture of debauched perfection.

I squeeze as I drag my hand up his length, twisting at the top to stimulate the sensitive head. "Come for me, sweet boy. Be my good boy. Come for Daddy."

It's not long before he does. His entire body goes taut as he shoots rope after rope of creamy liquid into the water where they float, momentarily buoyant beneath the faded remains of our bubbles. Then they sink down to the bottom of the tub, out of view.

I kiss his damp forehead as he rides out the afterglow. Eventually, he cracks his eyes open and smiles lazily at me, before widening his gaze and pushing off my chest. Water sloshes onto the floor as he awkwardly turns around to face me in the narrow tub.

"Your turn," he declares before I can ask what's wrong, and he wraps his hand around my still achingly hard erection.

He leans in to kiss me while he strokes me, swallowing my moans as he brings me over the edge, sending my cum to mingle with his at the bottom of the tub.

"Thank you," he murmurs minutes later, when we're rinsing off in the shower. "For everything today. I...I needed that. All of it. It was..." he struggles for the words, back to his Big headspace, but clearly drained from so much emotional expenditure. "Cathartic."

"I love you," I remind him. "I feel privileged that you trust me to be so raw and vulnerable."

"Well, I love you," he replies. "I never would have expected that I'd need a Daddy, that age play would be the thing to ease my stress, but I'm so grateful I met you, Gabe. I know it's still early days, and that we've got a lot to work out —especially once you graduate— but...I can't imagine not having this with you."

"You're stuck with me for as long as you'll have me," I tell him with a grin.

He's quiet for a moment. "Even if I want to experiment more with...um...with accidents and stuff?"

I've always imagined settling down with a Boy who trusts me to look after them, and I can't think of anything else that says 'I need you' quite as much as that request. It sends a thrill of love and excitement through me, just like it did the first time he raised the topic all those months ago.

"God yes," I tell him, holding him close. "For the record, I want everything with you. Whatever you want to try, I'm game."

"Really?"

The answer to that question is even easier. Justin tried out a whole new kink when he realized it was something I was into. Back then, I told him it didn't matter if we indulged or not, and that still rings true. I'm glad that he enjoys the age play, that he is happy to call me Daddy and to sink into a Little headspace. But if he wanted to stop tomorrow, I would still love him and want to be with him.

I might have thought I was completely fucked (or, as Mandy joked, completely pucked) when I first realized how serious I was about him, but now the thought only makes me feel stable in a way I've never felt before.

"Really," I insist, repeating, "I love you. Nothing will ever change that."

***

I felt bad for the guys when our team was knocked out of the playoffs. We didn't even get close to the finals. Our performance in the Independence Tournament had us sitting on the middle of the ladder, no thanks in part to me having to sit out a few games following my health scare, and the rest of the season played out just as poorly. It just wasn't our year, and that sucks for the other seniors who had big plans to make this their moment of glory.

Zach, especially, worked his ass off to make it to the pros and I was hoping we could get him there. His playing was awesome, though, so maybe his stats will still get him there, even if our team itself hasn't performed as well as a whole.

I try not to feel too guilty about my part in that. For the whole year, I had one foot out the door —off the ice? — and my team deserved better. Even before I met Justin, I was losing my passion for playing the game. It was a means to an end for me: play hockey, keep scholarship, graduate college. I don't think I was ever going to aim for the big leagues, or even the minor ones.

At the beginning of the year, I was convinced that I could balance everything. It took a lot of work, particularly once I agreed to be a stepdad as well as a Daddy, but I wouldn't have life any other way now.

And *now* is so damn perfect. I've graduated and, in a surprise to only me (apparently), Coach offered me a job with the trainers and physical therapists. Not working directly with Justin, which kind of sucks a little, but close enough that we see each other at work daily. And at home. In his house, which is now *our* house.

But the best thing? Mason and I eventually pitched his idea about hosting skating lessons and peewee hockey practice to Coach and to the college, and they loved it! So not only am I working with athletes, I've also got a part-time job working with cute kids, teaching them everything from how to skate to how to check someone into the boards (safely).

Owen was one of the first kids to sign up for both the lessons and the hockey team, which we've named the Peewee Penguins. Brian signed up with him, and so did a bunch of other kids from their school. They're the cutest thing ever on skates, and I couldn't be prouder that my (not legal, but close enough) stepson is among them.

A year ago, I could never have imagined that I would have this. A career. A serious boyfriend. A kid who considers me his second dad. I was happy being single and carefree, but that version of me had no idea how much better life was going to get.

"Mmm, Daddy," Justin rolls over and snuggles his face against my shoulder, "why are you awake?"

It's the weekend and Owen is staying at my sister's. We don't have to pick him up until after lunch. I smile.

"Just thinking about how awesome everything is."

"*Hmmph*," he grumbles, kicking at the light sheet which is tangled around our ankles. "It's hot already."

Summertime in Arizona is still not his friend.

I chuckle. "Well, we could go cool down in a shower?" I suggest, rubbing my hand over his naked back. "Or maybe we could get a bit sweatier first?"

I feel his dick twitch against my thigh, and I know before he answers that he's definitely happy with this new idea.

As our mouths come together, morning breath be damned, I can't help but think once again that this is exactly the way life is supposed to be. I am so lucky that I happened to be in Ma's diner the day he and Owen walked in and changed my life forever.

I was never completely pucked at all.

Epilogue

Justin

I RELAX ON THE sofa, sighing at the way the air conditioning hits my body and cools me off. The Arizona heat is no joke in the summer. I can only handle twenty minutes at a time before I feel like I need to guzzle a gallon of water. Owen, for what it's worth, is having a blast in this heat. I think his skin is finally acclimating to the blaring sun because, despite his red hair, he has a constant golden tan, whereas I still just burn.

I'm not facing the sliding door, but I can hear the celebrations continuing. Gabe and I decided to host a going away party for Marshall, who of course is the last to arrive now. Izzy was the first to show up, to help decorate for their friend (and I use the word friend loosely, because I have a feeling one or both of them are harboring some *feelings*). Then it was some of the hockey team, including Zach and Vincent. Mason showed up a few minutes after them.

Owen pulled Mason through the house the moment he arrived, and they've been playing since. Mason is a great guy. He works hard with Gabe coaching the peewee hockey team, on top of keeping up with his training for next season and getting a head start on his studies for his classes. I don't know how he's got the time for all of it, but he doesn't let anything fall through the cracks.

"You okay?" Gabe asks, startling me. With the laughter and other noises coming from outside, I didn't hear him. He stands behind the couch and massages my shoulders. It's relaxing, and I rest my head against the back of the couch with my eyes closed. It's only lunch time on a Saturday and I'm ready for bedtime.

"I'm great," I say after a second. "Hot. Sweaty. Tired."

"I can attest to the hot and sweaty," Gabe whispers in my ear. It sends a shiver down my spine. I open my eyes and tilt my head to look at his face. His hair is up in its usual bun, and I can see the tendrils of sweat at his temples too.

"This is the yucky kind of hot and sweaty." I add a pout to the words and Gabe chuckles. Before Gabe can say anything, the doorbell rings.

"I guess the guest of honor has finally arrived," Gabe says half sarcastically as he stands to go to the door, but a blur rushes past him before he makes it halfway.

I don't even know how Owen heard the doorbell from the backyard with everyone out there. Owen opens the door to a less-than-happy Marshall. It's only a second, a flash, before there's a smile on his face and he's holding his hand out for a low five. Owen smacks his hand in Marshall's and giggles.

"We're all playing outside! Want to join?"

I love that Owen is back to his silly, wonderful self. Since the court case, it's been radio silence from Karen and Harold, and Owen hasn't asked about them in two weeks.

However, because he's just turned six, he doesn't catch the switch in Marshall's express like Gabe and I do. I look at Gabe who nods in understanding. "Do you want to see my new toys? Daddy and Daddy Gabe got me a whole bunch of them for my birthday!"

"Of course! I want to see everything." Marshall grins, but his gaze slides up to us. It's a little pensive. "Can I talk to your daddies real quick?"

"Okay! Coach Mason and Izzy are playing firefighters!" Owen answers with a smile and runs back to the sliding door. He pushes his hair back from his face before sliding the door open just enough to squeeze himself through. I follow behind him with a sigh and close the door behind him. We're working on remembering that the hot air needs to stay outside.

"What's up?" Gabe asks. "You're not exactly screaming party mode."

"Not really," Marshall's reply has me feeling instantly concerned. He looks between me and Gabe. "How did you two know you liked each other? Or, y'know, guys in general?"

"That's a loaded question," Gabe tells him. I step outside to give them privacy. I know Marshall seems comfortable asking to talk to us both, but Daddy has known him for years, and, really, he's probably better at answering questions like that anyway. *Especially* if they might relate to another member of their friendship group, like I suspect they do.

The backyard isn't that big to begin with and it feels even smaller with the seven people standing around. Mason and Owen have Izzy cornered with water toys, Zach and Vincent are laughing while standing clear of any spray zones. Noah is sitting in the shade, at the little table Gabe bought when he moved in. I make the smart choice and sit next to him.

"Izzy is going to soak them," he says when I join him on the other side of the table. "I hope you're okay with that."

"He'll end up in the tub tonight anyway," I say with a shrug. "Mason, on the other hand, I have no idea if he has extra clothes but I'm sure I can loan him something."

Just as I say it, the water hose is aimed at Mason and soaks the whole front of his shirt. Owen's shrill squeal is music to my ears as I watch him run away from Izzy.

"Izzy the Grizzly!" Owen shouts, using the moniker he gave him last month. Despite Izzy being adamant that he isn't a kids kind of person, the moment Owen asks to play or starts asking a million questions, his patience is unlimited.

Living up to his nickname, Izzy lets out a roar, playing the grizzly bear, before dropping the hose and chasing after both Mason and Owen. It's all laughs and giggles from the two as they run around.

The playing is momentarily halted when Gabe and Marshall make an appearance. I turn to look at them, smiling at Gabe. He nods, letting me know everything is okay. I'm sure, if it's not too personal, Gabe will tell me later. Right now, we have a lot to celebrate.

"If it isn't the man of the hour...thirty minutes late!" Izzy says with a huge smile.

"I was at lunch with my family," Marshall shoots back, playful and definitely not faking the happiness now. Gabe motions for me to stand up so he can sit down. He pulls me back onto his lap and I snuggle close to his chest. To anyone else, it's just a bit of PDA, but I know that this is my Daddy holding me. I love having that little bit for ourselves. We haven't been to the club in a while, not with our schedules the way they are, but I do like having my Little time in private.

"Well, we have burgers, dogs, and be—"

"We're eating *dogs*?" Owen shouts incredulously, interrupting the whole moment. We all laugh at his worried expression.

"Hot dogs," Mason corrects. "Not actual dogs."

"Oh." Owen turns to look at me and Gabe with a wide smile. "Daddy, can we get a dog?"

"How did you get from hot dogs to an actual dog so fast?" I ask. I look at Gabe and he shakes his head quickly

"No. You two are not ganging up on me with this. We are not home enough to have a dog right now."

"That's okay, Owen." Mason is sitting next to Owen on the grass. "You can come hang out with my dog, Bakery."

I hear Marshall laugh the loudest. "You have a dog named Bakery?"

"I found him in the alley behind my favorite bakery with my favorite pastries." Mason explains it with a shrug like it makes total sense. "He's a little older now, because we found him when I was only fifteen, but I thought the name was perfect."

"Anyway," Gabe says, steering the conversation back, "no pets in this house right now. We can talk about it in a couple of months. Right now, we're celebrating Marshall on his internship, and Zach for getting drafted into the NHL."

"Congrats, again, on that." I look between both of them. Zach announced he signed the papers to play for a team, but he hasn't announced which team just yet. We're going to find out with everyone else during the announcements.

"I might have found out and congrats are definitely in order," Vincent says with a smirk to the rest of us. I'm surprised, but also not. Zach was captain for the Phoenix Penguins this year and he's passed that torch to Vincent now. I know, just by watching and being his physical therapist that Vincent is going to make the team proud next season. They had a rough go of it this year, but we'll bounce back and Gabe will be there cheering them on.

Marshall, on the other hand, was on the fence about his internship. He talked to everyone, including me, about what he should do. He was offered a paid internship in Chicago. It's a great opportunity, but it means leaving his friends and family so he struggled for a bit. We promised that none of us were going to drift apart.

"I'm getting excited," Marshall says. We're all sitting now, most of us finding the shade. Owen and Mason are in their own little world, though, playing thumb war. I don't know if it's me projecting, but I can totally see Mason being Little. "I packed up the final box last night and I start the drive tomorrow."

"And you'll call every couple of hours to let us know you're making it there safely," Gabe says pointedly.

"I'll be driving him," Izzy says. "We're making a road trip out of it before I head back home for the summer."

"Then definitely call and make sure you're okay!" I say with a snicker. Izzy shoots me a glare but the rest of the group laughs with me.

We decide to move inside and eat now that everyone is here. I loan Mason a new shirt and Gabe gets Owen changed before we all sit around the living room, chatting and laughing about nothing in particular.

It's nice, having our different circles mingle so easily. I'm grateful for this group, for Gabe coming over to our table that first day. I love him, my Daddy, so much, but I'm happy his friends accepted me too. I've barely talked to those I left behind in Virginia, other than the occasional happy birthday message or something.

"What are you thinking so hard about?" Daddy whispers against the shell of my ear. I can feel myself itching to sink into my Little space already. It usually comes out when I start getting sleepy and it's been a long day.

"Just how happy I am and how much I love you."

Daddy gives me a soft smile and kisses behind my ear, then down the side of my neck. I tilt my head down, giggling at the ticklish touch of his lips. "I love you too, baby."

I turn my head to look at him, smiling coyly before I ask, "Can we revisit the idea of getting a pet, though?"

"Oh no," he hangs his head and sighs. I hear someone laugh next to us. I turn to see it's Izzy.

"What about a cat? Or a goldfish?" I know that this is my house and I am an adult, but it feels so natural and right to get my Daddy's approval for such a big decision. Not just because we live together, but because I know that Daddy loves either making all the decisions or helping me talk about options. When I'm Little, I know that everything has to go through my Daddy and I fully trust that he knows best.

After our wetting scene, there isn't anything I don't trust him with. I can't imagine being with anyone else, ever. I know our relationship moved fast, but I remind myself that we have time now. It doesn't stop my brain from thinking about marrying my Daddy and how happy that would make me. I don't say any of that, though. Instead, I blink slowly at him.

"What about sea monkeys?"

"I want monkeys!" Owen shouts excitedly. Both of us turn and correct him at the same time. Gabe squeezes my knee and looks back at Owen. Our son.

"We can get a little fish aquarium," Gabe says. *That didn't take long*, I think to myself as he continues, "We'll go this week and get the supplies."

Behind me comes a whipping noise and the whole room cracks up in laughter. Izzy adds the motion to it, flicking his wrist like he has an actual whip in his hand.

Gabe reaches over my shoulder and smacks his friend's shoulder. "Wait until you find someone and see if you can say no."

The others are still talking and laughing, sharing stories of what their futures hold. I don't know what ours holds, but I know that Gabe will always be in it.

THE END

About the Authors

MJ BOOTH

I've been writing since I was eight-years-old. I remember writing my first story while watching The Notebook when it first came out (please don't do the math on how old that makes me). I love writing LGBTQ+ stories, putting a little bit of myself in each character. The book community surrounding this community is beautiful and I'm so grateful for everyone that picks up one of my books.

You can find all of my works, keep an eye out for future stories, and sign up for my newsletter here: linktr.ee/mjboothauthor

***

ANNA SPARROWS

I am a bi Aussie author living in Brisbane, Australia. I've been writing* for as long as I can remember. I started with silly short stories as a kid, moved on to fanfiction in my teens, and then to publishing original fiction in my thirties.

I have been an avid reader of MM romance my whole life. (Ask me about my beginnings with *Buffy* fanfic, haha!) I wrote a sweet and kinky MM romance novel in 2022 and the reader response changed my life. From there, I knew I had found my niche.

And thus Anna Sparrows was born.

*All of my writing is 100% my own. No part of it is generated by Artificial Intelligence (AI) software of any kind. Yes, that means that it's sometimes flawed, but I'm okay with that.

You can find my books and more at https://annasparrows.com/

Printed in Great Britain
by Amazon